cx

"Compelling and thought provoking, *Original* plucked from the police files, and Colton Parker is the kind of hard-nosed, bloodhound PI you'll want to follow from case to case. Brandt Dodson has delivered a strong, intriguing first novel."

MARK MYNHEIR,
former homicide detective and author of
Rolling Thunder and *From the Belly of the Dragon*

"*Original Sin* is a terrific read, packed with characters—both savory and otherwise—you couldn't forget if you tried. I'm looking forward to the next book!"

JOHN LAURENCE ROBINSON,
author of the Joe Box Mysteries:
Sock Monkey Blues and *Until the Last Dog Dies*

"I loved *[Original Sin].* A friend sent it to me as a gift. I had others in front of it...so I figured it would be a month or two till I read yours. Then I teased myself with the first chapter. Oops. From there, I was hooked and raced through the whole thing in a day and a half. The writing was clean and tight. The characters were intriguing. I liked the 'realness' of the characters, as opposed to much of the fiction in the Christian market."

ERIC WILSON,
author of *Expiration Date* and *The Best of Evil*

"This is a terrific beginning to what promises to be a great series of mysteries with a touch of inspiration. Rating: 4½ daggers."

JERI NEAL,
The Romance Readers' Connection

"As a mystery and detective story it was excellent, with an intriguing trail of crumbs to follow."

ARMCHAIRINTERVIEWS.COM

"…*Original Sin* is the first in a series that promises a bright future. Fans of Robert Parker's Spenser series will feel right at home. Recommended."

ASPIRING RETAIL MAGAZINE

"I love a good mystery, and *Original Sin* by Brandt Dodson has all the elements of a good mystery: a PI the reader can identify with, a believable cast of characters, and a plot that's right out of the daily paper. Highly recommended!"

LINDA HALL,
award-winning author of *Dark Water*

"*Original Sin* is full of surprises and will keep you turning the pages. Brandt Dodson comes from a long line of police officers, spanning several generations, and it shows. I enjoyed this one."

BARBARA WARREN,
Dancing Word Writers Network

"I picked up *Original Sin* and found myself unable to put it down after reading the first page. I loved the characters and the straightforward writing. The author gave me a greater world of feelings and emotions for Colton Parker. I'm ready to read number two…right now!"

JULIE SCUDDER DEARYAN,
review from the Harvest House website

"*Seventy Times Seven* deals with forgiveness and the consequences of lack of forgiveness. If Robert Parker's Spenser ever needed help in Indianapolis, Colton would be the man for the job."

ASPIRING RETAIL MAGAZINE

"Crisp. Wry. Honest. PI Colton Parker is as unexpected as a bullet hole in a brand-new Brooks Brothers suit. You're gonna like this gumshoe!"

CLINT KELLY, AUTHOR OF *SCENT*

THE ROOT OF ALL EVIL

BRANDT DODSON

HARVEST HOUSE PUBLISHERS

EUGENE, OREGON

This is a work of fiction. Names, characters, places, and incidents are products of the author's imagination or are used fictitiously. Any resemblance to actual persons, living or dead, or to events or locales, is entirely coincidental.

Cover by Garborg Design Works, Savage, Minnesota

Cover photo © MVal / iStockphoto; Jon Patton / iStockphoto; Helle Bro / iStockphoto

THE ROOT OF ALL EVIL
Copyright © 2007 by Brandt Dodson
Published by Harvest House Publishers
Eugene, Oregon 97402
www.harvesthousepublishers.com

Library of Congress Cataloging-in-Publication Data

Dodson, Brandt, 1958-
    The root of all evil / Brandt Dodson.
        p. cm.—(A Colton Parker mystery ; bk. 3)
    ISBN-13: 978-0-7369-1811-4 (pbk.)
    ISBN-10: 0-7369-1811-6 (pbk.)
    1. Parker, Colton (Fictitious character)—Fiction. 2. Private investigators—Fiction. 3. Fathers and sons—Fiction. 4. Adult children—Fiction. I. Title.
    PS3604.O33R66 2007
    813'.6—dc22
                                                                                    2006022288

Printed in the United States of America

07 08 09 10 11 12 13 14 15 / BC-SK/ 10 9 8 7 6 5 4 3 2 1

To Robert and Wanda Dodson
By the example of your lives, you have
given me the proper values.
I love you both.

Acknowledgments

In any endeavor—particularly writing—doubts arise that can only be overcome by the support of good people. I am blessed in having that support.

To Bob and Linda Lenn. Your patient reading of the manuscript has meant more than you know. Your suggestions are always on target. Your advice is always sound. Your friendship is unwavering. Thank you.

To Jeff and Ruby Goldberg. Thank you for your patience and advice. And for the research trip. Jeff, we tested their security and found it sound. The people of that fair city can sleep well.

To Christopher and Sean. No father could be more proud. No father has been more blessed.

To Mom and Dad. Check the dedication.

To the many readers and supporters of Welborn Clinic, Deaconess Wound Services, and First Christian Church of Newburgh. Thank you. Your faith in me has sustained me during many difficult days.

To Nick Harrison. Nick, what can I say? Thank you for taking a chance and for your patient editing. You have made a dream into a reality.

To the many professionals at Harvest House. I won't name you individually for fear I may miss someone. But you know who you are, and you have my undying gratitude.

And...

To Karla, who believed from the beginning. I love you.

CHAPTER ONE

"Do you own a gun, Mr. Parker?"

"Yes."

"Has the state of Indiana licensed you to carry it?"

"Yes."

"Then I can assume you are proficient in its use?"

"With either hand," I said.

The woman sitting across the desk from me was an attractive brunette with brown eyes that were clear and doe-like. And she was young. I placed her in her early thirties. Her face hadn't yet developed the lines that would later give it character.

She sat with her legs crossed as she bounced one foot, reviewing information from an open file folder that sat on her lap. She had taken her folder and Montblanc pen from an expensive-looking leather briefcase she had carried into my office. She was wearing a charcoal gray business suit with an understated pink blouse. A single strand of freshwater pearls hung around her neck.

"May I ask," she said, "why were you terminated from the FBI?" Her attention was focused on the open file.

"Abuse of power," I said.

She looked up from the folder. "Abuse of power?"

"I forced a confession out of a young girl's kidnapper."

7

"And how did you do that?"

"Abuse of power."

"I see," she said, turning back to her file. After another perusal, she said, "The information I have indicates you were also with the Chicago Police Department. Is that correct?"

"Yes."

"How long?"

"Five years," I said. "The Fourth District."

"I see." She made a note in the margin of the file and then rested the pen against her lower lip as she continued to review the dossier.

"That's the south side of Chicago," I said.

"Uh-huh," she murmured without looking up.

The room was silent as she continued to review the file, flipping to the second page with her left hand while her right hand kept the pen resting against her mouth. I watched as she continued to bounce her foot to a tune that only she could hear.

"Jim Croce called it the baddest part of town," I said, breaking the silence.

She remained unimpressed as she nodded and flipped to the third page in the file. Her demeanor was professional. And tough. Wall Street tough.

I glanced at the business card she had laid on my desk: "Elizabeth Carmichael, MBA."

"What can I do for you, Ms. Carmichael?" I finally asked, easing back in my chair and clasping my hands behind my head.

She held up an index finger in a "wait just a minute" gesture as she continued to scan the file. After a moment, she raised her head. "I work for Berger Hume, Mr. Parker. Have you heard of him?"

"Sure," I said. "Who hasn't?"

Berger Hume was a rich man's rich man. Listed annually in *Forbes,* he had been an instrumental figure in Indianapolis' revitalization efforts during the 1980s. Hume had been the primary driving force in turning what had been "Indiana-no-place" into a major metropolitan hub. A city with two professional sports teams, an international airport, and a thriving economy.

"He seems to have dropped out of sight, though," I said.

"Yes, that's correct. He hasn't gone public for more than two years now. He went into seclusion after his wife's death."

I could sympathize. Since my wife died eighteen months earlier, I too had often felt like withdrawing. But I didn't have that luxury.

She uncrossed her legs and crossed them again as she snapped the cap of her pen back into place. "Mr. Hume is dying, Mr. Parker."

"I'm sorry to hear that," I said. "How long?"

She shook her head. "We don't know for sure. The doctors are perplexed and haven't gotten a handle on his problem."

"I'm sorry," I said again, for lack of anything better to say.

"Yes."

Her response was followed by a barren stretch of silence that was accented by the hissing of my radiator.

"I don't mean to sound glib, Ms. Carmichael," I said, disrupting the stillness, "but how does that involve me?"

"Prior to his marriage to the late Mrs. Hume, Mr. Hume was engaged to another woman. They were within days of marriage when Mr. Hume broke off the engagement. Recently, we have begun receiving letters from someone who is claiming that Mr. Hume fathered a child with the other woman."

"Any idea who's writing the letters?"

She shook her head. "No. They've been anonymous."

"Are they accurate?"

"Perhaps. We've been able to determine that the woman did have a child eight months after Mr. Hume ended their engagement. We've also determined that the child's name is Miles Poole. We have not, however, been able to determine if he is Mr. Hume's son."

"Blackmail?" I asked.

"We don't know the motive behind the letters, but to be frank, that has crossed our minds."

"Blackmail," I said to myself.

"That's always the risk, isn't it? Particularly when one is as successful and as visible as Mr. Hume."

"That explains it," I said.

She tilted her head. "Explains what?"

"Why no one has tried to blackmail me."

She smiled. "At any rate, Mr. Hume was unaware of the child until the letters began to arrive."

"Where are the letters coming from?" I asked.

"We don't know. All we know is that they have Indianapolis postmarks."

"How many letters have you received?"

"Two. One came a month ago, the other two weeks ago."

I unclasped my hands and eased forward in my chair. "How does Mr. Hume feel about all of this?"

"He wants to know."

"If Miles is his son."

"Yes. And if he is, Mr. Hume wants to see him."

"Any idea where he might be?"

"None. We could have gone to the police, but given the circumstances we felt it best to do this as privately as possible. Which is why we have come to you."

"I'm not up to speed on all of my local business trivia," I said, "but it seems I read somewhere that Mr. Hume has children."

She nodded. "Yes. Denton Hume is the oldest son. He is the current president of Hume Enterprises."

"To succeed his father?" I asked.

"Soon. It is anticipated that he will be selected as CEO and chairman of the board."

"Mr. Hume is that close to passing?"

"Yes. Then there is Warren Hume. He is the younger son and vice-president of Hume Enterprises."

"Rivalry?" I asked.

"Of course."

I crossed one leg over the other as I clasped my hands around one knee. "How do the sons feel about the revelation of another sibling? Assuming, of course, that he is the genuine article."

"I would characterize them as less than thrilled."

"They are concerned," I said.

"That," she said, with a wry smile, "would be an understatement."

"What kind of business problems does this create for the family?" I asked.

She shifted slightly in her seat. "Denton and Warren are currently in negotiations to sell one of Hume Enterprises' subsidiaries. Specifically, the hotels."

"And a new son," I said, "particularly one that may have ulterior motives, could challenge the sale and tie it up for years to come."

She nodded. "Yes. The hotels are losing money, and the family wants to jettison them from their holdings as quickly as possible."

"So this new revelation becomes a wrench in the works."

"Yes."

"How close is the deal to being inked?"

"Close. Three, four weeks at most."

"Do the brothers want him found and exposed, or left alone?"

"If Miles is Mr. Hume's son, Denton wants him found and appropriate arrangements made prior to Mr. Hume's demise."

"Appropriate arrangements?"

"Settle with him."

"Throw a few dollars at him until he goes away?" I asked.

"Yes. Warren, on the other hand, is much less accommodating. He has made it clear that he desires to leave the whole thing alone."

"Lest Miles rock the boat," I said.

"Yes. Unfortunately, however, leaving him alone won't make the potential problem go away. Even if the sale is finalized, he could always challenge it."

"So Denton's plan to settle with him—buy him off—would make it much more difficult for him to challenge the sale later."

"Yes."

"And what if he can't be bought off?"

She shrugged. "He could create problems for the family regardless of how the situation is handled."

"But it's better to address the issue now than to let it fester and blow up later."

"Correct."

I stood and went to the coffeemaker that I kept on top of my file cabinet. I dropped a filter and some coffee into the basket, filled the carafe with water, and poured the water into the maker's reservoir before flipping on the switch.

"Why me?" I asked, settling back into my chair.

She tilted her head again.

"Mr. Hume has unlimited resources, Ms. Carmichael. He could hire half the federal government. Why me?"

She smiled. "You have come recommended."

"By whom?" I asked.

"By Harley Wilkins."

"Harley?"

She studied me for a moment. "Yes. Why? Does that surprise you?"

"In a way."

Harley Wilkins was a detective captain with IPD. Though we had known each other for a number of years and had worked together on several cases, his disdain for private detectives was palpable.

"Well, as you say, Mr. Parker, Mr. Hume is not without resources. He is a close friend of the chief of police. After a phone call asking for a recommendation, the chief mentioned that he thought the captain may know of someone who could help. Your name came up."

"The chief is apprised of the situation?" I asked.

A frown crossed her face as she shook her head. "No. Absolutely not. As I alluded before, until the situation can be properly developed, the family wants to keep this secret. It is imperative that we keep the police out of this. This is the one thing on which the brothers agree. The chief was only asked for his recommendation."

"Sure," I said. "And you're here today, asking questions, to see if I am worthy of Detective Wilkins' endorsement?"

She chuckled. "We've already checked you out, Mr. Parker. My visit today is to see if what we've heard is accurate."

"And what have you heard?" I asked.

"To be blunt? That you're a brash, insolent, and narrow-minded ex-cop who tends to be a bit of a loner. We've also been told that you often work with all the subtlety of a jackhammer in a funeral parlor." She slid the Montblanc into her briefcase. "The cliche 'a square peg in a round hole' came up more than once."

"Bull in a china shop?" I asked.

"We didn't hear that one, but I think it would have been consistent with the point they were trying to make."

"Nice to have friends," I said.

She continued. "Nevertheless, nearly everyone we spoke with said that you are honest, aggressive, and doggedly determined, and that you will get the job done."

"Kind to animals too," I said.

She ignored my last remark as she slid the file into her briefcase. "Your sense of subtlety does concern us, but it was counterbalanced by your determination. Mr. Hume would like to meet with you tomorrow morning. Would nine be okay?"

"Sure," I said.

"Because of the obvious urgency of the situation, we're going to need your full attention. We're prepared to offer ten thousand dollars in advance, plus expenses."

"In that case," I said, "I can clear my calendar and be there at eight."

"You forget, Mr. Parker. We've checked you out. Your calendar *is* clear." She stood with the briefcase in one hand.

"I'm in a slump," I said.

"At any rate, we didn't want someone else popping up at the wrong time and diverting your attention."

"No chance of that," I said. "I'm all yours."

She handed me a card with preprinted directions to the Hume home. "You must understand that time is of the essence. Miles must be found before Mr. Hume dies."

"I'll find him," I said, standing to see her to the door.

She smiled. "Tomorrow at nine?"

"Tomorrow at nine."

After she left, I poured coffee into my Chicago PD mug and sat down, spinning my chair around and resting my feet on the window ledge behind my desk.

Berger Hume was dying. A son he did not know existed had popped up at the most inopportune time. Or opportune, depending on which side of the fence you were on. And that was leaving his other sons, who seemed to have agendas of their own, to speculate about the trouble this could mean to them. Or their father's business. Or *their* business. Again, depending on which side of the fence you were on.

This was the sort of problem I usually tried to avoid. The kind of case I didn't like but that seemed to come my way. The family kind. In particular, the rich family kind. There was no way to win. The best I could do was to avoid trouble and try not to lose. Then again, they were offering ten thousand dollars. For that kind of money, I would be willing to drive to Amity and brush Jaws' teeth.

I blew on the coffee before drinking and watched as the previously clear September sky darkened with a sudden influx of churning clouds.

Narrow-minded?

CHAPTER TWO

B erger Hume had become a wispy shadow of a man. Previously robust with a booming James Earl Jones-like voice, he was lying in bed at nine the next morning, tethered to an oxygen machine by way of a tube that ran through his nose. His eyes were sunken and yellowing, his voice was raspy, and his skin had the pallor of the dead or dying. He extended a thin frail hand as I was ushered into the room.

"Thank you for coming," he said. "Please have a seat." He gestured to a nearby chair. I pulled it closer to the bed and sat.

The bedroom was elaborate. Hume's canopy bed was solid cherry, as were the chest of drawers, night table, and dresser. A large ornate rug overlaid an immaculate hardwood floor, and the draperies were tastefully done. At one end of the room, a large bay window gave an unhindered view of the spacious grounds. At the other end was an expansive fireplace that contained a glowing fire, but the crackling embers couldn't warm the chilling sight of a dying man.

"Has Ms. Carmichael filled you in on the details?" he asked.

"No, sir," I said. "She did tell me about the problem though."

He closed his eyes as he nodded. "Her name was Marian. Marian Collins. She and I were deeply in love. But I was a young man who was trying to make his mark." He paused to lick his parched lips before opening his eyes again. "Do you know what I mean, Mr. Parker?"

"I believe so," I said.

"I wanted success. I wanted to be known. I wanted to make a difference. To be somebody important in an important world." He breathed deeply before continuing. "Not long after Marian and I announced our engagement, I met Aurelia. I knew instantly that she was the one who could help me." He slowly shook his head. "It was the decision of a young man who was after the wrong things. What a waste."

"I wouldn't say your life has been a waste, sir," I said. "If it weren't for you, this city wouldn't be where it is today. You can be proud of your achievements."

He shook his head again. "No, Mr. Parker. I'm not talking about those things. I'm talking about losing Marian. I chased after success when my heart was really with her."

His last statement was suspended in air, punctuated only by the popping and snapping of the burning wood.

"You didn't love your wife?" I asked.

He sighed deeply. "Eventually, yes. We 'bonded' is how I think they put it. But…" He paused again to lick his lips. "We were never truly in love. Aurelia came from money. Lots of money, Mr. Parker. She was attractive, and she was connected."

"So you left Marian," I said.

He nodded. "Yes. I left Marian for Aurelia."

"Ms. Carmichael said you ended the relationship just a few days before you and Marian were to be married."

"Yes, that's true."

"Marian was angry?"

"Yes. And hurt. Very hurt and very angry."

"Why did you end the engagement so late?"

"Uncertainty. I loved Marian, but I also loved the idea of success. Or what I thought was success. I spent many agonizing months weighing the choices."

"Were you seeing Aurelia all along?"

He slowly shook his head. "Not at first. But as time went on, I became increasingly aware of her. I knew I had to find my place in the world. I believed I could do great things. And I believed Aurelia was the one who could help me achieve those things."

I looked around the spacious bedroom again. Like the entire house, it spoke of financial stability and societal position. Both were things that Hume had accomplished. But now, in view of his imminent death, they seemed more like the empty artifacts of a life gone off track.

"Did your wife know of Marian?"

He nodded. "Yes. I told her everything."

"Were there any problems with that? Did Marian's name ever come up?"

He shook his head. "No, but I often thought about her. Especially during the many times that Aurelia and I would clash. During those times I'd wonder if life would have been different with Marian." He closed his eyes as he placed a thin hand over his face and sighed. "Marian was always there," he said. "Always in the background."

"Aurelia knew?"

He let his hand fall to his side as he stared vacantly at the ceiling. "She sensed it."

"Did you have contact with Marian after your marriage to Aurelia?"

He shook his head. "No. We never spoke again."

"Have you made any attempts to speak with her since your wife died?"

He shook his head as he began to cough, and motioned for a glass of water on the nightstand. As I reached for it, my hand bumped the glass causing it to spill and roll off the night table, breaking into several pieces on the hardwood floor.

"I'm sorry," I said, standing. "I—"

The door opened immediately, and Ms. Carmichael entered. "Is everything all right?"

"Everything is fine," Hume said. "Mr. Parker inadvertently knocked over the glass."

"I'm sorry," I said again. "I—"

Hume waved a hand. "Please don't give it another thought." He glanced at Ms. Carmichael who was already approaching with a towel. She placed it over the puddle that had formed on the night table and then knelt to pick up the broken pieces of glass, dropping them into a nearby wastebasket. "I'll bring you another, sir," she said to Hume.

He was silent until she left and then resumed our conversation. "Marian died shortly after my wife's passing."

"I'm sorry," I said.

He nodded again as he licked his lips.

"Did you know she had a son?"

He closed his eyes and breathed deeply before answering. "When I told her it was over, she told me she was pregnant."

"And you left anyway?" I immediately winced, regretting the way I had asked the question.

He nodded as tears began to form in his eyes. "Yes," he said, his voice breaking. "I thought she was trying to force me to stay. I didn't believe her." He placed a hand over his face and began to sob. "I didn't want to believe her."

"I'm sorry about all of this," I said. "But I have to ask these questions."

He nodded as he kept a skeleton-like hand over his face.

"Her son's name is Miles," I said. "Miles Poole. Did you know she had married?"

"No."

Ms. Carmichael entered the room and handed a fresh glass of water to Hume. He drank slowly and handed the glass back to her. She set it on the night table. "Will there be anything else, sir?"

He shook his head. "No, thank you."

She glanced at me as she left the room, closing the door behind her.

"Any idea who might be writing to you?" I asked.

He slowly shook his head as he motioned toward a tissue box on the nightstand. I held the box out for him, and he took one from it.

"I have made mistakes in my life, Mr. Parker," he said.

"We all have," I said, placing the box back on the night table.

"Most of them I can't do anything about. Not now, anyway."

"You can be proud of your work," I said again. "The city owes you a great deal."

He slowly shook his head. "No. You don't understand. I've spent my life building and accumulating. And for what?"

I didn't have an answer.

"I have two sons, Mr. Parker. I am proud of both of them, of course. But I am not proud of the paths they have chosen. They are following the trail I blazed. An empty road that leads to regret." He closed his eyes and sighed. "I have not done well by them. But if this man, Miles Poole, is my son, I must know. I need to see him. I need to do what I can for him before I…" he began to cry again.

"I'll find him," I said. "But I'm sure you know that I can't make him come."

He dabbed at his eyes. "I know. I know all too well the limits of what you can accomplish here."

"Ms. Carmichael has alluded to the fact that Warren is not eager to find Miles."

He nodded as he gently folded the tissue before dropping it into the wastebasket near his bedside. "I know. Denton and Warren are good men, Mr. Parker. But I have not been the father they needed. Not for them or for Miles." He sighed. "Denton and Warren have secure futures. If Miles doesn't want to see me, I'll understand. But I must reach out to him." He turned on the pillow to look at me. His eyes seemed more focused than they had been since I entered the room. "Have you ever felt compelled, Mr. Parker? As though you are being directed? As though the thing you are doing…you *must* do?"

I thought of the kidnapped young girl and how I had felt compelled to find her. "Yes."

"Then you know how I feel. If I have another son, I must meet

him. I must make things right with him even if I can't make up for
a life of empty promises."

"Do you have the letters?" I asked.

He pointed a feeble finger toward the nightstand. "The letters are
in the drawer. Take them. Take whatever you need to find him."

I opened the drawer and extracted two envelopes that were bound
together by twine. Lying in the drawer beside them was a yellowing
clipping from the newspaper's obituary section. It was for Marian
Collins.

"May I borrow this too?" I asked.

He nodded. "Ms. Carmichael will see to it that you have anything you need."

"I understand," I said, standing. "I'll get right on this."

"Please keep me updated, Mr. Parker. And please hurry. I don't
have long."

CHAPTER THREE

What did he have to say?" Warren asked. He was sitting on the arm of an expensive-looking sofa. The others in the living room, Ms. Carmichael and Denton, were standing near the fireplace.

"Only that he wants me to get to the bottom of all this," I said.

"Meaning that he wants you to find this Miles Poole," Warren said. "Find him and cut him into the family."

"If he's your father's son," I said, "he is family."

Denton approached me and held out his hand. "Denton Hume, Mr. Parker. According to Ms. Carmichael, you've come highly recommended."

Denton had not been at the house when I arrived. I shook his hand.

"What Warren's trying to say," Denton said, "is that this man could cause a great deal of trouble for the family."

"I understand. And I'm sensitive to the situation. But I'm working for your father. He has hired me to find this man, and if he's your father's son, to tell him that your father would like to meet him."

"I don't think you're hearing us," Warren said, sliding off the arm of the sofa.

Denton held out a hand to his brother. "What Warren means to say is that this man can cause a lot of damage to some very important negotiations. If our father wants him found, you must find him. How we deal with him afterward is entirely a family decision."

At forty, Denton was five years older than his younger brother and seemed to revel in the family's success. Unlike Warren, who was dressed casually, Denton was decked out in an Armani suit with highly glossed, Italian leather shoes and a diamond-studded Rolex that had probably cost more than my entire wardrobe.

"The issues you two have with—"

"Whatever those issues are, they are ours. Not our father's," Warren said.

Denton cleared his throat and glared at his younger brother. "Warren, shut up!"

Warren glared at Denton but slowly sunk back onto the sofa. Denton turned to me.

"Our father is dying, Mr. Parker. In the meantime, I'm sure you can appreciate our position. We have to protect our family's interests."

"And what interests would those be?" I asked.

"Oh, come on," Warren said, clearly exasperated. "We—"

Denton held up a hand to stifle his younger brother. "What Warren means to say is that we were under the impression that Liz had explained the delicacy of our situation."

"Liz?" I asked.

"Ms. Carmichael," he said, nodding in her direction.

"Oh, that Liz," I said. "She did explain that you're undergoing sensitive negotiations to close an important deal, and that this new revelation could complicate matters."

"So what's the problem?" Warren asked.

"The problem," I said, turning to Warren, "is that your father is dying. He may have a son he has never met. If this man is your father's son, don't you agree that your father should have a chance to meet him?"

"Our father is not thinking clearly," Warren said. "There is simply too much at stake."

"For whom?" I asked.

"For Hume Enterprises," Warren said, "and for the two sons that have stood by him."

The conversation was deteriorating. It was time to leave.

I moved across the living room to the ornamental chair, where I had left my jacket.

"What good boys you are," I said, sliding into the coat.

Warren's face was turning crimson. "You could cause a great deal of harm here. Don't think for a second that we're going to let you destroy our family's business."

I zipped up my jacket. "If I were bent on doing that, I'd stay out of this thing and let you boys keep on keeping on. After all, don't you have a chain of hotels that are about to go bust?"

Warren slid off the sofa again and approached me in a manner that he thought would intimidate me. At five foot five and a hundred thirty pounds, he was seven inches and seventy pounds in the hole.

"Sit down, Warren," Denton said before I could react.

Warren glared at me before heeding his brother's advice. He moved back to his position on the sofa but didn't take his eyes off of me.

"Good boy," I said as I turned to leave.

"Mr. Parker," Denton said, "before you go, there is something you should understand. We love our father, but we will not sit idly by and allow him to chase a relic of some lost love while jeopardizing our family's security. My brother and I are committed to seeing that this man is not a risk to our business interests." He moved toward me and leaned forward, speaking under his breath. "Reason with him, Mr. Parker. I'm prepared to meet his needs for life *if* he is my father's son and if he stays out of our business."

"No."

Denton recoiled. "No?"

"No. I'm not your errand boy. If you have a message for Miles, tell him yourself."

"We will," Warren said. "We'll deal with him any way necessary to protect our family's interests." He stood again. "And we won't let you, or any other low-slung overpaid security guard, get in our way."

"Low-slung?"

"Now or later, tough guy," Warren said. "We can hire the best."

"No you can't," I said. "The best is already working for your father."

Sensing the mounting tension, Ms. Carmichael crossed the living room toward me and said, "I'll see you to the door." She glanced back at both brothers as she took my arm and steered me toward the foyer.

Once we were out of earshot, she said, "I'm sorry for their behavior, Mr. Parker, but as I mentioned yesterday, they will not make any of this easy. They see it all as a threat. They're simply trying to protect their interests." She handed me a white envelope that contained a check for ten thousand dollars.

"No problem," I said, pocketing the envelope. "It was easier than brushing teeth."

CHAPTER FOUR

Ten grand was a lot of money, and a lot of money wasn't something that I was used to seeing.

After leaving Hume's home, I headed straight for the bank and deposited the check, minus enough to create a bulge in my pocket.

The September weather, which had been seesawing back and forth for the past several days, had taken a decided upturn. As I drove away from the bank, I rolled the window down, pulled out my cell phone, and called Wilkins.

When he came on the line I said, "I didn't know you cared."

"I don't."

"That's not what Elizabeth Carmichael said."

"Who's Elizabeth Carmichael?"

"Executive assistant to Berger Hume."

"Oh."

"Thanks," I said. "I appreciate it."

"Sure. Thought you could use the business."

I could. My wife's death had come only hours after losing my job as an FBI special agent. In order to provide for myself and my daughter, I had opened for business as a private detective. The ensuing months had been difficult. Cases were as scarce as a bag full of donuts in a detective squad room. Any business that came my way was a welcomed relief, even if it was the rich family kind.

"How's it going?" Wilkins asked.

I balanced my phone between my ear and shoulder as I merged into the traffic of I-465. "I don't know. Just got started. I'm probably going to have to find out what I can on—"

"I mean the business. How's it going?"

"Okay," I said. "I've picked up a couple of steady clients. I'm doing some work for Benjamin Upcraft, and—"

"Upcraft?" There was disgust in Wilkins' voice.

"Yeah."

"Isn't he the lawyer who represented that guy you worked for a while back? What was his name?"

"Billy Caine," I said. "Yeah, it's the same guy."

"What're you doing for him?"

"Preliminary stuff. You know, background stuff for court."

He snorted.

"And I'm doing some work for American Mutual."

"Insurance work?"

"Yep."

"Man, oh man," he said. "How the mighty have fallen."

Since being promoted to captain, Wilkins was spending the majority of his days typing reports and keeping statistics. The result, was that he was no longer able to devote much time to field investigations. He excelled as a detective, making his move to a desk job a loss for the city, as well as for the victims of crime in Indianapolis.

"It pays better than writing reports," I said.

"Maybe. But the work is steady."

"True," I said. "Listen, I need to find who's writing these letters."

"What letters?"

"The ones that Hume has been receiving. The ones that claim he had a son with Marian Collins."

"I don't know what you're talking about, Parker. I just referred them to you. I didn't ask questions."

I explained the situation to Wilkins. He was an uninterested third party and a decent man, and I had no reason to fear he would leak the sensitive information.

"You think the old man is being blackmailed?" he asked.

"Yep."

"What's the son's name?" he asked.

I gave Wilkins the name. "You think he could be writing the letters?" I asked.

I could hear Wilkins' keyboard clicking in the background. "Sure. Don't you? Whether he's the son of this man or not, he stands to gain a lot by setting himself up as though he were. If he works it right, he can even make it look like he was dragged into the whole thing."

"An innocent victim of his birth," I said.

"More like the victim of a do-gooder."

"A do-gooder who, coincidentally, would just happen to be him," I said.

"Right." There was a pause, and then Wilkins said, "Miles Poole has a record."

"Con jobs?"

"No. He seems to prefer the direct route. He's been busted several times for assault. It looks like the sheriff's department might be your best bet. We haven't had any run-ins with him, but they have. A lot of them."

"Do you have an address?"

"It's 1220 Wicker Lane. DOB is August 10, 1965."

"He's a year older than Denton," I said.

"Who's Denton?"

"Okay," I said, ignoring Wilkins' last question. "And thanks again."

"I don't know, Parker. You might not be so critical of desk work when you get hold of this guy. He looks like a real winner. Do anything for a buck."

Sure, I thought as I exited onto I-70. *Just like his brothers.*

CHAPTER FIVE

Miles Poole was a thug. An equal opportunity offender who would mug an elderly grandmother as surely as he would a Wall Street banker. He had, in fact, done both—and more. Although he had no current wants or warrants, his record showed that he had been popular with the Indiana law enforcement community.

"Quite a list," I said.

"Ain't it though?" Dave Chastain, a detective with the Marion County Sheriff's Department, eased back in his desk chair and popped a stick of Juicy Fruit in his mouth. He rolled the foil wrapper into a tight ball and pitched it into the trash can on the other side of his desk.

"Lived in New York for five years," I mumbled, flipping through Poole's rap sheet. "Arrested four times for shoplifting. Once for mugging…moved back to Indiana where he was arrested for mugging again, but…charges were dropped?"

"No evidence. The old lady didn't see who beat her up, and there were no witnesses."

"You must have had some evidence. You didn't arrest him for no reason."

"We pulled in the net. Turned out he had her locket. Said he found it."

"Flimsy," I said. I was sitting on the edge of Chastain's desk.

"Sure. But so was our evidence. You've been there, you know how it is. You practically have to have video of them in the commission."

"I have an address for him," I said. "But I wanted to come here and talk to you first. See if—"

"Wicker Lane?" Chastain asked, wadding a blank piece of memo paper and shooting it into the basket.

"Yeah."

"Isn't there." He wadded yet another sheet of paper.

"How do you know?"

"We wanted to talk with him six months ago about some stuff we heard he was trying to fence." He shot the paper ball toward the basket. It hit the rim and bounced off.

"And he wasn't there," I said, picking up on the obvious.

"Right. We found him later, though, and he was clean."

I handed the report back to him and slid into the seat next to his desk. "Where can I find this guy?"

"He fancies himself a biker."

"Lot of those in town," I said. "Any particular location I should check out?"

He shot another wad of paper. This time, it landed in the basket. "Come on. I'll show you."

We drove to the near west side, to a house that sat on a mostly quiet, mostly deserted side street. The house was an older two-story that was in serious need of repair, with a concrete wall that rose from the floor of the front porch and created a protective barrier around the front part of the house. Several square holes had been cut into the wall, four in front and two on each side, with each measuring approximately six by six inches. Large enough to allow access for a gun barrel if the house came under sudden attack. Another opening, big enough to allow a man to pass, was covered with a section of plywood that also had a similar gun port cut through the center. The entire yard was encased in a six-foot high chain-link fence, creating a sort of biker fortress.

"The only thing missing is a moat," Chastain said.

"Or a fire-breathing dragon," I said.

Chastain turned to look at me as we began to get out of the car. "Don't kid yourself. These guys can make a dragon look like fun."

As we approached the gate, two Dobermans came charging forward. Their ears were fixed and their spines were straight, but neither was making any sound or showing any teeth.

"Hold on," Chastain said, going back to the car. He opened the trunk, fished around, and came back with a lug wrench. When he approached the gate, he held his badge high overhead with his left hand and began to beat on the gate with the wrench in his right. The dogs began to bark. The more they barked, the more Chastain beat on the fence.

"You've been here before?" I asked.

"Yep."

Before long, a curtain parted behind a second-floor window. Chastain held the badge higher so that whoever was behind the window could plainly see he was a cop.

"They don't like the police," he said. "But they don't like the other gangs a whole lot more. It's better to let them know we're the good guys and didn't come here to shoot the place up."

"Sure," I said.

"What do you want?" a voice yelled from the open window.

Chastain quit beating the fence. "Detective David Chastain, Marion County Sheriff's Department," he yelled, over the barking of the dogs. "I want you to open this gate and let us in. We want to ask you a few questions."

The curtain remained open as the dogs kept barking. After a moment or two, a different voice said, "'Bout what?"

"Open up."

The dogs were beginning to froth as they continued to bark. A minute passed, and then the second voice said, "Go away."

Chastain slid the badge into his pocket and looked at me. "Ain't this a blast? Really. Can you honestly say you would rather be doing something else?" He turned back toward the house. "Open up, fellas. I don't want trouble, I just want to talk. But if it's trouble you want, I can come back with my friends and a warrant. I can give you all the trouble you can handle."

"Warrant?" I asked. "For what?"

Chastain shrugged. "Who cares? Whatever I list on it is probably in there. Drugs, guns...whatever."

"You can get a judge to sign off on that?"

"Friends of this bunch raped a judge's daughter once. They're not on good terms with our friends in the judiciary."

"Hold on," the second voice said.

Chastain went back to the car and dropped the wrench into the trunk. When he came back to the fence he said, "There used to be more with this group. Most of them are either dead, in jail, or members of rival gangs. There are only a couple of guys left now, and they're strictly small time."

We waited silently at the gate. After a few seconds, the plywood covering swung open, and two men appeared. One of them was short and very round with a long, scruffy-looking gray beard. He wore a bandanna over his head, a leather vest over a blue T-shirt, and jeans with boots. The other man looked younger, maybe midthirties, with a partially-shaven face, and greasy blond hair. He was wearing a black T-shirt and jeans and was smoking. As they approached the gate, the shorter man took the dogs away, eyeing us cautiously as he did.

"What do you want?" the younger man said. His voice was the second voice that we had heard from the window.

"I want to know where I can find Pork Chop."

Pork Chop?

"I dunno, man. How am I supposed to know that?" He inhaled deeply on the cigarette, causing the embers to glow a deep red.

"'Cause you know," Chastain said.

"Why do you want him? What's he done now?" The man exhaled

the smoke, having the decency to turn his head to one side as he did. He kept his eyes focused on Chastain.

"Maybe he hasn't done anything."

The man grinned.

"Then again, maybe he's done everything," Chastain said. "Right now, none of that matters. I just want to talk to him."

The man studied Chastain for a minute, drawing again on the cigarette as he did. He looked at me. "Who're you?"

Before I could answer, the detective said, "He's with me."

The man narrowed his eyes and kept them fixed on me. "I don't want any trouble," he said, turning his gaze back to Chastain.

"Me either. Like I said, I just want to talk with Pork Chop."

The man exhaled and then flipped the cigarette to the ground, crushing it underfoot. "I don't know where he is, man. I really don't. He's a loner. Drops in once in a while to do some business and then disappears until he's ready to work again."

"Who would know?" Chastain asked.

The man thought for a minute, then shook his head. "Don't know. Nobody really knows where he is. He just sort of shows up." He paused as he thought some more. "Maybe Ernie."

"Ernie?" Chastain asked.

"Yeah. Little guy who runs a bike repair shop. He's not attached, but he does some work for guys who probably are. It'd be a long shot, but…"

By "attached" I knew he meant affiliated with a particular gang.

Chastain scribbled some directions and then glanced at me. "Okay," he said. "Thanks."

"Hey," the man said, as Chastain and I headed toward the car. "If the Chop's done something that's going to cause us trouble, we can take care of him for you. Save you the hassle. You know?"

"I know," Chastain said. "But I just want to talk to him."

The biker crossed his arms. "Okay. But if he *is* doing something, we don't need him drawing the heat on us."

Chastain looked at me. "Honor among thieves."

CHAPTER SIX

Chastain drove us back to the sheriff's office, where I picked up my car and took another look at the picture of Miles. The photo came from the sheriff's department files and showed Pork Chop to be a short man with a bushy unkempt beard, a thinning hairline, and a bulbous nose. In the picture, he appeared to be wearing the requisite black leather vest over a black T-shirt. His profile revealed a large round belly.

I burned the picture into my memory and thanked Chastain for his help before leaving the Marion County Jail.

I now had a lead on Miles—or Pork Chop, depending on which name he preferred—and based on what I knew of him so far, I couldn't see him meshing very well with either Denton or Warren. Bringing him home would be a lot like letting a battle-worn alley cat go to work on two poodles.

I left the downtown area on my way to interview the lead I had on Miles, stopping at a local McDonald's on the way. It was a late lunch, and the double cheeseburger, fries, and Coke filled the void. Most of the normal lunchtime crowd had thinned out, leaving only a smattering of young mothers and their kids.

I watched as the young women clustered together and talked about their common issues while the kids climbed on the indoor playground equipment. The play area contained an indoor maze and an enclosure filled with multicolored plastic balls. Simple things that provided immense pleasure for toddlers.

I watched as they giggled and played, argued and made up, and dived headlong into the ball-filled arena. I wondered if Marian Collins had been like the mothers I was watching. I wondered if she had been filled with the same hopes for her son. And I marveled at how quickly a giggling toddler, easily satisfied with a Happy Meal and an hour at McDonalds, could grow up into someone who would mug old ladies.

As I finished lunch and tossed the wrappers and cup into the receptacle, I felt a sense of urgency. Berger was dying, and if he was Miles' father, could that mean Miles would have a chance at a better life? Could a man who had slid off the rails so far get back on the right path so late?

I left the restaurant and drove to the address the biker at the house had given us, a mechanic shop on the near north side. When I arrived, I saw a building that appeared to be an abandoned gas station but that was now being used to repair motorcycles, scooters, and mopeds. The pumps had been removed, and the holes that were left by their removal had been plugged with concrete retainers. Weeds were growing through large cracks in the asphalt lot, and the sign that had once advertised the price of gas was now gone. In its place was a handmade sign that had been painted to read, BIKER HAVEN—ALL BIKES—ALL THE TIME.

I pulled into the lot and parked near the front of the shop. As I got out, I immediately smelled oil, rubber, and exhaust fumes. From the garage, I heard the whirring sound of a pneumatic wrench.

I walked into the office and saw a tall counter pasted over with Harley-Davidson and Pennzoil stickers. A cash register and credit card scanner sat on top. Two chairs were off to my right, along with a heavily stained coffeepot and a stack of biker magazines. A wall phone was ringing, but no one was in the room to answer it.

I moved through the door that led from the office to the work area. A man that I guessed to be in his late twenties was hunched over a bike, using the pneumatic wrench to adjust a tire. A set of headphones over his ears and the wrench prevented him from hearing the phone.

I noticed an extension hanging on the wall of the garage, so I picked it up, walked over to the man, and tapped him on the shoulder with the receiver. The action startled him, and he jumped when he saw me. The wrench in his hand was still going full tilt. He shut the wrench down and pulled the earpieces away from his head, letting them slide down around his neck.

"Phone," I said, offering him the receiver.

He didn't say a word but kept his eyes on me as he stood and took the receiver.

"Ernie," he said, followed by a pause. "Yeah. I'm on it now. Almost done." He looked at a clock on the wall. The hands said it was almost two o'clock. "You can pick it up at four." Pause. "We take all credit cards." Pause. "Okay. We close at six." Pause. "See you then." He handed the phone back to me, and I walked over to the wall and hung it up.

"Who are you?" he asked.

"I'm looking for Pork Chop," I said.

"He ain't here."

"I can see that. Do you know where I can find him?"

"Nobody knows where you can find him."

"I was told you might."

"You were told wrong."

"I don't think so," I said.

He studied me for a minute. "I don't want no problems."

"You don't have any. At least not with me. I just want to talk to Pork Chop."

"Who are you?" he asked again.

"Colton Parker," I said.

"You a friend of the Chop's?"

"Yeah."

The man set the wrench down and moved toward the office area. "I gotta smoke," he said.

I followed him as we stepped from the office to the parking lot outside.

He lit up a cigarette and shook the match out before tossing it to the ground. "The Chop hasn't been around for days."

"He work here, or just hang out?"

Ernie took a long drag on the cigarette and exhaled. "He worked here once, for about a day. But the grind got to him."

"The grind? One day?"

Ernie smiled. Mostly to himself. "That ain't the kind of question a friend of the Chop would ask."

"I didn't say we were close friends."

He shook his head. "You ain't a friend at all. You a cop?"

"No."

He grinned. "Yeah, sure you ain't."

"If I were, wouldn't I admit it? I'm not out to arrest the guy. I just need to talk with him."

He took a few drags while he studied me. "That it?"

"That's it," I said.

After a few moments and a few more drags, he nodded. "Okay. You got a number?"

I gave him my cell and office numbers.

"I'll tell him," he said. "But I can't promise he'll call."

"Sure," I said. "But you can tell him this. If I don't hear from him, I'm going to keep looking."

The man shook his head and tossed the cigarette to the ground. "I don't think he cares about that," he said. "A lot of people are looking for the Chop. You'd be the least of his worries."

CHAPTER SEVEN

B etwixt and between," I said. "That's where I am. A rock and a hard place. Between the devil and the deep blue sea."

Mary shook her head. "If you don't go easy on that rosemary, your chicken is going to get up and walk out of the pan."

"Sorry," I said, sprinkling the spice onto the chicken. Mary had finished work early and was trying to teach me how to cook.

"You might want to ease up on the clichés too," she said. "Too much of a good thing ceases to be a good thing."

I flipped the chicken breasts over and shifted them around in the pan. "Too much rosemary?"

She shook her head. "No, but you were leaning that way. Think of spices like clichés. Too much spice will spoil the taste." She watched as I repositioned the chicken. "That's good," she said. "Let it brown evenly."

I turned down the heat.

"Berger wants you to find his son—"

"*If* he's his son," I said.

"*If* he's his son," she said, correcting herself. "But the other two boys don't want the guy found."

"Close. Denton, the older son, isn't all that keen about finding the guy, but he knows it's going to happen. He'd just rather throw a few bucks at the problem and move on." I opened the refrigerator and pulled the broccoli from the crisper. "What do I do with this?" I asked, closing the door.

"Cut off the stems and set them aside," she said, setting a pan of water over the burner. "When this heats up, we're going to dump the broccoli into the steamer and set it over the pan."

"Of course we are," I said. "Then what?"

"The baked potatoes should be done soon, and then we can pour the cheese over the broccoli just in time for Callie to come home from school." She smiled.

I pulled a knife from the block that I kept on the counter and began cutting the broccoli in a methodical sawing motion. Mary chuckled.

"Here, let me show you," she said, taking the knife. "Let the tip of the blade rest on the cutting board like this." She demonstrated. "Then all you have to do is feed the broccoli into the rear of the blade and chop." She displayed her technique.

"Just like Emeril," I said.

She smiled and handed me the knife. "Now you try."

I took the knife and chopped the broccoli as I had just been taught, although not as smoothly as Mary had done. "This should be the easiest money I've ever made," I said. "Find the guy, tell the old man where he is, and walk away."

"What if he doesn't want Hume to know where he is?"

"That's a possibility," I said. "I can't force him to meet his father."

"*If* he's the father."

"That's correct," I said. "But I did promise Berger I would find the guy. And I will keep my promise. Beyond that, there's little I can do. Which is one of the reasons this *isn't* the easiest money I've ever made."

"You can't make him come, so Hume may die without ever really knowing."

"Right. On the other hand, if he agrees to meet with Berger, I'll need to confirm him as Berger's son before I take him to meet his father."

She lifted the lid on the skillet, wrinkled her nose, and turned the chicken over again as she turned the heat down a little more. "Any leads?"

"I know that Marian Collins had a son. His name is Miles Poole, and he's a biker."

"Poole? She must have married." She inspected the pan of water. Satisfied with the temperature, she set the perforated steamer on top of the boiling water and dropped the broccoli into the pan. For good measure, she poked at the vegetables with a fork before adjusting the heat. "Do you know where to find him?"

"Maybe. I have an address that hasn't checked out, but I know the gang he tends to hang with, and I know where he works sometimes. I have one of his coworkers trying to get in touch with him as we speak."

"Watch the chicken," she said. "If it burns, the whole thing was for naught."

I smiled and watched as Mary kept check on the steaming broccoli. At thirty-five, Mary Christopher had the build and athleticism of a woman ten years younger. During my ten years with the FBI, all of them in the Indianapolis field office, I had gotten to know her as a dedicated law enforcement officer and as a friend. But the fact that she was also an attractive woman was not lost on me. I found myself being drawn to her more and more.

"Any idea who's writing the letters?" she asked, replacing the lid over the broccoli.

"No."

"Maybe someone is blackmailing Hume," she said.

"Wish I had thought of that," I said, flipping the chicken again.

"That's what I do—think of things like that for you." She smiled. Rachel Ray with a gun.

"I could probably think of things like that too if I set my mind to it. But it takes all my mental powers to stand erect and keep my knuckles from dragging the ground."

She opened the freezer side of the refrigerator. "Any ice cream?"

"I think there's a half gallon of vanilla," I said, putting a lid over the skillet.

She dug through the freezer and found the carton of ice cream. She opened it and wrinkled her nose. "You have about a teaspoon left," she said.

"Sorry. Why?"

She pulled a spoon from the drawer and ate what was left of the ice cream before tossing the carton into the trash. "I was thinking of dessert."

"I have some Pop-Tarts," I said.

She gave me one of those looks that show pity and disgust at the same time. "I'll go to the store." She grabbed the jacket she had draped over one of the kitchen chairs.

"Don't, Mary," I said. "We can live without dessert. Besides, you've done enough. If you want something, I'll get it."

"I don't mind going," she said.

"I know you don't. It's just that I owe you a lot. You've been great since Anna died, and I don't want to impose any more than I have." I turned to face her. "In fact, let me buy you dinner. Tomorrow night?"

A slight frown creased her face. "I can't, Colton." She dropped the jacket back onto the chair.

"Sure you can," I said. "It's the least I can do."

She shook her head. "No, I can't. I…have a date."

"A date?"

She nodded her head as she went back to forking the steaming broccoli.

"Oh," I said. "Well, another time then."

She nodded. "Sure, that'd be fine." She glanced at her watch and said, "When does Callie get home?"

Her last words were punctuated by the screeching of the school bus' brakes. "Right about now," I said.

Moments later we heard the front door open as Callie came into the house. Mary went into the living room to greet her.

I heard Callie return the greeting as the two of them caught up on events since their last conversation. Less than a month shy of her fifteenth birthday, Callie had developed a bond with Mary that was based largely on their common love of soccer. Their friendship was strengthened by what they lacked—Callie a mother, and Mary a child.

"Hey, babe," I said, coming into the living room and hugging her. "How was school?"

She ignored my question and asked, "When are we moving?"

I glanced at Mary. "Moving?"

"Yeah," Callie said.

"Honey, we're not moving."

Callie looked at Mary and then back to me with a look of confusion. "The house is for sale."

"For sale?" I asked.

"There's a sign out front," Callie said.

I went to the door and opened it. There was a For Sale sign in the front yard.

"See?" Callie said.

Mary joined me at the door. "Colton, that wasn't there when I got here."

"It must've just gone up," I said.

"Are we moving?" Callie asked again.

"I don't know, honey," I said. "I didn't know the place was for sale."

After Anna's death, Callie had gone through a rough time that culminated in a halfhearted attempt to harm herself by taking a handful of her grandmother's medicine. Although the doctors had described it as a "cry for help," neither they nor I could ignore the fact that it had happened. Anna's death had come on the heels of an argument with me. An argument that Callie felt had led to her mother's death. The result was a daughter who blamed her father for the situation in which she found herself. Now, this new change—the sale of the house—could mean another move and another school. Coming as close as it would on Anna's death, it would not make things any easier.

"I'll find out what's going on tomorrow." I closed the door. "How was school today?" I asked, changing the subject.

"The same."

"Homework?"

"A little."

"Guess what?" Mary asked.

Callie arched an eyebrow.

"Your dad has fixed dinner."

Callie's countenance fell. "Eggs?"

Eggs were one of the few things that I could cook. Scrambled, over easy, fried, or hard-boiled, if it came out of a chicken, I was a culinary artist second to none.

"Rosemary chicken, broccoli with cheese, and baked potato," Mary said.

Callie glanced at me and then looked at Mary. "You helped, right?"

Mary put an arm around her. "Would I throw you to the wolves?"

CHAPTER
EIGHT

Part of the trouble with lifting weights in your basement, as opposed to a real gym, is the lack of fresh air. So by the time I had gotten Callie off to school and finished lifting, a three-mile run in the crisp September air was a welcome relief.

I left the house and shot across the street toward Garfield Park, entering the park from the north side, near the fire station.

The park was a long-standing Indianapolis fixture that had been allowed to spiral into decay before being rescued by a significant renovation. The park's makeover had its intended effect. Instead of remaining an attraction for drug dealers and other ne'er-do-wells, it became the focal point of one of the city's older communities. The rehab of Garfield Park sparked a renovation of many of the area's homes and businesses, and the subsequent result was a sense of community pride that had been missing for a long time.

As I began my usual trek, the traffic around the park was light, and the park itself was empty, which left the whole place to me. One of the many benefits of an early morning run.

I worked my way across the grounds, around the bandstand, past the pool, and then back up along the south side. The run was nearly effortless. Years of exercise, essential for my line of work, had kept me in the condition of a younger man. I wasn't sure if the effort was going to extend my life on earth, but it would sure make me feel better while I was here. But the workouts had other benefits too. Benefits that were outside the cardiopulmonary area. Running allowed time to think. And that morning, I was allowing my mind time to ruminate over the case I had been hired to investigate. So far I had a lot of speculation but few facts.

I suspected that someone was trying to blackmail Hume. If so, the plan had backfired. Far from being ashamed or reluctant to face a man who may be his son, Hume was eager. In fact, he had made it clear that his shame had been in *not* knowing about the child. But that could also provide leverage for the letter writer, assuming his motive wasn't blackmail but something more permanent. Like a role in the family business.

All of this left me with the question of where the writer would go next. And for that matter, who was the writer? Or did it matter? And what about Hume's other sons? How much trouble would Miles bring into their lives? Or Berger's? Or did any of that matter? After all, I was hired to find Miles and tell him about his father. I hadn't been hired to roll him and his brothers into one big happy family.

On its face, the case seemed easy enough. But things are rarely as they appear. There were hidden undercurrents. The kind that can quickly become too strong to manage and can pull under even the most adept. Which, of course, I prided myself in being.

I finished my run through the park and was on my way back to the house when I noticed an unmarked squad car parked at the curb. As I approached the car, detective David Chang of the Indiana State Police stepped out. He was not alone. Another man, taller than Chang and dressed in a dark suit, got out on the passenger side.

"Why is it," I said, approaching the pair, "that you can always spot squad cars? Marked or unmarked, they stand out like clowns at a state funeral."

"We need to talk," Chang said.

I didn't know Chang all that well. In fact, I didn't really know him at all. We had butted heads alongside US 41 in Terre Haute on one occasion, and the meeting had left me with the impression that we weren't going to be swapping recipes anytime soon. The other man didn't look like he had spent much time in the kitchen either.

"I'm flattered," I said, continuing to run in place. "A busy lawman like yourself, taking the time to talk with someone like me. And bringing your friends along too."

Chang leaned against the car and folded his arms across his chest. A thin yet perceptible smile crossed his face. "This is Simon DeGraff."

The man nodded.

"We have a bit of a problem," Chang said. "Or rather, you have a bit of a problem."

"You could've called. You didn't have to come all the way out here to tell me," I said. "Don't think I don't appreciate it, though."

"I've been appointed by the superintendent of the state police to the Private Detective Licensing Board." He paused for a reaction. I didn't have one to give him.

"DeGraff," Chang said, nodding to the other man, "is a private detective, appointed to the board as well. It seems that there has been a bit of a discrepancy on your application."

"What discrepancy?" I asked, halting my stationary jog.

Chang smiled. "It would appear that when you applied for your license, you falsified your application."

I glanced at DeGraff, who stood motionless. "Are you for real?"

Chang looked at DeGraff. "Are we?"

"Absolutely," DeGraff replied.

Chang pulled a folded photocopy of my license application from inside his jacket. "Here," he said, flipping to the second page of the document. "Under employment history, you list the FBI under the 'current employment' section."

"Yeah. So?"

"So," Chang said, "you weren't employed by the FBI at the time of your application."

Technically, he was correct. I had been fired, but I had mentioned that on my application. "I may have placed the information on the wrong line, but I explained my position farther down."

Chang nodded thoughtfully. "Yes, I see your point," he said, in mock concern. "But I must tell you that Mr. DeGraff and I, as representatives of the licensing board, cannot allow errors like this to slip past. We'll hold your license until a formal hearing has been arranged. At that time, if you can show just cause why we should reinstate your license, you'll be reinstated."

I looked at DeGraff and then back to Chang. "You've got to be kidding."

Chang turned to the man and said, "Are we kidding?"

"Most certainly not," DeGraff said.

Chang handed me a copy of the court order requiring me to turn in my license. Then he held out his hand. "We're not kidding. Your license card, please."

I pulled the card from my billfold and handed it to Chang. "And when is my hearing?" I asked.

He looked at DeGraff. "Any idea?"

DeGraff shrugged. "Eight weeks. Maybe ten."

Chang slid my ID card into his pocket. "Let me point out that we are acting under IC 25-30. If you conduct business without a license, you will be prosecuted. Understood?"

"Sure," I said, feeling the heat beginning to rise. "Now you need to understand this. I don't know why you two are playing games, but I'll find out. And when I show at that hearing, I won't come alone."

Chang smiled but didn't say a word as he and DeGraff slid into the unmarked car and drove away. I stood on the curb and watched helplessly as the license that allowed me to do my work drove away with them.

Without a license, I had no job. Yet I had work. But accepting payment for it was now illegal. Which meant that I would be committing a crime, since I had no intention of rolling over for either Chang or DeGraff.

I moved up the steps toward my house, intent on handling this threat the same way I would handle any other. I would ignore it for the time being.

CHAPTER NINE

I was showered and in the office by ten with my feet on the desk and a chocolate long john from Long's Bakery in my hand. Marian Collins'—or rather Marian Poole's—obituary was in my lap.

> Marian Poole, age 64, passed away on Tuesday after a long illness. A dedicated wife and mother, she was employed as comptroller of the Easton Corporation for nearly forty years, retiring to enjoy her garden and traveling.
>
> Her son, Miles, survives her.
>
> Arrangements are pending.

There was no picture of Marian, but the obituary mentioned Miles. Then again, Poole wasn't Berger's name. And since Berger didn't believe Marian when she told him she was pregnant, he probably didn't give Miles a second thought. Not until the letters began to arrive.

I tossed the obituary onto the desk, took a healthy bite of the donut, and reached for the letters.

I examined them before reading and found that they had several things in common.

Both of them were handwritten on quality stationery. Both were postmarked in Indianapolis, both were stamped instead of metered, and both were unsigned.

I read the first letter.

47

Mr. Hume,

You have a son. His name is Miles Poole. He was born to
the late Marian Collins.

I read the second letter.

Mr. Hume,

Why the delay, Mr. Hume? Your son has the right to know
his father. When will you do the right thing?

Where there is a crime, there is a motive—however weak it may
be. And blackmail, being one of the oldest and most dependable of
all motives, certainly seemed to be hinted at in the letters. If so, the
writer was in for a big disappointment.

I tossed the letters onto the desk and finished the long john.

If someone wanted to blackmail Berger Hume, why do it now?
The man was within weeks of dying. He had more important things
on his plate than a black mark on his reputation. Why not strike
when he was more likely to care?

I tossed the empty donut bag into the wastebasket and reread
the letters.

But if blackmail wasn't the motive, what was? Concern for the
child of Berger and Marian? And if that was the reason, when did
the writer discover the existence of a child? And how? And why the
concern? And why not just tell Miles who his father was instead of
playing cat and mouse with Berger?

My mind was starting down the same trek it had begun during
my run in the park when the phone rang.

"Parker?" a nasal-sounding voice asked.

"You've got him."

"You looking for me?"

"Depends," I said. "Are you Miles Poole or Mr. Goodbar?"

"What do you want?"

"To talk," I said.

"How'd you know my name?"

"I saw the movie," I said. "I've always liked Diane Keaton. She's—"

"How do you know my name?" he asked again, more sternly this time.

"I was having a hard time picturing Pork Chop on a birth certificate," I said.

"If you want to talk with me, you better cut the jokes."

"We'll talk, Poole. Now or later, but we'll talk."

"Who sent you?"

"I can't tell you that until we talk."

There was a brief silence on the other end before he said, "What do you want to talk about?"

I didn't want to have the conversation on the phone. Since I had no way to tell if it was actually Miles I was talking to, I didn't want to tip my hand to someone who may have unrighteous motives for finding out why I would want to talk with him. "I'll tell you when we meet," I said.

There was a long pause. I strained for background noise but heard nothing.

"Who're you working for?"

"You've already asked me that. The answer hasn't changed."

Another pause.

"I can meet you tonight. Eight o'clock," the voice said.

Eight o'clock wasn't good. Callie would be home alone, and although she was almost fifteen, I was reluctant to leave her without supervision, given her past events.

"How about now?"

Another pause. "No, I don't think so. It's tonight or never."

"Not never," I said. "I will find you. Be a lot easier for both of us, though, if we could meet now."

"Nope. Tonight at eight."

"Look," I said, "I—"

"Eight or forget it. Behind the old Eagle Glen strip mall. Know it?"

"I know it," I said.

"Be there at eight in the alley between the stores," he said before hanging up.

CHAPTER TEN

After a dinner of precooked frozen lasagna, I put the dishes away and went into Callie's room. She was sprawled on the bed with her schoolbooks and notepaper spread before her and a phone in her hand. She paused from her conversation and placed a hand over the receiver's mouthpiece when I entered.

"I have to go somewhere for a while," I said.

"Okay."

"You going to be all right?" I asked.

"Yeah. I'll be fine."

"I called Grandma and Grandpa to see if they could come over, but they said they couldn't make it. Something about—"

"Dad, I'm okay. I'll be fine."

I was skeptical, but I didn't want it to show.

"Really," she said. "I'll be fine."

"Okay," I said, relenting. "But I'll have my cell on if you need something. And—"

"Mrs. Rengel is next door too," she said.

"Who?"

"Rengel. She's the lady who moved in next door a couple days ago."

We lived in half of a rented duplex. Next door meant on the other side of the wall.

"Oh, right," I said. "I haven't had a chance to meet her yet."

"I'll be fine. If I need to, I can go next door."

It was getting late, and if I missed my meeting with Poole, it might be days again before I could get a handle on locating him.

"Okay," I said as I was leaving. "But I want you to lock the door behind me when I leave. And don't stay up too late. Tomorrow is a school day."

I left her room to head for the front door. She followed me, and I turned to kiss her before leaving.

"I'll be fine," she repeated as she closed the door and turned the dead bolt behind me.

Ten minutes later, I was heading north on US 31, keeping time with jazz musician Benny Carter. *Ahead of his time,* I thought as I floated along.

Carter had been prominent in jazz for eight decades, beginning his professional career in the 1920s and finishing in the 1990s. Through it all, he had been a soloist, an arranger, and a big-band leader. Known mostly for his skill with a saxophone, he was also an accomplished trumpeter and clarinetist. Although I had enough trouble playing a radio, I knew good jazz when I heard it, and hearing it didn't get any better than Benny Carter.

The music lightened the trip, and before long I was pulling into the Eagle Glen strip mall, a concrete and asphalt version of an old west ghost town. The only things missing were the tumbleweeds.

The mall's anchor store had pulled out a number of years ago, leaving the smaller stores to fend for themselves. They couldn't, so the whole thing went belly up. The buildings remained, but the businesses that had given them life did not. Like corpses, the structures stood muted against time as time began to claim its due and dissolve them to ashes and dust.

I pulled around to the back of the mall and into an alley between two rows of stores. Except for a dumpster that had long since been abandoned, the alley was bare and dark. The two street lamps that stood at each end had long ago been extinguished. The only available light came from the full moon, which cast an unearthly glow on the dead asphalt artery.

I rolled the window down as I eased into the alley, straining to hear anything that might indicate I wasn't alone. But all was quiet except for the sound of my tires against the pavement.

I stopped about a third of the way into the alley and killed the engine. As I waited, I checked the Ruger to be sure I had a round chambered. I did.

Fifteen years of law enforcement, almost a third of it spent in dark alleys like this one, had given me a sixth sense. An ability to recognize the uncomfortable feeling that nearly always conveyed a sense of impending danger. It wasn't a feeling I took lightly.

I sat in the alley for almost ten minutes and was about to start the car and drive away when I saw a figure emerge from behind the dumpster seventy feet ahead. The narrow swath of light cast by the moon was insufficient to illuminate the end of the alley from which the figure was approaching. All I could see was a dark silhouette and the glowing embers of a cigarette.

"Parker?" a voice called.

I pulled the Ruger from its position under my left arm and slid it into the right hand pocket of my jacket. I kept my hand on the gun as I got out of the car.

"Poole?"

The figure flicked the cigarette to the ground and crushed it underfoot. The trail of glowing ash resembled a firefly in summer after it has met a similar fate.

I moved to the left-front of my car. "I need to—"

My words were cut off by a sudden flash, the blast of a large-bore handgun, and the sound of a breaking headlight.

I ducked in time to avoid being hit by the second shot, which slammed into the fender, rocking the Escort.

I spun to my left as a third shot careened off the pavement where

I had been standing only a few seconds before and whined off into the distance.

I rolled back toward the car on my right, sliding under it as I pulled the Ruger from my pocket.

A fourth shot rang out, slamming into the grill of my car. The Escort shuddered as the radiator began to spew antifreeze with all the force of Old Faithful.

I slid out from under the car on the right side just as another shot hit the car again. I was able to get off a shot of my own. It went wild but was enough to force the figure back behind the dumpster.

I scrambled to my feet and moved around to the rear of the car, firing in the direction of the dumpster as I did.

I saw another flash from the opposite end of the alley and felt the car rock again as another bullet struck the grill of my car. That was six shots. Assuming from the blast that he was using a Magnum, he would now be reloading. But if he was experienced with a handgun—and if he had a speed loader—he could reload in less than three seconds. Not enough time to rush him, but enough to shed some light on the subject.

I emerged from behind the rear of my car, firing toward the area of the dumpster. The nine millimeter does not have the stopping power of a Magnum. And I only had one magazine with me, so I didn't have the ammo to continue this type of fight. But I did have one headlight left, and it could help even the score.

I kept firing as I went around the driver's side of the car and turned on the headlight. The shooter's end of the alley was suddenly awash in blessed light.

Another shot rang out from behind the dumpster and struck the car in the grill again. He was trying to put out the other light, but from his position behind the dumpster he couldn't hit the right headlight without exposing himself.

I hustled back to the protection of the rear of the car and returned fire. My shot rang off the dumpster, spewing a few sparks but doing little damage otherwise.

During my training with the Chicago PD, and later with the FBI at Quantico, I had learned that when engaged in a firefight at night, shooting instinctively when possible is most effective. Aiming a gun in the dark will cause the shooter to experience temporary blindness from the muzzle flash. I was glad to have had the training. It kept me from sighting the gun and helped me to react without having to think. It was probably one reason I was still alive.

I held my fire and kept a watch for the figure to either return fire or emerge. But as I waited, I suddenly realized the alley was quiet.

A brisk breeze began whipping up, stirring a cloud of dust and dirt. I wiped the debris from my eyes with the back of my left hand as I kept the Ruger trained on the dumpster with my right. Tired of waiting, I fired again in an attempt to draw him out. It didn't work.

I could feel the pounding of my heart as I eased from behind the relative safety of the car and began to move toward the dumpster. I inched my way forward until I was within ten feet of the shooter's hiding spot. The dumpster sat squat on the ground, so I couldn't approach him from underneath. It sat against the building to my right, so I was going to have to come around the left side, using the same approach he was going to have to use to hit my right headlight. The approach was as dangerous for me as it had been difficult for him.

I could climb over the top, but that wouldn't go unnoticed. Besides, I would have to tuck my gun into its holster or my pocket in order to use both hands to hoist myself up. That would guarantee a clear shot for him and a really bad evening for me.

"I just want to ask a few questions," I said.

Nothing.

"Toss the gun out. Toss it out and let's talk."

Nothing.

My palms were beginning to sweat, making it difficult to hold the gun. I wiped my left hand on my left pant leg and then switched the gun from my right hand to my left. I crept to the left corner of the dumpster and paused to listen. I heard nothing.

Taking a deep breath, I held it as I charged around, leveling the Ruger with both hands.

The shooter was gone. Except for a few spent shell casings on the pavement and my bleeding radiator, there was no evidence he had ever been in the alley.

I knelt to pick up some of the brass and stood to examine it in the light. He had been using super velocity .357 Magnum load and had reloaded behind the dumpster, ejecting the spent casings when he did.

"This explains a lot," I said, recalling the fierce impact of the shots that had struck my car.

I dropped the spent casing and eased out of the alley from the direction the shooter had entered.

Except for the vacant parking lot and the abandoned businesses surrounding it, there was nothing.

I jammed the Ruger into its holster and went back to my car.

CHAPTER ELEVEN

I paid two fees to the tow-truck driver. The first was to drop the car in the alley behind my house so I could get Callie off to school the next morning without her noticing that the Escort had more holes in it than a window screen in downtown Baghdad. The second was to keep the driver quiet about the condition of the car.

After arriving home, I draped the vehicle in a bedsheet and anchored it with duct tape. One nosey neighbor, or one squad car driving by and seeing my shot-up car, could create more of a stir than I needed.

The next morning, after seeing Callie off to school, I called a cab. Thirty minutes later, I was talking with Larry Lemmings.

"It's only got a hundred and ninety thousand on it, Colton," Larry said.

"Gee," I said, "it's practically still new."

"It's got new brakes, new tires, a new alternator, and a new battery." He lit a cigarette and blew the smoke upward. Larry Lemmings had been the proprietor of Dashing Auto (DASH IN—DASH OUT. NO CREDIT? NO PROBLEM.) for more than a decade. I had bought the Escort from him after selling my other car to help finance the new business. And the car had actually run quite well—until Poole pumped it full of lead. Getting the Escort fixed—and avoiding the questions that would inevitably come as a result—was going to cost me more than the car was worth.

"Great," I said.

"The air works fine, the heater gets hot, and the windows are power."

"Sure. But do they go up and down?"

He tried to look hurt. "Of course. What do you take me for?"

"What's the downside?"

He hesitated as he flipped some ash to ground and then said, "The previous owner's girlfriend ran it into a concrete retaining wall at the county jail when she was going to visit her old man."

"How bad?"

"A dent in the right front fender about the size of a small plate." He moved aside so that I could see the damage.

"And?"

"And some paint missing over the dent. See?" He moved farther away to give me a broader view of the car.

"Nothing else?"

"And it tends to run on a bit."

"Anything else?" I asked.

"No."

"Lights work?"

"Sure."

I opened the driver-side door. It creaked, but inside, the upholstery looked clean and appeared to be in good shape.

"How much?"

"For you? Say...a thousand?"

"How about seven hundred," I said.

He grinned as he inhaled on the cigarette and blew the smoke out the corner of his mouth. "I'm going to have to have eight."

"Seven-fifty," I said.

He smiled and nodded. "Okay. Sold. When do you want it?"

"Now."

"Follow me."

I followed him into a small trailer that sat on the lot. After another twenty minutes of completing the paperwork, I said, "I have another car that I need to unload."

He filed our papers into a cabinet behind his desk. "Trade?"

"No. I just need to get rid of it."

"Why? What's wrong with it?" The end of the burning cigarette dangled in time to his moving lips.

"It's shot," I said.

"Can't drive it?"

"Not as is."

He leaned back in his chair with his hands crossed behind his head. "I can give you fifty bucks for it."

"You charged me five hundred for it a year ago," I said.

"A year ago it was still running."

I sighed. "It'll need a tow."

He nodded. "No problem. I'll tow it for free."

The sum of the parts was greater than the whole. Larry would place the car in a salvage yard and sell off the parts for an amount that was many times greater than the fifty bucks he was giving me. But I needed to get the car off of the street before anyone saw it. When I considered that, plus fifty dollars and a free tow, I knew he had a deal. He knew it too.

"Sign here," he said, smiling as he crushed the cigarette into an ashtray.

CHAPTER
TWELVE

I was back at Biker Haven by noon. This time, Ernie was working on a bike frame. He had a welding torch going and was wearing a welder's mask.

I pulled the Ruger from its holster and tapped Ernie on the helmet. He stopped welding, flipped the visor back, and stood up.

I put the barrel of the gun under his chin.

"What do you want?" he asked, rolling his eyes to the gun.

"How's it feel?" I asked, keeping the gun pressed against him as I walked him backward and deeper into the garage.

"How's what feel, man?"

"Having someone put a gun in your face. How does it feel?"

His head was tilted back, but his eyes were focused on the gun. "What're you talking about?"

I pushed harder on the gun. "I'm talking about how you set me up. About how Pork Chop tried to ambush me."

"I didn't set you up, man. I just—"

"Save it," I said. "I'm not interested in lies. I want to know where to find Poole."

"He told me he'd kill me if I talked to you."

"I'll kill you if you don't."

He licked his lips and rolled his eyes again toward the gun. "I need to smoke."

I shoved him back with my free hand while I lowered the gun with the other. "Go ahead," I said. "But if your hand comes out of that jacket with anything other than a cigarette..."

"No way. Okay? I just want to smoke." He pulled a pack of cigarettes from inside his denim jacket and a book of matches from his pocket. He shook the pack into his hand, extracted a cigarette, and slid it between his lips. His hand trembled as he slid the pack back into his jacket.

"Thanks," he said, blowing smoke through his nostrils as he dropped a spent match to the floor.

"Where do I find Poole?"

"I don't know, man. I really don't. He never stays in the same place more than a few days."

"How do you find him?"

"He has a number. I call it and he checks for messages. Sometimes he gets back with me, sometimes he don't."

"A number? You mean like an answering service?"

He brought the cigarette to his mouth in a trembling hand and inhaled deeply. "No, man. It's a...pager. One of them kind that shows the message." As he spoke, smoke billowed from his nostrils. "He likes to keep low."

"Call him."

He shook his head. "He don't want to talk with you."

"I want to talk to him," I said.

He inhaled again and then pulled the cigarette from his mouth with one hand as he exhaled. "What if he don't call back? Sometimes he just doesn't." Ernie was growing increasingly nervous.

"You'll have to convince him."

He worked the cigarette faster.

"Why does he give you his number?"

"'Cause he don't stay in one place. He gets his mail here. If he gets something important, I call him. Sometimes he checks to see if something came in."

"Call him. Tell him you've heard from Ed McMahon. Tell him anything. Just find out where he is."

Ernie was nervous. He kept bouncing on one foot as he puffed on the cigarette in a rapid, inhale-exhale sequence. "He'll know you got the address from me."

"Maybe, since you're the one he used to ambush me."

He continued bouncing as he smoked and thought over the possibilities. "You're not as bad as him. I can maybe take my chances with you."

"You'll lose," I said.

He was thinking. Whoever Poole was, he had Ernie scared. I decided to take a different tack.

"I won't kill you," I said. "But when I find Poole, I'll tell him how I found him. I'll tell him you handed him over to save your own skin. That is," I said, "if I have to find him without your help."

His eyes were pleading and filled with despair.

"On the other hand," I said, "if you help me, I'll never mention your name."

There was a momentary flicker in his eyes, before he glanced outward toward the street. He continued to work the cigarette like it was his last. "Okay. Okay, I'll help you find him."

"There we go," I said, sliding the Ruger back into its holster. "See? We can work together after all."

He shook his head. "We're not working together. I'm just going to tell you where he is. Okay?"

"Sure," I said.

"And you'll keep it secret. Right?"

"Cross my heart," I said.

CHAPTER THIRTEEN

I left Biker Haven and was heading back to the south side of town when my phone rang. It was Mary.

"What's up?" I asked.

"Does something have to be up?"

"Something usually is."

"Well, not today. Things are quiet around here. Want to have lunch?"

I glanced at my watch. It was twelve thirty. "Sure. Where?"

"How about Steak 'n Shake? Downtown."

I was passing through the downtown area on my way to my office on the near south side. "Sure. I can be there in about five minutes."

"Great," she said. "I'll see you then."

I was sitting at a booth when Mary walked in smiling and with a bounce in her step.

"You're looking radiant," I said.

"Yes I am, aren't I?" She slid into the booth. "Have you ordered?"

"Not yet," I said.

She pulled a menu from the rack on the table. "I think I'm going to have a salad."

"Wow," I said. "Really going out there on a limb, huh?"

"I've got to watch my figure."

"Everybody watches your figure," I said.

She smiled. "What are you having?"

"Double steakburger."

She wrinkled her nose. "Seems like you're the one who's going out on a limb now."

The server, a young woman whose name tag said Tiffany, approached the table and took our orders. Within a minute, she was back with two drinks. She set them on the table, along with a couple of straws, before moving away.

"How did your date go?" I asked.

She smiled. "Great."

"Anyone I know?"

"Steve Flynn. Know him?"

Steven Flynn was a Secret Service agent with the Indianapolis office. About the same age as Mary and me, he had served on White House detail before coming to Indianapolis. The Service, as its members liked to refer to it, had been charged by Congress with a much wider expansion of duties than most people realized. Protection of government officials was the most visible of their tasks, but others such as the investigation of counterfeiting, credit card fraud, and other treasury issues, were equally important. Steve was a good agent and a decent man.

"Sure," I said. "We've worked out together a few times."

She smiled. "That's him," she said.

"Going out again?"

"Tonight."

Before I could respond, Tiffany brought our food. "Is there anything else I can get for you?" she asked.

We told her no, and she told us to enjoy.

"Are you okay?" Mary asked.

I had been reaching for the ketchup bottle and stopped mid-reach. "Okay?"

She nodded. "You know, with Steve."

"Why wouldn't I be? I'm not seeing him."

"But I am," she said. "Are you okay with that?"

"Am I okay with that?" I asked, opening the ketchup bottle. She nodded.

"Why wouldn't I be?" I asked again.

"Well…I don't know. I just…"

I was shaking the bottle, but nothing was coming out.

"Why don't you try tapping it?" she asked.

I began thumping on the bottle.

Mary smiled. "You don't have to beat it to death. Just tap it a little."

I continued to smack the bottom of the overturned ketchup bottle. "So where are you and Steve going tonight?"

She had just forked some salad out of the bowl but paused to say, "I don't know. We went to dinner the other night. I don't know what he's got planned. Dinner, I guess. After that, I—"

I cursed. "This stuff just isn't going to move." I began beating on the side of the bottle. "He sounds like a real thoughtful guy," I said.

"Here," she said, taking the bottle from me. "You're beginning to attract a crowd."

I looked around and noticed that several patrons were staring at us.

Mary stuck a knife into the bottle, tapped it, and the ketchup began to ooze.

"There," she said, handing the bottle back to me. "All better now."

All better now, I thought as I soaked the fries in ketchup. Mary had another date. Good for her.

CHAPTER
FOURTEEN

After lunch, I drove to the south side. The address Ernie had given me was on a street off of Troy, just east of the US 31–Madison Avenue split.

I worked my way through the maze of perpetual construction that had seemed to exist at the intersection since the beginning of time, and turned east from Madison onto Troy. I drove about an eighth of a mile before turning north. The street I was looking for was just ahead.

I turned east onto Milner and began looking for the address. It wasn't hard to spot. A Harley chopper was parked in front. The frame had been dramatically extended, and the handlebars rose high above their original design. The gas tank had been painted in a "tongues of fire" motif.

I parked in front of the house.

The neighborhood was quiet and consisted of older, well-maintained homes. The city's garbage strike, though, had not added to the area's image as bags of rotting refuse lined the streets.

I pulled the Ruger from its holster, ejected the magazine, and pulled back on the slide. The chamber was empty. Replacing the magazine into the butt of the gun, I pulled the slide again, feeding a round into the chamber before flipping the de-cocking lever, allowing the hammer to drop harmlessly back into place. I holstered the gun and got out of the car. Since Miles had seen me at night under partial light, I wasn't sure he would recognize me in broad daylight. But I wasn't going to take a chance.

The air had gotten decidedly chillier since I had left Mary, and a brisk wind rustled the leaves overhead. Some of them had begun to change color, but most were still green and still on the trees.

The sidewalk that led from the street to the house was cracked and uneven, but for the most part, the house itself appeared to be as well maintained as those around it. When I reached the front step, I knocked on the aluminum frame of the screen door and took a couple of steps back off the stoop to allow the door to swing open. It didn't.

I knocked again.

Nothing.

I opened the screen door and knocked hard on the front door.

Nothing.

"They're not home."

I turned to see an elderly man dressed in a plaid flannel shirt and jeans. He was holding a rake and standing in the yard next door.

"Do you know where they are?" I asked.

"You the law?"

"No."

"Too bad."

"Why's that?" I asked, closing the screen door as I stepped off the stoop.

The man shrugged and lowered his eyes.

"I'm not a friend of theirs," I said. "I don't mean them any harm, but I'm not a friend. What you tell me, stays with me."

The man had a hard time making eye contact. He seemed to be holding the rake more for protection than for raking the few leaves that had fallen.

"I don't know much about them," he said. "I just know they're no good, that's all."

"Sounds like you know them about as well as I do," I said.

The man nodded as he began to lean on the rake. "Party all the time. Drinking, loud music, and them motorcycles," he nodded toward the one parked out front. "They're a rough bunch."

"Have they ever given you any problems?" I asked.

The old man lowered his eyes again and began pushing a couple of leaves around with the rake. "I'm an old man," he said. "I'm not as strong as I used to be."

"Happens to all of us eventually," I said.

He nodded. "I used to be. Strong, that is. I used to work the coal mines before I retired and moved up here."

"Up here?"

"I'm from Kentucky," he said.

"You have family up here?" I asked.

He nodded. "Yeah. But I don't see them much anymore. Adele died a few years back, and the boys are working a lot. Don't have a lot of time for their old man," he said. "But I guess I can't blame them. I worked a lot too. Man's got to take care of his family. You only have so many money-making years."

"Sure," I said. He needed to talk, and I needed to find Poole. Our meeting could be mutually beneficial.

"Sometimes, I just get scared. You know?" he said.

"We all do," I said. "It's one of the things that makes us human."

"A man that doesn't get scared," he said, "isn't normal."

I agreed.

"I asked them to turn it down once. The music, I mean. You know?"

"I know," I said.

"They shoved me off the steps. There were three of them. Big guys." He lowered his eyes to the ground again and began to shuffle a couple of leaves around with the rake. "I couldn't do anything. Just had to take it."

"There's not much you can do with three of them," I said.

He nodded. "I know. But I just got scared. You know?"

"Sure."

"What's a man to do?"

"Let others help," I said.

He didn't say anything as he continued to play with the leaves.

"Any idea where I can find them?" I asked.

He shook his head.

"Can you call me when they come home?"

He quit raking and began leaning on it again, using both hands. He seemed to have a need to think about whether or not it would be wise to help me. I offered him a card.

"You can call me," I said. "He won't know."

The old man took the card and tucked it into his shirt pocket. "Be careful," he said. "They're a rough bunch."

I know, I thought as I walked back to my car. *But this time, they'll be dealing with someone who'll shove back.*

CHAPTER FIFTEEN

I arrived home a few minutes before Callie and discovered a disheveled, middle-aged woman sitting on the steps that led to my side of the duplex. She stood as I parked at the curb and seemed genuinely angry as I came up the short walk.

"Are you Callie's dad?"

"I am."

She stuck out a pudgy hand. "Hi. I'm Pat Rengel." Pat was short and round but not fat. She wore a denim jacket, jeans, and house shoes. Her hair was orange and pinned back on top of her head. There was a ring on every finger.

I shook her hand. "Colton Parker."

"What are you and Callie going to do?"

"About what?"

"About the house." She slid both hands into the pockets of her jacket. "I just moved here, and I'm mad. I admit it. Just fuming mad."

I took a step back and looked at the house, giving it the once-over. I gave a quick glance at the roof, the siding, and the gutters. Everything seemed to be intact. "What about it?"

"What about it?" she asked, with a tone of unbelief. "You mean, you don't know?"

"I guess not."

"Burkett is selling the place. Moving to Florida."

Carl Burkett was my landlord. An elderly man whose wife had passed away a couple of years before Anna, he kept a few rental properties to supplement his pension and social security. He had spoken often of his daughter who lived in Florida, and apparently he decided to move and be with her. His decision to sell had apparently caught Rengel as off guard as it had me.

"Oh sure," I said. "Callie told me about that the other night. He must've put the sign up after I came home."

"You don't care?"

"Sure. But I guess he has a right to sell his property."

"But what're we going to do?" she asked. "Where're we going to go?"

I started to tell her that there wasn't a *we* in this, but I didn't want to inflame her any more than Burkett's decision already had.

"Why don't you call him?"

"I did," she said. "About an hour ago."

"Did he mention if he had any lookers?"

"Not yet, but he will. What're we going to do?" she asked again.

"Move. Or stay. Depends on what the new owner wants to do with it, I guess."

"That's it?"

I nodded. "Yeah, pretty much. Listen, it's getting kind of chilly out here. Want some coffee?"

She turned to look at the house again and then looked at her watch. "Sure," she said. "But I gotta go talk to Burkett. He said he wouldn't be home until five."

"Didn't you just talk to him?"

"On the phone. But I need to give him a piece of my mind—in person."

I motioned for her to follow me.

We went into the kitchen where I put on a half pot. We sat while the coffee brewed.

"Where you from?" I asked.

"Encino," she said.

"What brings you this way? Indy's a long way from California."

"My ex used to live out here. When we first got married we lived here for a while, but things didn't work out so I moved back to Encino. Then I find out my daughter is pregnant, so I moved back here to be with her." She shook her head. "Her old man is no better than mine. Soon as he found out she was pregnant, he ran. Just up and left."

"Happens," I said.

She shook her head again. "It shouldn't have happened to her. She should've learned from my mistakes."

We made more small talk for a few minutes, and when the coffee was done, I stood to get two cups from the mug tree on the counter.

"Just black," she said before I had a chance to ask.

I poured two cups of "just black" and offered her one.

"You're going to talk to Carl this evening?" I asked.

She nodded as she drank the coffee.

The information my neighbor had given me did not hit me as hard as it would have just a couple of days before. In fact, it could provide an opportunity.

"You know, you may be able to stay," I said. "Just because he's selling it doesn't mean he's tearing it down."

"Yeah," she said. "That's true."

"Why don't you talk to him first and see what he has to say?"

"Yeah, I could do that," she said. "Probably would be the smart thing."

"Probably," I shifted slightly in my seat. "I don't mean to pry, but how much are you paying in rent?"

She told me. It was the same as I was paying. A plan was beginning to form.

She glanced at her watch. "Sorry Parker, but I have to go. I told

Burkett I'd come by, and he should be home by now." She stood, downing the last of the coffee.

"Sure," I said. "It was nice to meet you."

Callie and Rengel passed like two moles in the ground. As soon as Callie came into the house, she grabbed the phone and headed for her room. I followed her.

"I have something to tell you," I said before she could call whoever she was going to call.

"What?" She was already sprawled across the bed with the phone in hand. Her book bag was sitting on the floor.

I sat on the edge of the bed next to her. "I met Mrs. Rengel today, and she's upset about the sale of the house."

"Are we going to move?" There was angst in her face.

"Maybe not. I was thinking about trying to buy the house."

A flash of relief. "Buy the house?"

"Sure."

"With what?"

Callie knew of our precarious financial position. Our lifestyle had made it clear to her even if I hadn't.

"I got a client who paid me a large fee. I think we might have enough to make a down payment on the house."

She shifted on the bed as she paused to think. "Did you call Mr. Burkett?"

"Not yet. I wanted to talk with you first. I wanted to see if you still want to live here or if you want to move somewhere else."

"Where else could we move?"

"We probably couldn't afford to move back to where we lived before Mom died, but we could find another house."

"Would I go to the same school?"

"Yes. We could stay in this area."

"Then it's okay. Wherever we live is okay if I can still go to the same school."

It was a reasonable request.

"I'm going to call Mr. Burkett and see what he's asking," I said. "If we can afford it, I'm going to make him an offer."

She nodded. "Okay."

I stood to leave her room.

"Dad?"

"Yes?"

"How will we pay for it?"

It was a question that was beyond the knowledge base for a fourteen-year-old. I was proud that she was thinking that far ahead but ashamed because she had to ask.

"Let me worry about that," I said.

CHAPTER SIXTEEN

I was in my office early the next morning, using a rubber band to flip paper clips into the wastebasket I had set on top of my file cabinet. I learned that if I used the thick rubber bands that came wrapped around the mail every morning, I couldn't get as far as with the thin ones. There was a physics lesson in there somewhere, but I wasn't up for it. I had my hands full trying to decipher a case with only a few leads, and I had managed to upset nearly everyone involved.

Marian's son, Miles, who might also be Berger's son, had tried to kill me the other night. Both of Hume's other sons were unhappy with me too, which meant that three quarters of the Hume family were either angry with me or trying to kill me. Typical for a case that involves family issues. Especially when that family was worth well over a hundred million.

But I was determined that the morning would not be a total loss. I had called Carl Burkett after dinner the previous night and found that he was asking a reasonable price for the duplex. The fee from this case would provide enough to offer a down payment on the house. For a reasonable upgrade in rent on the other side, I could pay the house payment on the rental income alone. The money from this case was going to ease my financial burden, even if the case itself overloaded me in other ways.

I called the bank that Anna and I had worked with in the past and made an appointment to speak with a loan officer for later in the afternoon. As soon as we had agreed on a time and ended the call, the phone rang. It was Ms. Carmichael.

"I wanted to call, Mr. Parker, first to extend my apology for Warren's behavior."

"No need," I said.

"Yes," she said. "there is."

I told her to consider the apology accepted.

"As I told you in your office, you can expect some opposition."

"You did not mislead me," I said. "Was there another reason for your call?"

The tone of her voice grew more serious. "Mr. Hume has taken a turn for the worse. He has been placed on dialysis."

"I'm sorry to hear that," I said, detecting the sense of urgency. "Still no explanation for the problem?"

"None so far," she said. "Tell me, Mr. Parker, have you found Miles Poole? Are you any closer?"

I told her about Miles. I told her that he was a biker and that he had a police record. I also told her that I had an address for him on Milner. I did not tell her about the gun play in the alley.

"I've run into another bit of trouble," I said. "More mine than yours, but it could present a challenge under the right conditions."

"That is?"

"My license has been suspended." I didn't want to tell her about my troubles, but if I continued on this case long enough, she was going to find out the truth. "But," I quickly added, "I am continuing to move forward despite the obstacle."

"Who suspended your license?"

"I was served with the papers a couple of days ago. A state trooper named Chang and another man named DeGraff met me at the house. They sit on the licensing board."

There was a long silence followed by an "I see."

"But as I said, this will not deter me from moving ahead."

"Our faith is in you, Mr. Parker. License or no, we want you to continue. Mr. Hume is not without influence. If the need arises, call us and we'll see what we can do."

I thanked her for her confidence.

"If he is who you say he is," she said, steering the conversation back to Miles, "he will not fit well with the brothers."

"I think we can agree on that," I said.

"But of course, we did not hire you for family reconciliation, did we?"

"No."

Another pause. "Have you been to the address?"

I told her that I had and that I had come up empty-handed. "But," I said, "I'm heading back there as soon as I'm done here." I flipped another paper clip, which hit the wall before landing in the wastebasket. "If he's there, I'll find him. If not, I'll continue looking until I do."

"Please hurry, Mr. Parker. Mr. Hume does not have long."

After my conversation with Ms. Carmichael, I slid into my shoulder rig and drove to the house on Milner. The chopper that had been parked in front was now gone, and I saw no sign of the elderly man who approached me on my last visit.

I parked in front of the house as I had before and approached the door. This time I got an answer when I knocked.

"Yeah?" A tall lean man with a bushy mustache and long hair answered the door. He was wearing a pair of jeans, no shirt, and a crucifix around his neck. An earring hung from one ear.

"I'm looking for Pork Chop," I said.

"Who are you?"

"A friend."

The man studied for a minute and then said, "Hold on," and closed the door.

I stood on the step as a gentle breeze blew the few leaves that had fallen into a neat pile, only to shift them around again into a confused mosaic. The door opened.

"Sorry," the man said from behind the closed screen door. "He ain't here."

I took out a card and slid it through the door jamb. "Tell him that I have to talk to him. It's very important," I said. "I may have some good news for him."

The man smiled and said, "Sure thing." He closed the door without taking the card.

I went back to my car and drove four doors down, turned around in the driveway, and parked, facing Poole's house.

For the next two hours, I watched as nothing happened. Not even a mail delivery. Finally, as the time drew closer to my appointment with the bank, I started the car and drove away, counting my losses. Losses which so far included a shot-up car, several hundred dollars to buy another one, and one count of attempted murder—mine.

CHAPTER SEVENTEEN

"Your paperwork is in order, Mr. Parker, but we do have some concerns."

She was a middle-aged woman with thick gray hair and long fingernails that were painted a vivid red. She wore a dark business suit and a gold chain with matching earrings. The nameplate on her desk identified her as Ms. Crutcher.

"What concerns?" I asked.

"Well, to be frank, your income. We see that you're in the process of starting a new business. That can take time."

"Sure," I said. "But if you notice on the form I just completed, the income from the rental side will take care of the mortgage payment. And I've been able to develop some sources of steady income."

"American Mutual," she said, holding her glasses to her face long enough to read the paperwork, "and a Mr. Benjamin Upcraft?"

"Yes."

She allowed the glasses to dangle about her neck as she set the paperwork down on her desk and set her clasped hands on top of it.

"Mr. Parker, your income from Mr. Upcraft is new and sporadic at best. Your total source of income from American Mutual has amounted to less than three thousand dollars to date."

"To date," I repeated.

"And renters move, sometimes leaving you without a source of income for weeks—maybe months—on end."

"Of course," I said. "But I'm not dependent on renters. That income would be an additional source of revenue." I smiled, and gave her my best "let me assure you" look. "I've never missed a rent payment, and I have a greater income than when I first began my business a short while ago. For just a few dollars more a month, I can make a mortgage payment." I leaned across her desk and lowered my voice for emphasis. "And I can get the few extra dollars a month that it will take."

She sighed. "Mr. Parker, I have no doubt you are an industrious individual. But I believe there are several things you're not taking into consideration."

"I've bought a home before," I said.

"Of course. But—"

"And I have an excellent credit rating."

She nodded. "Yes, you do."

"Then what's the problem?"

She pushed the paperwork to one side. "There are taxes. Property taxes that you are not paying now."

"Of course. As I said, I've bought a home before. I—"

"And," she said, counting the fingers of one hand, "there are the hidden costs such as general maintenance costs, higher insurance premiums, the costs of repairs, the legal fees you will incur when collecting overdue rent…" she sighed as she allowed her hands to fall to her desk. "Your income just doesn't support all of that."

There was a look of pity in her eyes. It was the same look I had seen at Anna's funeral. It was the same look that I had seen as a child when I was shuttled back to the Guardian's home after yet another foster family had rejected me. It was a look I didn't like.

"Who makes the final decision?" I asked, hearing the agitation in my voice.

She glanced over her shoulder at a balding middle-aged man

who was sitting in a corner office. "The final decision is up to Mr. Dimond. But I can tell—"

"Take it to him," I said. "Take it to him and let him make the decision."

She sighed again. "Okay, Mr. Parker. I'll take your paperwork to him. But my advice is to not get your hopes up."

Now, why would I do a thing like that? I thought.

CHAPTER EIGHTEEN

I left the bank with little hope of securing the loan. Crutcher had not been encouraging, and unless Dimond saw things differently, my chances were all but dead.

I drove through a Hardee's drive-through, picked up a small coffee, and drove back to the house on Milner. When I turned onto the street, I immediately saw a phalanx of IPD patrol cars with their light bars going in full color and a grouping of uniformed officers standing near the house. Some of the officers were taking notes as they talked with the neighbors, others were putting yellow CRIME SCENE tape around the yard, and still others were scouring the area for evidence. A couple of detectives were directing the crime lab technicians toward locations that needed to be tested, sampled, or photographed. I parked along the curb several houses down and got out of the car.

I walked to the crime scene with my coffee in hand and got as close as I could before a uniformed officer stopped me. I was behind the tape line, watching as two body bags were carried out of the house, when I spotted the elderly gentlemen I had spoken with earlier. He was wearing a flannel shirt again, but it was different from the one he had on the last time. He nodded in recognition as I approached him.

"What happened?" I asked.

"Somebody shot the place up. Looks like they killed a couple of them too."

I didn't want to tell him I had been at the house just a couple of hours before. If he repeated it to the police, I could be in for a lot of time-wasting questions. The fact that I didn't currently have a license would then inevitably come out, and I would find myself neck deep in bureaucrats.

"When did it happen?" I asked.

He glanced at his watch and did a quick calculation. "About forty minutes ago."

"Did you see what happened?"

He nodded. "Sure did." He pointed toward the end of the street. "I was in my yard and saw a van come from over there." He slid his hands into the pockets of his jeans. "They were coming real slow, and I said to myself, 'Now, what's going on over there?' Then, first thing I knew, the van stops in front of the house. But they didn't park. Just kind of stopped. Right there in the center of the street." He shook his head. "I knew there was going to be trouble 'cause I saw the engine still running. I could see the exhaust coming out of the tailpipe."

"You're observant," I said. "Most people would see all of that and not give it a second thought."

He smiled, pleased with himself. "I knew them boys was no good. I knew they were going to come to a bad end."

"Looks like they did," I said, wondering if the van load of hit men had found Miles for me. "By the way, my name's Colton Parker." I offered my hand.

"Right. I remember your name from the card you gave me." He shook my hand. "Ted Michaels. Anyway," he continued, "I knew that there was going to be a shooting. Then two men got out of the van and went into the house. Next thing I knew, it sounded like Patton's third army had invaded the south side of Indianapolis."

"What did these men look like?" I asked.

"Big. I don't think either one of them was any less than six feet. And dirty looking. Long beards, long hair. One was wearing a ball cap."

"Ball cap? Did you get a look at the name of the team?"

He shook his head. "No. I was trying to stay out of sight."

"Sure," I said.

"Anyway, like I was saying, the two of them got out and marched right on into the house just as bold as anything."

"Could you see the guns they were carrying?"

He nodded as he talked. "Sure. That's what I mean." He paused to shake his head. "I just don't understand how a guy can be so brazen as to walk right into someone's house and shoot it up in broad daylight."

"Sign of the times," I said.

He nodded. "Drugs too. Everybody's either selling them or making them."

"What kind of guns were they carrying?" I asked, trying to get him back on track.

"One of them had a sawed-off shotgun. Looked like a twelve gauge. Another one had a handgun, probably like the one you have under your jacket right now."

His comment made me aware of the bulge under my arm. "My gun show that bad?"

He smiled. "Yep. I saw it the other day when you was here. That's why I asked if you were the law."

"I could've been one of them," I said, gesturing toward the house. "You took a chance."

He smiled. "No I didn't." He raised his shirttail to reveal a thirty-eight tucked in his waistband.

"I thought you were planning on using the rake."

He laughed. "The rake?" He shook his head. "No. I may be older than I used to be, but I'm not stupid." He nodded again toward the house. "Them boys play for keeps. I don't take no chances living around here."

I looked at the house. The police were still moving in and out, but the crowd had begun to disperse. "Did you tell the police everything you told me?"

"Yeah. I was the first one to talk with them."

"Any idea who got hit?" I asked. I didn't know if the man knew Miles by any name other than Pork Chop or if he knew him at all. But if Miles was hit, I needed to know.

He shook his head. "No. I didn't know any of them other than by sight. I know that two of the three that shoved me before were in the house earlier today."

"One of them wear a crucifix around his neck?" I asked.

"Yeah. How'd you know that?"

"I think I saw one of them the other day," I lied.

He nodded. "Yeah, one of them wore a crucifix."

"I only saw two body bags," I said. "Were there more before I got here?"

He shook his head. "Nope." Then he smiled. "Two down."

CHAPTER NINETEEN

I drove back to the office to wait it out. I wanted to give the coroner time to ID the bodies, and then I was going to call and see if either one of them was Miles Poole. If so, I would have to break the word to Berger. If not, I had more work to do.

I arrived at the office, got a Coke out of the small refrigerator I kept next to the file cabinet, and pulled a Robert Crais novel out of one of the drawers where I kept a stack of books for "emergencies"—the kind of emergency that required waiting. It's the worst part of the job.

I had just settled in when I noticed the blinking light on the answering machine. I had bought the machine to replace the expensive answering service I had when I first opened. The cost-cutting move was just one of several that would help me come up with the extra money I would need to make mortgage payments.

I punched the Play button and heard a familiar voice.

"Mr. Parker, I wanted to call and apologize on behalf of my brother and myself. We were out of line. However, I would like to meet with you and explain the delicacy of our situation in better detail. Would this afternoon be okay? If so, you can reach me at…"

I wrote down the number. The machine beeped and reset itself as I called Denton. He answered on the first ring.

"Colton Parker here," I said.

He thanked me for returning his call, told me he was in the area, and asked if he could come to the office. I agreed to meet with him, explaining it would be a one-way conversation. Everything in the investigation was considered confidential and would be given only to his father. He told me he understood.

Fifteen minutes later I was sitting on my windowsill, watching as Denton arrived in a late-model, black Mercedes. He parked curbside and eased out of the car, obviously uncomfortable with his surroundings. When he entered my office, I noticed he was wearing another Armani suit with shoes that gleamed as they had before. He had nary a hair out of place. He shook my hand and sat across the desk from me in the same chair Ms. Carmichael had sat in just a few days earlier.

"What can I do for you?" I asked.

"As I mentioned earlier, I wanted to apologize for my brother's rude behavior. It is not indicative of our family."

"Sure," I said. I waited for him to continue. Discretion may be the better part of valor, but silence is the better part of discretion.

"And," he said, picking invisible lint off the legs of his pants, "I wanted to explain the reason for his outburst. While not intended as a justification, it may help you to better understand my brother."

"Understanding is the key," I said.

"Yes, well, I'm sure that Ms. Carmichael has told you of our desire to unload the hotels."

"She did."

"There are five of them. All five-star, and all with great potential."

"Sure," I said. "Potential is a great thing."

A frown momentarily creased his face before he continued. "Unfortunately, we have taken Hume Enterprises in a different direction. We are unable to manage the hotels in the way they need to be managed, so we have decided to...cut and run, as they say."

"You're losing money."

"Yes."

"A lot?"

"Yes."

"Who runs that part of Hume Enterprises?" I asked.

He smiled. "I think you know the answer to that, Mr. Parker."

"Warren?"

He nodded.

"So Warren is VP, but he is also over the hotels?" I wasn't sure if "over" was the correct business term or if Warren had another title relative to his position with the hotels. Nevertheless, Denton got the message.

"Yes. Warren is VP of operations, which includes, among other things, oversight of the hotels."

"What other things?" I asked.

He crossed his legs and began picking at the invisible lint again. "He is largely responsible for oversight of day-to-day operations."

"The person who is charged with oversight of the hotels is also overseeing general operations?" I asked.

He continued to pick at the imaginary lint as he said yes.

"Are you losing money in any other areas?"

He looked up from his lint picking. "No. In fact, we're doing quite well."

"What is little brother going to do when you sell off the hotels?"

"Continue overseeing his other areas of responsibility."

"Which are what, specifically?" I asked.

"The day-to-day things. Recruitment, training, and retention. Cost-cutting, business development, things like that."

I put my feet up on my desk. "Uh-huh," I said. "And what does Ms. Carmichael do?"

"She is an employee of my father. She helps him with his responsibilities, both personal and professional, but has no official position with Hume Industries."

"Do you have a suitor for the hotels?"

"We do. An offer has been made, and we expect to sign off on the deal as soon as the attorneys are finished preparing the documents."

"Who's made an offer?"

"I am afraid that's confidential."

"Sure," I said.

"Mr. Parker, it's important for you to understand that even though I'm here to apologize for my brother's behavior, I'm not apologizing for my brother. We have differences regarding the best way to deal with Miles Poole, but we have no differences when it comes to the harm that this man could bring to Hume Enterprises."

"I understand," I said. "But I have a job to do, and I'm going to see it through."

"I see." He stood. "Well, as I said, I apologize for my brother's behavior. He tends to run on pure emotion, and there is very little that he will not do when cornered." He extended his hand. I rose to take it.

"Sure," I said. "Me either."

CHAPTER TWENTY

Seeing it through" meant another trip to Biker Haven. Prior to leaving the office, a call to Harley Wilkins had netted the fact that Miles was not among the two who were killed in the hit. But the identities of the two who did make it to the morgue revealed a little more about Miles than I had known before.

The man who had greeted me at the door was named David Wayne Likens, AKA "the Priest," which was probably why he wore the crucifix. The other was identified as James Albert Kennedy, AKA "Buster." The identification was preliminary because both Buster and the Priest had to be identified by way of their driver's licenses. Each of the men had taken several shotgun blasts to the head, which meant that the most reliable means of identification was fingerprints, and the results from them wouldn't be back for a day or two.

Wilkins had given me a rundown on the two victims, and as I made my way across town, I tried to connect the dots between Miles and the two men that were laying on slabs in the morgue.

The Priest had been involved in gun running—selling large weapons to larger and larger inner-city gangs. The ATF had been on him for some time, suspecting that he had cached some fully-automatic weapons somewhere in the city and was due to unload them soon.

Buster had focused on drugs. He had been busted twice for dealing, but in both cases the amount on him at the time of his arrest was minimal.

Both men, like Poole, had a proclivity to violence, and neither of them, like Poole, had any problems exerting their influence on the elderly or disabled. That would probably ID them as being two of the three who shoved the old man off their porch. I was betting that the other was Poole.

As soon as I pulled onto the lot of Biker Haven, Ernie bolted out the back, hopping a chain-link fence for the freedom of the nearby alley. I immediately pulled out of the lot and headed east, turning onto the side street that ran alongside his shop. The alley emptied onto the side street, which caused quite a look of surprise on Ernie's face when I turned and began heading directly for him. He stopped, jumped over the same fence again, and began running across the parking area from which I had just come.

I killed the engine, jumped out of the car, and hopped over the fence in pursuit of Ernie.

Having never seen the man without a cigarette in his hand, I knew he wouldn't be able to maintain his run for long. With each step, I closed ground as he wheezed his way down the busy side street, across the vacant parking lot of what had once been a used car dealership, over a wooden privacy fence, and back down the first alley he had jumped into.

We ran down the unpaved, pothole-filled alley as Ernie flipped over each trash can he passed in order to slow me down. It didn't work. I was less than twenty yards behind him and gaining.

"Too many cigarettes," I said. "You need more time in the gym."

He kept running, but his speed was slowing, and he was running out of garbage cans.

As he moved past a small building, he saw another alley that intersected with ours. He turned left into the next alley and I followed him, only to discover that the alley dead-ended into the back of a garage. He stopped midway into the intersection and turned, frantically, only to see me blocking his way out.

"You've got to give up the smoking," I said, moving toward him.

He pulled a knife from his rear pocket. The blade flipped open almost instantly, much like a switchblade. But this knife was spring loaded and had a blade that was less than two inches long.

"Get away, man," he said, with barely enough breath to get the words out. "Just leave me alone."

"I can't do that, Ernie," I said. "Two men are dead, and I need to find Pork Chop. You're going to help me this time."

"No, I'm not," he said, managing to elevate his voice half an octave over his normal pitch. He wiped the sweat from his brow with his left sleeve as he waved the knife from side to side with his right hand. It was a pitiful attempt at intimidation, coming from someone who had learned it from seeing too many movies.

"Put the knife down," I said, pausing my advance on him. I opened my jacket, revealing the Ruger. "If I wanted to mess with you, I'd just do it here and take the knife."

He continued his labored breathing. He wasn't a threat, and I didn't want to hurt him. I just wanted to find Poole and be done with it. Ernie was still my best option.

"Put the knife down," I said. "Put it down and take me to Pork Chop. Then I'll be out of your life."

"Get out of my way," he said, huffing.

I shook my head. "Put the knife down, Ernie. Put it down—now."

He waved the knife again as he crouched and tried to circle past me. I felt sorry for him.

"Out of my way, man," he said. "Get out of my way."

I didn't have all day. If I let this thing drag on, the police would show, and this would turn into a trip downtown and two hours of questioning.

I moved in on Ernie. His expression revealed his dismay that his display of machismo had failed.

He slashed at me with the knife and I sidestepped it, allowing the blade to pass harmlessly. When it did, I hit him hard on the left side of his head with a right hook. He sank to the ground.

I knelt and picked up the knife, closed the blade and slid it into my hip pocket. Then I pulled Ernie to his feet by grabbing the back of his denim jacket. I held him against a building until he cleared his head.

His eyes were glassy as he massaged his face with one hand. "Did you have to hit me so hard?"

"Sorry," I said. "But you had a knife." I let go of his jacket but stood in front of him so he couldn't run again.

"It's just a little one," he said, crouching against the garage as he continued to rub the side of his face.

"Sure," I said. "I probably should have taken that into account."

He fumbled for his pocket. I grabbed the hand.

"It's just cigarettes, man," he said. "I need a smoke."

I fished the pack of Camels from his pocket and handed them to him. He pulled some matches from a pocket in his jeans, shook out a cigarette from the pack, and lit it in the same way I had seen him do before. When he exhaled, he seemed to relax, and some of the glassy look left his eyes.

"You okay?" I asked.

He nodded as he continued to half-stand, half-crouch along the garage wall. "Yeah. I'm okay."

"I need to find Poole," I said. "And you're the best chance I have."

He shook his head. "I don't know where he—"

"Yes you do," I said. "You know how to contact him. You did it when he tried to kill me. You did it when you gave me his address later. And now he has someone after him. Someone other than me."

He eased back and then stood straight as he inhaled on the

cigarette. "He has a lot of people after him," he said. "He's not taking any chances."

"He's taking a chance by not meeting with me," I said. "If he's in trouble, I might be able to help." I wasn't sure what kind of trouble Poole had gotten himself into, but I was willing to guess it had something to do with a deal gone sour. If I could keep Poole alive long enough to confirm whether he was Hume's son and get him to meet with Hume, I would have earned my fee. If not, I was going to have a hard time keeping the money that I had been trying to spend earlier that same morning. Money that would give Callie and me a better life.

"He won't meet with you," Ernie said.

"He doesn't have a choice," I said.

He looked at me through the eyes of a man who knows he's trapped.

"You said his mail comes to your shop."

He nodded.

"Is he expecting anything?"

He started to answer, then hesitated.

"I'm going to find him, Ernie. And when I do, I'll make sure he knows how I found him."

His eyes reddened. "He's expecting a shipment."

"Drugs?"

He shook his head. "Guns."

"Call him. Tell him they're in but that I keep hanging around."

"He'll kill me," he said, drawing on the cigarette again.

"He'll get killed if you don't."

There was a momentary pause as Ernie thought it over. Whatever the process was that he was using to mentally balance the scale, it gave him the only possible answer. He nodded as he flicked the cigarette to the ground, exhaling smoke through his nose. "Okay. I'll call him. But don't expect a welcoming party."

I don't want one, I thought, recalling my last meeting with Poole.

CHAPTER TWENTY-ONE

Ernie made the call. Miles took nearly an hour to return it. Ten minutes later, we were on our way.

"He's going to be mad," Ernie said.

"He'll get over it," I said, turning south onto I-465. The address that Pork Chop had given Ernie was just a few miles from my office.

He turned to face me. "He might be *really* mad. Know what I'm saying? He'll think I set him up."

I glanced at Ernie as I merged into the flow of traffic. There was genuine fear in his eyes.

"I'll reason with him," I said.

The fearful mechanic redirected his attention to the road ahead. Under his breath he said, "Take a lot of reasoning."

For the next few minutes neither of us said a word. Ernie didn't have to. His nervous energy, expressed through the incessant tugging on his jacket, the continual shifting in his seat, and his extensive repertoire of facial twitches, shouted of his fear of Miles. By the time we had exited onto Raymond Street from I-65, he came very near to bouncing around in the car like a balloon with the air suddenly released.

We drove east on Raymond for a couple miles and came to the apartment complex where Ernie told me we would find Miles. I pulled the car to the curb and parked. I dug into my jeans and handed a folded ten-dollar bill to Ernie.

"What's this?" he asked.

"This is where you get off. The money is for a cab back to the garage." I gestured toward one of the few free-standing pay phones that were still in existence. "You can call one from there."

"You're not going to make me come with you?" he asked.

I shook my head. "No reason for you to go any further. I just needed to be sure you didn't tell him I would be coming."

"How do you know I won't go over there," he nodded toward the pay phone, "and call him anyway?"

"Will you?" I asked.

He sighed and slid the money into his pocket. "No, man. I won't." He opened the car door and paused, turning to look back at me before getting out. "Thanks, man. Thanks for trusting me again."

After Ernie got out of the car, I pulled away from the curb and drove into the Village Square apartments. I turned into the complex, followed the directions that Miles had given Ernie, and found Miles' building near the rear of the complex.

I drove around the aging brick building, circled back a street to the south, and parked in an area that was two buildings down from the one in which Miles was waiting. Just as I had at the house on Milner, I chambered a round in the Ruger and slid it back into my holster before getting out of the car.

The September air was still unseasonably warm, but the brisk breeze gave it an edge that made the jacket I was wearing seem appropriate for something other than a cover for my gun. Men like Miles, who live their lives looking over their shoulders, tend to recognize the techniques for gun concealment. Wearing a jacket is the technique of choice, but if the weather doesn't require it, a jacket can stand out like an air raid siren in a convention of Tibetan monks.

I came up the front side of the building and entered the small foyer through a metal door that was covered by more graffiti than paint. None of the mailboxes had names on them, which was a strong indicator that no one in the building stayed put for very long.

I pushed the first buzzer. No answer. I pushed another one. Again, no answer. I continued to buzz until I finally got a response from an agitated woman.

"Yeah?"

"I have a delivery for you."

"For who?" she asked.

"Mrs. Kemp," I said, pleased with my quick response.

"There ain't no Mrs. Kemp here," she said.

"Look lady, I've got to get to my sister's wedding today, and I can't do that until this delivery is done. It's a DVD player. All I've got to do is deliver it. I don't care if you're Mrs. Kemp or not. Want it?"

Her greed got the better of her, and she buzzed me into her building, hoping for a DVD player that didn't belong to her. I entered the building and immediately went to Miles' apartment.

I paused to listen at the door. From inside, I could hear the irritating noise of a TV game show. I pulled the Ruger from its holster.

The last time Miles and I had met, he had gotten the drop on me and had almost blown a hole through my head. This time, I wanted to turn the tables. I kicked in the door.

Miles was sitting on the sofa with a can of beer in his hand, watching the game show I had heard. His gun was on the coffeetable, surrounded by cleaning supplies.

Our eyes locked for a second, but I saw no spark of recognition. Instead, I saw the fear that anyone would have who has just had their home violently invaded. In Miles' case, the weapon he would have relied on for protection was now lying on a table, as clean as any weapon can be, but also as unloaded as any weapon can be. He reacted in the only way left open to him. He threw his beer at me.

I ducked as the alcohol-laden projectile flew in my direction. It bounced off the door frame behind me and landed on the carpet, where it immediately began to foam. By the time I had straightened up, Miles had opened the patio door and taken off, sliding the door closed behind him.

I cursed and jammed the Ruger into my holster as I jerked the door open and took off after him.

Like Ernie, Poole was out of shape. Unlike Ernie, he didn't know it.

He glanced over his shoulder at me as we ran along the courtyard, turning between two apartment buildings and heading north. I was fifty yards behind him but gaining. By the time I rounded the corner, I had closed the distance to less than thirty yards.

He turned again, rounding the corner of the building on his right, glancing over his shoulder again as he did.

"Two foot chases in one day," I said. "Two in one day and I'm still gaining on you. Why don't you stop? All I want to do is talk."

He turned right again, around the same building he had just rounded and back toward the courtyard where we'd started.

He appeared to be older than I knew his age to be and much rounder than his mug shot had shown. He was dressed in a dirty gray T-shirt, jeans, and tennis shoes. Like his friends, who Chastain and I had talked with previously, he had a large leather wallet chained to his belt and a sheath for a small knife.

When he entered the courtyard he paused, seemingly confused about what to do, and then suddenly took off toward his left.

I turned the corner with him and was now less than ten yards away.

"Give it up, Pork Chop," I said. "You're making this harder than it has to be."

He was beginning to slow, and by the time he reached the midway point of the courtyard, he came to a complete stop. When I reached him, he was leaning forward with his hands on his knees as he tried to get his breath.

I approached him cautiously, keeping an eye open for a hidden weapon. Other than the knife, I didn't see any telltale bulges.

"I need to talk," I said.

"Then...why...did...you...try...to kill me?" he asked, still huffing.

"What're you talking about?" I asked.

He coughed and struggled to get his breath. "Ernie said you... you've been talking to him. Then...you found the house and hit them." He slowly straightened up and glared at me.

Full-on, Miles looked much older than his age. He had a ruddy complexion, a bulbous nose that was reminiscent of W.C. Fields, and a long scraggly beard. His eyes were puffy and bloodshot, and his dirty T-shirt was much dirtier than it had appeared from a distance, with large stains around the neck and under his arms.

"I didn't hit anyone," I said.

"You were by there early today." He was still puffing. "I saw you. I saw you when the Priest answered the door. I was there the first time too."

"You were there? Why didn't you just come to the door? I told the Priest that I might have some good news for you."

"Somebody shows up at my door, and for the first time in my life, it's good news? I'm supposed to buy that?"

I needed to gain his trust. Allay his fears. "I didn't hit your friends."

He studied me for a moment. "Maybe."

"Were you there when the hit went down?"

He shook his head.

"Who's after you?"

He shook his head as he continued his labored breathing.

I looked around the courtyard. Miles and I were standing in an open area. If someone wanted him enough to come gunning for him, it wasn't wise to be standing where we were.

"Look," I said, "why don't we go back to the apartment. I have something to tell you, and I don't think being out here in the open is the best place to be."

He was still uncertain. Still wary. He glanced at the bulge in my jacket. "You packing?"

"Yes."

He kept his focus on the bulge. His eyes told me he was debating whether it would be smarter to run or to try and jump me.

"You're safe, Miles. You're just going to have to believe me. After all, if I wanted to waste you, why not do it right here?"

He nodded after thinking it over. "Okay," he said. "Okay, we can go back. But when we talk, I don't want to be seeing you again."

"After we talk," I said, "the feeling will be mutual."

CHAPTER TWENTY-TWO

"What's his name?"

"I can't tell you that. Not yet," I said.

"What do you mean, 'not yet'?"

"Until I know with reasonable certainty that you're his son, I'm not going to divulge his name to you—or your location to him."

He got out of the dilapidated chair to pace the room.

The apartment was as unkempt as its occupant. Paint was peeling from the walls, large stains were on the carpeting, and in some areas, large segments of carpeting were missing altogether.

"This guy is saying he's my father?" Poole asked, turning to look at me.

"Not exactly. Someone else is saying it."

He shook his head and gave me a lopsided grin as he went to the refrigerator. "Want a beer, man?"

"No."

He opened the refrigerator, got a can of off-brand beer, and popped the top as he pushed the refrigerator door closed with his foot. "He wants to take me to ball games and buy me cotton candy?" He chuckled as he chugged the beer.

"He's dying," I said.

Pork Chop belched. "So?"

"So the man is trying to do the right thing. You do remember the difference, don't you? Between right and wrong?"

"Yeah, I remember." He sank into the chair again. "I remember my mom telling me that my dad was dead. That he died in Vietnam." He narrowed his eyes as he looked at me. "That sound like the right thing to do to a little kid?" He drank more of the beer.

"No. But it wasn't your father's fault," I said. "He didn't know about you."

"*If* he's my old man."

I nodded. "Sure. *If* he's your father."

He guzzled the remainder of the beer and crushed the can. For the next few minutes, he was silent as he thought about what I had just told him. "What do you want me to do?"

"Nothing, for the moment. I'll have to contact the family first, tell them I need a sample from…the man, and then I'll need a DNA sample from you. If we get a preliminary match, I'll connect you two."

He paused again to think, then nodded his agreement. "Okay. It might be nice to have an old man. Even if he's not going to be around long."

I stood to leave. "Weren't you ever curious?"

"About my dad?"

"Yeah."

He shrugged. "Yeah, sometimes. But life goes on. You forget about the things you never had." He got up to get another beer, and I watched as a man who was aged beyond his years continued down the road that would surely bring him up short. In a way, I almost felt sorry for him. Almost.

"Why did you try to kill me?" I asked.

He popped the top on the beer and took a long drink as he kept watch on me over the rim of the can. "I thought you was setting me up."

"For what?"

"A hit."

"Are you expecting one?"

He shrugged. "Hard to live my life and not have someone after you. Goes with the job."

"Someone in particular?"

"Nobody you need to know about."

"Sure," I said. I looked around the apartment. "Do you live here, or on Milner?"

"Here."

"Then why did you send Ernie to the house on Milner?"

"'Cause that's where I was when he called. I live here, but we hang out there."

"We?"

"The Priest, Buster, and Freeze."

"Freeze?"

"Yeah. Jimmy Rossi. We call him Freeze."

"Why?"

"'Cause he don't care, man. He don't care about nobody or nothing. He's just...cold."

I laughed. "And you consider this guy a friend?"

The flatness of his expression made it clear that he saw neither the humor nor the irony. "I can't afford friends. It's how I stay alive. Freeze is someone I can do business with. I can trust him. But it's business. That's as far as it goes."

I shook my head. "A guy who cares so little for others that he's known as Freeze, and you can trust him? You live in a mixed-up world, Poole."

"And you don't?"

"Nobody's messing with me," I said.

"You sure?" he asked, moving back into the living room and sinking into his chair. "Every time you pay an insurance premium, where do you think it goes? To be there when you need it?" He cursed. "And you call me a thief." He drank from the can. "But when some company bigwig does it, he gets a slap on the wrist, goes to club Fed for a few weeks, and keeps the money. See a problem there?"

"Sure," I said. "But that—"

"Them guys is worse than the worst gangbanger." He was getting loud, and his ruddy complexion transitioned to bright red. "The head dude lets the other dudes go to jail for him, and he keeps the money and lives well for the rest of his life. And you pay for it." He drank from the can. "Sure, we might go after each other, but it's for the honor. Somebody messes with you—you mess with him. No one's going down for no one else. You play, you pay."

"Semper Fi."

"Huh?"

"You pay a lot," I said. "The Priest and Buster were hit today, remember? They're both dead."

His expression fell, as he raised the can and drank slowly.

"Thanks for telling me about my old man."

"Sure." I turned toward the door. Part of the jamb was broken, and the lock wasn't working, but the door was still useable. "I'm going to need a blood test. Can you do that?"

He shrugged. "I guess."

"If you're a match, my client is going to want to meet with you."

He laughed. "That's going to go over big, ain't it?"

I had to laugh with him. "I think so. Should be interesting to say the least."

He nodded.

"Miles, you're not going to run again, are you?"

"No, man. I ain't running. Not unless I have to, you know? I can't stay in one place too long."

I moved through the doorway and stepped into the hall. "By the way, do me a favor. Take it easy on Ernie."

He waved a hand. "Ern's safe. Besides, I owe you an apology anyway. I'm sorry I tried to kill you," he said. "I just thought you was setting me up."

"I'm not sorry I fired back," I said.

He nodded again. "I understand. If things was the other way around, I'd have been trying to kill you too."

CHAPTER TWENTY THREE

I took Callie to a south side Mexican restaurant for dinner that evening, after helping her with what was left of her homework. Her grades had began to steadily climb, and I wanted to help her maintain the momentum.

The drive to the restaurant went well, and by the time we were seated, we were having a conversation.

"You want to try out for soccer?" I asked.

"Yeah. I think it's time. Don't you?"

We had already ordered and were working on a bowl of chips and salsa while we waited for our food.

"Sure. If you feel up to it, I think it's definitely time. When are tryouts?"

"Well, technically they're over, but when I told the coach about my other school, she called them. She said she would test me, and if I was as good as they said I was, she would field me."

This was good news. Before Anna's death, soccer had been Callie's primary reason for living. Playing again would go a long way toward getting her life back on track.

"Do you want to test?"

She nodded, and looked around the room. "Yeah."

"Well, I—"

The server brought our dinner: two tacos, rice, and beans for me, and a wet burrito for Callie. After determining that we didn't require anything else, he left.

"I don't see any reason why you shouldn't. Do you?"

I dribbled hot sauce across the tacos.

"Mary said it might be the best thing for me."

"When did you talk to Mary?"

"The other night, when she was at the house," she said, in one of her "don't you remember?" tones.

"You mean when I was teaching her how to cook?"

She gave me a quizzical look, then smiled. "You mean when she was teaching *you* to cook."

"Oh, that's right," I said. "She was teaching me."

We ate for the next few minutes with neither of us saying a word. Since Anna's death, Callie had been withdrawn, sullen. But over the past few weeks she had seemed to be coming around. She was more like the Callie I had known when Anna was alive.

"What would you think," I asked, "about going down to the Smoky Mountains over Christmas break?"

She nodded approvingly. "Yeah, that would be great. We haven't been there in a long time."

Each year after Christmas, Anna and I would travel to the Tennessee mountains and get a cabin in Gatlinburg before hitting the shops in nearby Pigeon Forge. By the time Callie came along, it had become tradition to shop for next year's Christmas decorations in one of the Christmas-themed stores. There was never a shortage of things to see or do, and although Callie couldn't remember, she had often posed in several "antique" photos, dressed as the daughter of a bank robber, a saloon girl, or a gun moll. It had been one of the better parts of our family life. A trip there this coming Christmas would be our first one in more than two years.

"Well, I wouldn't say it's been a long time," I said, "but it has certainly been longer than it should've been."

She nodded as she spread sour cream along the burrito. "Yeah, that's for sure."

"So," I said, steering the conversation back to soccer, "when is your coach going to test you?"

"She said I should talk with you first and that she wanted a note from Dr. Sebastian. Then—"

"A note from Dr. Sebastian?" Sebastian had been the psychologist who consulted on Callie's case shortly after Anna's death. He had suggested we keep Callie's life as normal as possible. I didn't think the doctor would have a problem writing a note that cleared Callie for soccer. In fact, I was convinced he would heartily recommend it. But I was curious that the coach needed him to.

Callie nodded as she ate. "Yeah. She said that since he was treating me, she would need a note from him and one from you, saying it's okay for me to play."

"I don't see why not."

"Great," she said. "The sooner the better."

"Okay," I said before finishing the last of the tacos. "I'll call Dr. Sebastian tomorrow. Will that work?"

I had bit into the taco before I realized that I hadn't gotten an answer. She was looking toward the door, where a small crowd was beginning to gather as the restaurant grew busier. There was an elderly couple who appeared to be accompanying a young woman and her baby, two young girls that I guessed to be about Callie's age, and a young man in his early twenties who was dressed in hip-hop clothing and who had a pony tail protruding from the rear of his hat.

"Will that work?" I asked again.

Her faced turned red.

"Something wrong?"

She turned back to her plate, and lowered her head.

"You okay?" I asked.

She shook her head. "No. Dad?"

"What's wrong?"

"I want to go home."

I glanced back at the doorway, but the people at the door were all being shown to their tables.

"Did you see something?"

"No," she said, looking up from her plate. "I just don't feel like being here. I want to go home."

I motioned for the server and asked for the check. As he tore it from his pad, Callie stood and left the restaurant.

CHAPTER TWENTY-FOUR

The next morning, Callie seemed more down than she had been the night before but still up from where she had been most of the past eighteen months.

"You feeling any better?" I had asked during breakfast.

She said she was fine and ate with all the enthusiasm of someone who was heading to the gas chamber.

Anna's parents, the Shapiros, had asked if Callie could spend the weekend with them. They planned a short excursion to Chicago and wanted to take Callie along for the trip. They promised to be back by Sunday evening, and I agreed.

After Frank and Corrin picked Callie up, I put away the dishes and called Ms. Carmichael. I also made a note to talk with Callie again when she came back home.

"I've found Miles," I said.

"Excellent. Where can we find him?"

"We may have a bit of a problem."

After a moment of silence, she said, "Such as?"

"I don't think Mr. Hume is going to want to invite someone into his home and his life until there is at least a reasonable chance that Miles is the person that the letters claim him to be."

There was a pause. "I agree. But if you're after more money, Mr. Parker, let me point out that…"

"No. I'm not after more money, Ms. Carmichael. I'm after the facts. Before I introduce Miles to Mr. Hume, I'm going to run tests on both of them to support the contention that he is your boss' son."

"Are you talking DNA? That can take quite a long time, and I'm not sure—"

"No, it doesn't. There are companies who specialize in this, and the results can be back in five to seven days."

A pause. "What do you want us to do?"

"I'll contact the company and ask them to come to Mr. Hume's home. They'll draw a small amount of blood, or take a simple swab of his mouth, and test it. They'll do the same for Miles and then compare the results."

"And if they're a match, you will tell us how to connect with him?"

"Yes."

Another pause. "I'm sure Mr. Hume will agree."

"It's why he hired me," I said.

"Yes." Another pause. "Okay. Call them."

"I'll need Mr. Hume to give them permission to give me the results of the test. If they're not a match, then there's no reason to pursue this further."

"I believe he will agree to that."

"I'll also need his agreement to be responsible for the costs incurred," I said. "It's the 'expenses' part of 'ten thousand dollars plus expenses.'"

"Of course," she said. "How soon can you arrange this?"

"I'll set it in motion today and contact you as soon as soon as I have the green light."

"Excellent."

After ending the call, I telephoned GenTec, a local lab that specialized in paternity testing. Their ad indicated that they had Saturday hours available, which meant we could complete the tests that day. After explaining the situation, they reacted as I had expected. They wanted written authorization from both Hume and Miles, releasing the lab from liability for giving the results to me. Once the paperwork was completed, the testing would begin, and the results would be available in just a few days. That was better than I had expected.

The arrangements were made, and I was told to have Miles in the lab by nine thirty that morning. They also promised to have a technician visit Hume at his home and obtain the sample from him there.

I poured the last of the coffee into my plastic travel mug and left the house for Pork Chop's apartment.

The morning was sunny with a strong wind out of the southwest that was beginning to clear the trees of their leaves earlier in the season than was typical. The resulting cascade of autumn color was vibrant, making the drive as scenic as it was enjoyable. One of the few things in life, I thought, that was still free.

I drove through the morning traffic with relative ease and made it to the Chop's apartment in less than ten minutes.

The complex was quiet when I arrived, and the metal security door I had encountered on my last visit was locked just as it had been then. This time, though, I didn't need to offer a DVD player to gain access. I rang Miles' apartment, and he buzzed me through.

I didn't figure the Chop as an early morning type, and when he opened the door I saw that I had been right.

"What time is it?" he asked, scratching his head as he stepped aside and allowed me to enter.

"Almost eight thirty," I said. "Get dressed."

He shook his head, but not out of disgust. It was to rattle whatever marbles he needed to rattle in order to get the day started. "Where we going?" he asked.

"I'm taking you to a local lab. They're going to take some blood or a swab of your mouth."

His face was swollen and his eyes were bloodshot. I saw a few more empty beer cans in the trash.

"Can we get something to eat first?" he asked.

"Afterward," I said.

He paused to look at me with an expression that told me he was having second thoughts, but he relented and said, "Okay. Let me get dressed," before disappearing into another room. When he did, I took advantage of the unattended time to learn more about him.

From his refrigerator I learned that he drank more than he ate. From his bookshelves I learned that he preferred men's magazines and comic books, and from his wardrobe I learned that he had a penchant for T-shirts and jeans. No startling revelations there. But when I glanced out the window, I learned a little more.

A dark van was sitting on the street that ran alongside the building. The engine was still running, judging from the escaping exhaust. Three men inside were looking toward Miles' building. I couldn't see their faces, but I could see them talking to each other before refocusing their attention on the apartment. They did this a couple of times before slowly driving away. I stepped away from the window as Miles came into the room.

"Okay," he said. "I'm ready. Let's get this thing over with."

He was clean but was dressed the same way he had been when I chased him down. Jeans, boots, and a T-shirt that was imprinted with a beer slogan.

"You didn't have to get all decked out for this," I said.

"I didn't."

I led the way outside as Miles followed behind. I glanced around for the van as obliquely as I could but didn't see the vehicle or its occupants.

"These people who are after you are killers," I said as we got into my car.

"Yeah, that's right. You just figuring this out, man?"

We pulled out of the complex and onto Raymond Street. "I'm wondering if you've figured it out, Miles. There may be a solution to all of this."

He laughed. "There is a solution, man. It's called 'killing Pork Chop.'"

We were silent for a while as I drove back toward the interstate.

"Do you owe them money?" I asked, breaking the silence as I moved onto I-65 northbound.

He turned to look at me. "I'll give you two guesses."

"Look," I said, as I merged into the flow of interstate traffic. "I'm here to do a job. A man who is dying has been told that you are his son. He wants to see you."

"Sure, I understand. My old man wants—"

"He wants to see his son alive. That means I have obligations here. I can't just show up with you and say, 'Here you go. Dad, meet your son. Son, meet your dad.' I need to do three things. One is to determine with reasonable certainty that you are his son. Two is to keep you alive long enough for him to see you. And three is to see to it that you don't drag your baggage into his life."

"You going to be my bodyguard, man?" He laughed at the thought.

"I'm going to keep you alive. It's part of what I'm getting paid to do. So if you'll tell me who you're in trouble with, I might be able to help you."

He shook his head and laughed again. "Man, you're one for the books, you really are."

"Tell me, Miles. Tell me who they are and what you've done."

He rolled the window down a bit and lit a cigarette, blowing the noxious fumes out the window. "I don't need your help, man. I can take care of myself."

"Like your dead buddies did?"

He rested his right hand on the door frame, with the tip of the cigarette hanging out the window as he flicked off some of the ash. He seemed to be thinking. He didn't say anything as he took another long drag and flicked more ash out the window.

I worked my way onto I-70 east.

"You ever heard of Satan's Posse?" he asked, looking ahead as he continued to smoke.

"No."

He flicked the ashes out the barely opened window. "They're a bad bunch."

"They have a problem with you?"

He nodded. "Yeah, you could say that." He took another long drag and exhaled. "We've had some disagreements."

"Have they had disagreements with your friends too?"

"I told you, man, I don't have friends."

"Right. You did, didn't you?"

He nodded. "Yes, I did."

We worked our way toward the Shadeland Avenue exit. Traffic was light.

"You think they were behind the hit on Buster and the Priest?"

He exhaled again as he slowly nodded, keeping his gaze fixed forward. "Yeah. I do now."

"Now?"

"Now that I know it wasn't you."

"And now you think it's Satan's Posse that's after you?"

"It's them at the moment." He turned to look at me. "Like I said, I ain't got no friends."

"Ernie seems to be looking out for you," I said.

"Ern's Ern. He ain't looking out for me. He's just afraid I'll rat him out for all the stuff I know he's doing. I used to work there."

"For a day," I said.

"Yeah, well, it was enough."

"You walk a tightrope."

He nodded.

We drove a little longer in silence before we exited off the interstate and headed north on Shadeland Avenue toward the lab.

"That makes you dangerous to be around," I said.

He turned to look at me, flipping what was left of the cigarette out the window. "Yeah."

Miles did as well as could be expected. Despite the stares of the others in the waiting room, he maintained decorum with the staff and was cooperative when asked for his DNA sample. Regardless of his chosen lifestyle, he was like anyone else in wanting a connection to his roots.

I paid for the test and kept the receipt and a copy of the registration form to give to Hume later.

We left the lab and stopped at a small mom-and-pop diner for breakfast. After ordering steak and eggs with coffee, Pork Chop lit up again. The restaurant was nonsmoking, but no one seemed willing to tell the biker he would have to step outside.

"I need to know," I said again, "that when I introduce you to my client, he won't be jeopardized." I was pumping him for information. Something that would give me a leg up on trying to keep the Hume boys safe from their wilder, more degenerate sibling.

He shrugged as he puffed on the cigarette. "Can't promise that. Being around me is a risk."

"It's a risk I have to eliminate," I said. I hadn't counted on Pork Chop having a trail of hit men fighting to get to him. Maybe it would have been easier to brush Jaws' teeth after all.

"You can't eliminate it," he said.

"I have to keep you alive."

"No you don't. I can do that myself. I've done it for years."

He was right, of course. He had done it for years. I wasn't his babysitter. My sense of duty could not exceed another man's boundaries. But I did have obligations. Obligations to protect the Humes from those who wanted Miles dead. If I couldn't eliminate the risk, I would at least have to minimize it, even if that meant stepping over the line.

"Keep your head down," I said, "My client wants to meet you in one piece."

The waitress set his breakfast and the check on the table before moving away without saying a word.

"Tell that to Satan's Posse," he said.

CHAPTER TWENTY-FIVE

The remainder of the weekend was quiet. I spent most of Saturday and all of Sunday going through the house, inspecting for repairs that would need to be done before I could upgrade the rent. Assuming, of course, that I qualified for the loan.

Callie came home very late on Sunday, so talking with her wasn't possible. After getting her off to school the next morning, I drove to the Marion County jail.

I met Chastain in the detectives' squad room. He was alone and working on pre-trial preparations when I sat in the chair next to his desk.

"Find Poole?" he asked, glancing at me.

"Yep."

He raised his head and eased back in his chair. "No kidding?"

"No kidding."

"Did that guy at Biker Haven turn out to be a good lead?"

"Eventually," I said.

"Good."

"Thanks for your help."

"Sure. You ever do much with the biker world?"

"No. Most of my Chicago time was street work," I said. "I did a little undercover stuff, but no gang work—biker or otherwise."

"The bureau get into anything like that?"

"Sure. The bureau tends to focus on gangs when larger issues are involved. Interstate transportation of stolen property, guns, women—whatever. If there are those kinds of problems, the bureau moves in under RICO."

RICO—Racketeer Influenced Corrupt Organizations Act—had been passed by congress in 1970 with the intent of destroying organized crime. The act was controversial in some quarters, but it gave the government teeth in combating organized crime and other gang activity.

He nodded as he drummed his pencil on the arm of his chair. "Why?"

"We have several gangs in Indianapolis, but none them are big players," he said. "I was just curious if any had attracted the attention of the FBI."

"How big is Satan's Posse?"

"Big. If we had any group in town that might draw the sustained attention of the Feds, it would be them."

"Who's the boss?"

He laughed. "You'll like this. Name's Percy Rogers."

"I assume Percy doesn't ride his bike with that name stenciled on the frame."

Chastain shook his head as he tossed the pencil onto his desk. "Not hardly. In those circles he likes to be called 'the Hammer.'"

"Because he rules the club with an iron fist?" I asked.

Chastain's expression grew serious. "Yes, he does that to be sure. But the name comes from the fact that he nearly beat a man to death with a…" he pointed a finger at me.

"Hammer," I said.

"There you go. He's what I would call *dangerous*."

I stretched my legs out and folded my hands behind my head. "Where would I find the Hammer?"

Chastain shook his head. "No. Sorry, Colton. I can't do that."

"Why? You have an active investigation going on this guy?"

He hesitated for a moment and then nodded slowly. "We have an investigation open on him all the time."

"Active?"

He hesitated again before slowly shaking his head. "I wouldn't classify it as active, but I'd say it's ongoing."

"So what's the problem with telling me where I can find this guy?"

He eased forward in his chair with his hands resting on his desk. "The problem is that I have a conscience."

"I don't follow."

"If I tell you where this guy is at, you're going to wind up dead. Can you follow that?"

"I can take care of myself," I said.

"I don't doubt that you can—if you know when it's coming." He stood and gathered his depositions, reports, and other paperwork. "I have to be at the prosecutor's office in twenty minutes. We're getting ready for trial, and we need to go over this stuff."

I stood with him. "You're not going to help me?"

He slid the paperwork into a briefcase and then punched me on the arm as he moved past me toward the doorway. "I am helping you."

CHAPTER TWENTY-SIX

I was back at the same house where Chastain and I had encountered the two men in the window and the two Dobermans in the yard. But this time I didn't have Chastain's badge. All I had was a business card without a license to back it up.

As I got out of the car I noticed that the house seemed eerily quiet. Serene. For all the security the house displayed, the surrounding neighborhood appeared to be quiet and relatively safe. I wondered if the fear of imminent attack was more psychological than real.

I opened the trunk of the Beretta, and like Chastain had a few days before, I used my car's lug wrench to get the attention of whoever might be home. I began banging on the fence and was immediately greeted by the two iron-spine Dobermans. The growling and barking didn't deter me from my appointed rounds. I continued my banging for a couple of minutes before someone finally appeared from behind the plywood door at the front of the porch.

"You want something?" It was the older of the two men who had approached the fence the other day. The one who had taken the dogs away.

"I want to talk," I said.

He jumped off the porch and came toward the gate with a look on his face that was meant to intimidate. Probably practiced it in front of the mirror.

I started to speak, but he grabbed the two dogs by their collars and dragged them to the unattached garage at the rear of the property. After locking the two in the building, he came back to where I was standing. Over his shoulder and through the garage door window, I could see the Dobermans jumping up and down in and out of view. I could still hear their muffled barking.

"'Bout what?" he asked, returning to the fence.

"A mutual problem." I wasn't sure how the Hammer related to these guys, but if they worked often with Miles, I was willing to bet they weren't friends of the man who may have been trying to kill him.

"What problem?" He was standing four feet away from the fence and kept his eyes on my hands. His own were in his hip pockets, and I figured that he probably had a weapon.

"I'm looking for someone, and I was told that you're the man to see."

He maintained his stance, but his eyes narrowed as he looked from my hands to my face. Like Pork Chop, this man lived in the dark alley of life, where everyone he met was a potential enemy. An enemy who wanted something and would stop at nothing to get it.

"You was here before, wasn't you?"

Since most of our conversation had been with the younger of the two, I wasn't sure if this man would remember me. He did, though, and that was going to give me an advantage.

"I was here."

He pulled his hands from his pockets and crossed his arms. His perceived need to maintain a grip on his weapon was gone. Although he probably hated the police, he also knew he had no fear of being openly gunned down by them. Knowing I had been with Chastain, he was probably figuring that I was a cop, which lessened his heightened sense of fear.

"Yeah," he said, nodding his head slowly, "you and that other cop was here looking for Pork Chop."

"Right," I said.

"Did you find him?"

I decided to ignore the question. I still wasn't sure what kind of relationship existed between Miles and this group, so I didn't want to open avenues that were better left closed.

"We're looking for the Hammer," I said.

The man's eyes narrowed. "The Hammer?"

"Yeah."

His eyes shifted again, following the same pattern as before. "You're in the wrong place."

By "wrong place," it was probably reasonable to assume that this man was not the Hammer's friend.

"We were told you know where to find him," I said.

He was hesitant to answer, as his searching eyes paused to bore holes through me.

"I'm not wearing a wire," I said, opening my jacket and raising my shirt.

He seemed to relax. "What do you want with the Hammer?"

"To talk."

He grinned. "Cops. You people sure like to talk. First you want to talk to Chop, and now you want to talk to the Hammer. You ever actually do any police work?"

"I'm getting a donut as soon as I'm done here," I said.

His grin broadened into a smile. "No doubt."

"Can you help us out?"

He sighed as he scratched his head and looked back at the house. "Maybe."

"I just need to know where I can find him."

He nodded as he dipped both hands into the side pockets of his jeans. "You don't want to go looking for him at the clubhouse. That would be a serious mistake."

I didn't know where the clubhouse was, but I could agree that looking for a man like the Hammer in his own backyard would be like dancing with the devil while the demons fiddled.

"Where can I find him? Where else does he hang out?"

"He don't hang out anywhere. He's all about business."

"What's his business?" I asked.

He shook his head. "Everything, man. The Posse is into drugs, women—everything. But most of their business is meth and guns."

"Meth?"

"Yeah. They cook that stuff everywhere. It's easy to do and pays good."

"What about the guns?"

"What's there to tell? Guns is guns. Lot of gangs in this town. Lot of gangs in every town. Somebody's got to keep them armed."

"And the Hammer?"

"The Hammer *is* the Posse. What he wants them to do, they do."

I recalled what Wilkins had said about the guys who were hit on Milner. How guns and drugs were their things too.

"How do I get this guy alone?"

He pulled both hands from his jeans, slipping his right hand back into his hip pocket as he leaned on the fence with the other hand. He shifted his weight from one foot to the other, with his head down as he paused to think. "I don't know, man," he said, finally raising his head to look at me. "I just don't. I know he's at the clubhouse most of the time, but other than that…"

"How many in the house at one time?"

He shrugged.

"What does the Hammer look like?"

A quizzical look crossed his face as he straightened from his leaning position. "Don't you have a mug shot of him?"

"Sure," I said. "But people change. The picture is old." I was hoping that this man didn't know the Hammer well enough to know when he had last been arrested.

He studied me for a moment. He scratched his head again. "Look, my people aren't going to take too kindly to me standing out here all day, chatting with the law. So how about we say that I tell you what the Hammer looks like, and you just go and do whatever it is you need to do. But away from here. Okay?" He shot a glance back to the house.

"Sure."

He glanced back at the house again. "The Hammer is big. Maybe six five, or six six, with black hair combed the way Elvis used to comb his."

"Pompadour?"

"Yeah, whatever you call it. Just up on his head, up and back, like Elvis. He's got a tattoo of a hammer on his left forearm," he paused, "or maybe it's his right...and he don't take anything from anybody. Understand what I'm saying?"

"Understood."

He turned to leave.

"Hey," I said.

He paused to turn in my direction.

"Thanks for the help."

He shot another glance back to the house. "I didn't help you. I helped me. I owe him one," he said.

CHAPTER TWENTY-SEVEN

The clubhouse was located in the twelve hundred block of North Tibbs in what had probably once been a nice home for a nice family. Now it was headquarters for a group of outlaw bikers who identified themselves with Satan and who were led by an Elvis look-alike.

I drove past the house at the posted speed limit to see if anyone meeting the Hammer's description happened to be standing outside or sitting on the concrete porch. I didn't see anyone matching his description, so I decided to drive around the block and look for a place to park.

Finding the clubhouse hadn't been easy. I couldn't ask the man I had talked to without tipping my hand and letting him know I wasn't the law enforcement officer he thought I was, and Chastain had already declined. A call to Mary hadn't been fruitful either since she was out of the office, so I had been relegated to the gumshoe's tried and true—research at the public library. My visit there had also clued me in on some of the club's history.

For example, I knew that they had been the subject of several IPD and sheriff's department investigations. Several raids had been conducted on the house over the past twenty years, one of those resulting in the death of IPD patrolman Horace McDonald.

According to one of the articles I read, Horace had been the first officer through the door in a raid that had taken place almost eighteen years ago and had been gunned down in the process by two shotgun blasts from someone inside the house. At twenty-nine, he had come up short, leaving a wife who was due to deliver the couple's first child in two months.

As I circled the block, I couldn't help but think that McDonald's child would be graduating high school in a year and wouldn't be able to share the occasion with the father.

I also learned that the group's leader had never been arrested but was under suspicion for several hits that had gone down in the city. Some of them were in full view of witnesses who could never seem to recall what they had seen. No weapons were ever found either, so charges were never filed. All of this pointed to the fact that Satan's Posse was violent and protective of their turf. It also meant that Pork Chop could be in profound trouble.

I found a place to park where I could keep the house in view and turned off the car. The engine continued to run on as it pinged and dinged itself into submission.

My position on a side street gave me an angled view of the house. From where I was parked, I could see two-thirds of the front and one entire side. The house was a two-story clapboard with a wraparound concrete porch that had been allowed to deteriorate, a roofline that sagged, and windows that were in dire need of work. Despite the desperate conditions, it wasn't hard to imagine how the house might have looked when it was new, probably sometime in the 1930s.

Stakeouts had never been my forte, and as the minutes crawled along, I recalled my disdain for sitting in cars and watching other people live their lives. During the first two hours, I didn't see so much as a curtain move or a door open. By the time the third hour rolled around, I was entertaining myself with a "here's the church, here's the steeple, open the door and see all the people" structure with my hands when I saw a car park in front of the house. I closed the church and took notice.

The car was in worse shape than mine, and two men were in the front seat. They sat motionless until a tall man with Elvis-like hair came out of the house. When he approached the car, a short, fat man with a ponytail and a red bandanna on his head got out of the car and slid into the backseat. The Hammer got into the car and sat next to the driver.

The Hammer didn't fit the mold of the others in his entourage. He was as tall as I had been told—I placed him at six foot six— with a lean, muscular build and an agile, catlike walk. The man was physical. No pushover. And he had the air of someone who was in command. Not just of others but of himself as well.

He was dressed in black jeans, black boots, and a short-sleeved black T-shirt. A silver chain hung around his neck, and he was carrying a leather jacket in his hand. From where I sat, I couldn't identify any weapon. But then, he *was* a weapon. A confrontation with him was going to require that I get an early upper hand.

The driver started the car and made a U-turn on Tibbs, heading south. I started my car and pulled out after them.

We drove to Michigan Street, where the trio turned east. I followed them, maintaining as much distance between my car and theirs as I could. From where I sat, I could see that the three men weren't interested in conversation. The Hammer rested his arm on the frame of the open window as he watched the world pass by. The man in the rear seemed to be asleep with his head reclined on the backseat, and the driver kept his focus straight ahead.

As we continued moving east, I slowed, encouraging the cars behind me to pass and insert themselves between my car and the Hammer's. I wanted enough barrier to maintain my anonymity but not enough to lose my suspect.

The trio turned south onto Warman Avenue, and I followed, grateful that one of the two cars between us did likewise. I wanted to talk with the Hammer, but I didn't want a confrontation in the middle of the street.

As their car approached US 40, it turned right and begin to pick up speed as it moved west with the traffic. I turned with them, as did the car between us, and picked up speed as well.

We continued west for ten minutes before the trio turned south onto High School Road. The Hammer and I appeared to be heading toward Indianapolis International Airport. The car that had been between us continued westward, leaving me directly behind the biker and his bodyguards.

I dropped back in order to maintain a safe distance between myself and the Hammer's car. I could see well enough to tell that none of the men in the car had turned around to see if I was tailing them, but I wasn't close enough to tell if the driver had glanced into the rearview mirror to do the same. Overall, I was reasonably certain they hadn't identified me, but not so sure that I could relax without concern.

The Hammer's car slowed as it approached the outer fringe of the airport, where the long-term parking lots begin, and turned into the first lot they came to. I was far enough behind that by the time they had entered the lot, I could do the same with minimal chance of looking like anything other than another air traveler.

I punched the automated ticket dispenser, and the gate swung upward, allowing me to enter the lot. From my position, I could see that the trio had moved toward the south end of the parking area and were beginning to slow down. I moved to the left, eased down a row of cars, and then turned right again, which put me in a position that was headed their direction.

I watched as they pulled into one of the parking stalls. From the lack of exhaust, I could tell they had turned off the car. None of them got out.

I pulled into a slot just to the north of them with enough cars and minivans between us that they wouldn't notice me, unless, of course, they already had. To hedge my bets, I pulled my gun from its holster and set it on the seat next to me.

I watched the trio for the next twenty minutes. For the most part they seemed docile with little in the way of head movement or observable conversation. Occasionally, one or the other of them would light a cigarette, but just as often as not, would soon extinguish it by flipping it out a window. Although the day was still unseasonably warm, the temperature had begun to dip, making the air a little chillier than when we had first arrived. Nevertheless, I wasn't in a position to turn on the heater without drawing attention to myself, so I sat with cold feet and watched as I waited to see what would happen next. I didn't have to wait long.

I saw a plume of exhaust exit from the car's tailpipe just as one of the airport's shuttle buses came into the lot. The bus looked to be a fifteen seater and was full of commuters.

I watched as the passengers, who were partially obscured by rows of vehicles, disembarked and moved to the various spots around the parking area. As the last of them got off the bus, I heard a short burst of the horn coming from the Hammer's car. One of the bus passengers held up a hand and began to move toward my suspect's vehicle. When he emerged from behind a row of cars and his previously obscured face came into view, I knew I had hold of something big.

CHAPTER TWENTY-EIGHT

The Hammer got out of his car and shook hands with State Representative Rolly Hutchins. The representative, who was chairman of the powerful Ways and Means committee, was dressed in a dark suit, highly polished black shoes, and a tan cashmere overcoat. I was guessing he had just come back from a colder climate and had lost track of the warmer weather in his home district. Judging by the company he kept, he had also lost track of the values of his home district.

The man who had been riding in the backseat got out of the car and leaned against one side as the Hammer and Hutchins got in. For the next five minutes, the two men talked as the biker stood guard and smoked. As the conversation ended, the representative got out of the car and glanced furtively about the lot as he shook hands with the Hammer. He quickly headed toward his own vehicle—a black late-model BMW.

The trio in the Hammer's car backed out of their stall and began to work their way toward the exit. Their action left me in a bit of a jam. Do I follow the known criminal or follow the suspected criminal? Since I already knew where to find the Hammer, I decided to follow my new suspect and see just how far the reach of Satan's Posse could extend.

Besides, I had been a cop too long to ignore the obvious. When one of the most powerful men in Indiana state government appears to be connected with one of the capital city's most violent gangs, I naturally had questions. And at the moment, they would best be answered by following Representative Hutchins.

The BMW moved out onto High School Road and turned east as it rapidly moved into the lane that would allow easy merging onto I-465 southbound.

I followed and watched as the representative talked on his cell phone while merging into the flow of the traffic. By the time he had successfully integrated himself, he was doing well over seventy, putting him above the posted limit.

We continued moving south and soon exited onto I-70 eastbound. Within minutes we were moving off that interstate and onto Morris Street. Within a few minutes more, the BMW was parked outside a seedy-looking bar that promised "Nightly Attractions." I parked across the street, several doors down, and watched the chairman of the Ways and Means committee exit his vehicle and enter the bar.

I wrote down his tag number and waited. He emerged ten minutes later, got into his car, and began to move back toward I-70. I followed.

Twenty minutes later, we were at a convenience store on south Meridian, and I watched again as the representative went into the store. Unlike the bar, however, the store's windows weren't covered over with dark paint. I watched as the representative and the man at the register moved toward the back of the store. Like the visit at the bar, the meeting didn't last long, and I soon saw Hutchins exit the store. He got back into his car and began heading deeper south along Meridian Street.

After another five minutes, he parked in front of another convenience store, this one attached to a gas station. Within minutes, he was out of the store and in the car, moving north toward the I-465–US 31 interchange.

Rolly Hutchins was an Indianapolis native. He had been born, raised, and educated in the city before moving east to attend the Wharton Business School. After graduation, he returned to Indianapolis to work for one of the city's most prestigious accounting firms, Chaney, Kline, and Smith. His rise within the firm had been rapid. But squabbles soon developed, so he broke out on his own and established himself as the primo financial advisor to the city's elite. He soon entered politics, succeeding on his first bid for the hotly contested house seat in the Indiana General Assembly. A few election cycles later, he became chairman of Ways and Means. His story was well-known, thanks to a flurry of campaign commercials he ran during his failed attempt at obtaining the governor's mansion.

We merged back onto I-465 and moved east. Within a few minutes we were on the east side of the city, heading toward the I-69 interchange.

I continued to follow as the car moved onto I-69 and drove to Allisonville Road, where it turned onto Eighty-second Street. A few minutes later, it pulled into the parking lot of the Bonefish, an upscale seafood restaurant.

I watched as he left the car and entered the restaurant alone. I was tempted to follow him but resisted. I could wait. The company he kept and the places he visited had kindled my interest, and I knew I would see him again. Soon.

CHAPTER TWENTY-NINE

The evening didn't go as planned. The Shapiros called and asked if they could take Callie out for dinner. I reluctantly agreed.

I had wanted to talk with her about what had happened at the restaurant and the mood change that had occurred. But since Anna's death, the Shapiros had sought a deeper relationship with their granddaughter, primarily as a way to stay connected to Anna, but also as a way to help Callie navigate her way through a sea of difficult changes. I was glad for the help, and I understood their need for the relationship, but I was also forced to put our talk on hold.

I was slipping into my jacket, preparing to go out for dinner, when Dale Millikin appeared at the door.

Millikin was the Shapiros' pastor and had been Anna's pastor, prior to her death. Millikin led Anna to Christ. After her conversion, she became more reflective, and we often talked late into the night about what she called "the eternal consequences for the choices we make." I loved my wife, but I didn't buy into her newfound philosophy. Still, the members of her church had been supportive since her death, and the pastor had helped keep Callie as grounded as possible. We got along well, but he often seemed to need to interject himself into my life at the worst possible time.

His hand was poised to knock when I opened the door. "Going out?" he asked, looking at my jacket.

"Callie is with Anna's parents tonight, and since I haven't gotten this cooking thing down yet, I thought I would drive over to Armatzio's."

He looked disappointed. "I didn't mean to come by unannounced, but I had tried to call earlier and see if the two of you wanted to join me out tonight. I was hoping to see Callie. She's been on my heart."

I had learned some of the Christian lingo since Anna's conversion. "On my heart" was another way of saying, "I've been thinking about" but with the added weight of concern.

"Gee, sorry, Dale," I said. "They just left."

He slid his hands into the pockets of his windbreaker. "I don't want to eat alone. Mind if I go with you?"

It wasn't what I had planned, but I didn't want to eat alone either. It was one of the reasons I was going to Armatzio's. The owners, Tony and Francesca, were close friends and served the best Italian food in the city, even if the restaurant's physical structure left a lot to be desired.

"Sure," I said. "Armatzio's okay?"

He told me that was fine, and we left in my car. Ten minutes later, we were seated at a booth in the crowded restaurant.

"I noticed you got a new car," Millikin said, making small talk as we waited for our order to arrive.

"I wouldn't call it new," I said. "Just new to me."

"Run okay?"

I shrugged. "So far."

"The other one give out?" he asked, emptying a packet of Sweet'N Low into his tea.

"You could say it was shot." I still liked the pun.

"Got any new cases?" He stirred the confection into his tea.

I told him about the case I was working and the nice fee I had collected. I told him of my intention to buy the house I was now renting.

"Sound's like you're doing okay," he said. "Buying the house is a good move."

"Security," I said.

He nodded. "Yes. In a sense it would be."

"In a sense?" I dropped a wedge of lemon in my tea.

"I don't mean to cast a cloud over your good fortune, Colton." He sighed. "It's just that we are needing to replace the roof of the church and, well, we don't have the money."

"Sorry," I said. I seemed to be saying that a lot lately.

He nodded as he sipped the tea. "Well, God will provide. He always has."

"Sure."

He glanced at me before dropping a second packet of Sweet'N Low into his tea. "We trust that He will take care of us."

"Well, it looks like Callie and I will be taken care of. If we can get the house, we'll have our first real piece of security since Anna died."

"I'm glad for you, Colton. I really am. But whether you're renting or buying, the means to do either comes from Him." He drank some tea, wrinkled his nose, and reached for another packet of Sweet'N Low. "And as you know, probably better than most, it can all go away in a second."

I could agree with him on that. My life with Anna had been the most secure family structure I ever had. Years of being moved from home to home as a foster child had left me with the realization that I would never be able to depend on anyone or anything other than myself. But with Anna, I had developed ties. Ties built from love that were designed to bind us together forever. But of course, they hadn't. It had all come crashing down one rain-soaked evening.

"Still," he said, "as I said, I'm glad for you. As long as we live in this world, money is necessary."

I smiled. "You don't like money, Dale?"

"I—"

"Can you run your church without it?"

"Of course not. But we look to Him to be the source of the money. And if He decides to cut off the flow, we know that it's in His will to do so."

"Sure," I said. "And don't get me wrong. I can recognize that there's a God. And I agree that money can't buy happiness. But as long we live in this world, it can sure smooth the ride."

He nodded. "Yes. It can. But—"

"A new roof would solve your problems, wouldn't it?"

He nodded. "Yes. It would solve the problem of a new roof."

"And I'll bet," I said, "that there isn't one person in your church who would turn down a pay raise."

"Of course not. But as I was about to say, money becomes a problem when we love it for its sake."

The waiter approached our table. He set up a folding stand and set our plates on it. "Let's see now," he said, turning first to Millikin. "You had the spaghetti and meat sauce?"

Millikin nodded as the waiter set the plate in front of him.

"So you must have had the linguini," he said, setting my plate in front of me. "Will there be anything else?"

"Is Tony in tonight?" I asked.

The young man shook his head. "No, sir. He and Mrs. Armatzio have taken the evening off."

He folded his serving stand and went back toward the kitchen. I was about to dig in when I noticed Millikin bowing his head. I bowed mine too as he said grace. When I opened my eyes, I shot a quick glance around the room to see if anyone had been watching.

"You were saying?" I said, as I moved the steaming pasta around with my fork.

"It's when we cease to see money as a tool and start seeing it as the end in itself that we take our first misstep."

"You must be talking about the rich. They're different. But guys like me never have enough money to fall in love with. I'm just eking by. And so are you. I think guys like us are safe."

We were silent for a moment as each of us ate. Millikin eventually broke the silence.

"You don't need a lot of money to lose perspective about it," he said. "It's the *love* of money that's the root of evil." He spooned some Parmesan cheese over his spaghetti. "You see, God must be first. But recognizing the power that money has, and the hold that it can have over us, Jesus often taught on the subject, warning us to keep it in its proper place."

I was getting a sermon. "Is your spaghetti good?" I asked.

He took a bite. "Yes, it is. In fact, I'd say it's *very* good."

"Great." I took another bite of the linguini. *Money bought it,* I thought.

CHAPTER
THIRTY

B y the time we finished dinner and arrived back at my house, it was a few minutes shy of seven o'clock. When we parked in front of the house, I saw a modified Harley sitting curbside. Miles Poole was sitting on the front step.

"Who's that?" Millikin asked.

"The subject of my investigation," I said, looking at the man on my front step. I turned to Millikin. "Dale, I'm going to have to call it a night. Something tells me I've got work to do."

He looked at Pork Chop again and then turned to shake my hand. "Thanks for dinner. Tell Callie I came by," he said, climbing out of the car.

I watched as Millikin drove away before I moved up the sidewalk and toward the steps. "How did you find me?" I asked.

"When you pulled out your billfold and paid for the test, I saw your address on your driver's license."

"What do you want?"

I didn't see Miles as a threat anymore, but I also didn't see him as someone whom I could completely trust. I kept an eye on his hands.

"I have a problem."

"Yes you do," I said. "I've spent most of the day tailing your problem."

He shook his head. "No, not that." He stood. "Can we go inside?"

I hesitated. I didn't like the idea of letting Miles into my house. It was the one place that was safe from the world. A haven for Callie and me.

But it was getting cold, and I didn't want to jaw jack with Miles all night long on the front step.

"Come on," I said, as I led him up to the front door.

I unlocked it and stepped aside, allowing him to pass.

I told him to have a seat, and he sat on the sofa. I sat in the recliner, opposite him. "What's the problem?" I asked.

He scratched his head. Under his jacket, I could see the hint of a shoulder holster and guessed he was probably carrying the same .357 he had used in the alley.

"There's a chance I might be killed."

"You mean as in 'someday' or as in 'imminent'?"

"Someday. Maybe soon."

"I can agree with that."

He licked his lips. "You got anything to drink?"

I slid off the chair and went into the kitchen and opened the refrigerator door. It was nearly empty. "Milk, Coke, and juice. Or coffee."

"That's it?" He sighed, and then muttered something under his breath. "Coke," he said.

I pulled two cans of Coke from the refrigerator and went back into the living room. I handed him one as I set down and popped the top on mine.

"Who'd you tail?" he asked, opening the can of soda.

"The Hammer."

He drank some of the Coke. "Find out anything?"

"Just enough to make me want to go out and do it again."

He nodded.

"What's his beef with you?" I asked.

He drank more Coke. "I'm not affiliated."

"With anyone?" I asked.

"Yeah. I don't join. But I have friends who do, and sometimes they don't all get along. That leaves me in the middle."

I knew how he felt.

"And sometimes I have to do things that can set one club against me and turn another one for me. Sometimes I have all the clubs working with me, and sometimes I have all of them after me. I don't always know where I stand. Keeps me looking over my shoulder."

"Sure," I said. "I think we've established that as one of the reasons you tried to waste me in the alley."

He grinned. "Yeah, sorry about that."

"No harm, no foul," I said.

"But just because I'm not affiliated, doesn't mean I'm a RUB."

"RUB?"

He had just started to lift the can again, but stopped midhoist. The expression on his face told me that he thought he had overestimated me. "You don't know what a RUB is? And you was a cop?"

I shrugged.

He shook his head and finished his hoist. After drinking he said, "RUB. Rich urban bikers. Wannabes."

I recalled that Chastain had said that Miles fancied himself as a biker. "You know," I said, "at least one cop I know sees you as a wannabe. I'm not sure about the rich urban part, though."

"Who?"

I shook my head.

He laughed. "It don't matter. I couldn't care less what anyone thinks. I live my life for me and…"

"And what?" I asked.

He drank some more and set the can down on the nearby end table. His expression had changed. It was solemn—sad. "For my daughter."

My own facial expression must have spoken loudly. He grew defensive. "You don't think I can have a kid?"

"Having a child and being a father are two different things,"

I said. "Most men can do one, but too many men don't do the other."

"Well, I do." He picked up the can and swigged more of the pop. Somehow, I couldn't help but think that his imagination was turning the Coke into a beer.

"Okay," I said. "So you have a daughter. I meant no offense. But I didn't see her at the apartment. Does she live with her mother?"

The lines on his face seemed to visibly deepen. "Her mother don't want her. Her mother is a crack…" He stopped midsentence, sighing heavily. "Anyway, her mother don't want her."

"Who does she live with?" I asked.

"Hope House."

Hope House was a group home, designed and funded to provide care for the mentally handicapped. "How old is she?" I asked.

"She'll be twelve on her next birthday." He finished the soft drink. "She's mongoloid," he said.

"You mean she's been diagnosed with Down Syndrome?"

He nodded. "Yeah, right. She can't take care of herself."

"How do you provide for her?" I asked. "Hope House is expensive."

He nodded slowly. "About forty grand a year." He crushed the empty can. "I do what I do. What else is there for someone like me?"

Miles was a strange mix of man, but I'd seen others like him before. On the one hand, he was an outlaw biker who would rob an elderly lady of her last nickel. On the other hand, he was doing his best to provide for a mentally challenged child.

"Is she the problem you came here to talk about?"

"Her name is April. Because, you know, she was born in April."

"Sure."

He fidgeted with the can. "We knew right away that she wasn't right." He shook his head and sighed. "The old lady and me weren't married, but I thought we could make a go of it for the baby. One look at April, though, and her mom said no."

"Just like that?" I asked.

"Yep. I didn't know what to do. My mom helped me with her for a while, but then she died. So I put April in Hope House. People say it's the best place around."

"It is," I said.

He fixed a vacant stare at the wall behind me. "I just put her there, and when the money started to run out, I knew I had to do something. Something big."

"What money?" I asked.

"Before my mother died, she wrote her will, leaving everything to April. The money was put in a trust."

"How long ago was that?"

He rolled his eyes upward as he calculated. "Little over two years ago."

That would correspond to the time that Marian died. Still no indication that he was Berger's son, but certainly an indicator that I had the right man.

"I read your mother's obituary," I said. "There was no mention of a granddaughter."

"Yeah. That's right. No need for my enemies to know."

"Don't you think they probably did?"

He shrugged. "Maybe. Still, no reason to advertise it."

We were both silent for a moment as we mulled over the existence of a daughter. Each of us, though, saw the newly revealed information from a different perspective.

"You never knew your father?" I asked, breaking the silence.

His eyes narrowed as he looked at me. "Yeah. I said that before."

"Sure."

"After Dad died in Vietnam, Mom married some dude before I was born. His name was Poole." He shrugged. "He bailed on us later."

"Did your mother take care of April?"

"Until she died."

"How much did she leave?" I asked.

"With the house and everything, it was around a couple of hundred grand."

Given what I saw of the way Miles lived, two hundred thousand could have upgraded his lifestyle significantly.

"And your mother put all of that in trust for April?"

"She had to. How else was I going to take care of her?"

"And now the money is running low, and you've gotten yourself into a jam."

He nodded. "And I'm not going to live long. Somebody's got to look in on April when I'm gone."

"Whoa," I said. "Listen, I would like to help. But—"

"Not you," he said. "I'm not asking you to take care of her. But I was wondering, if this man is my dad, do you think he might be able to look in on her? At least until he dies?"

Berger could more than provide for April's needs. And if Miles knew that, and if he knew of Berger's connection to his mother… then it was possible I had the letter writer in my living room, which brought blackmail back into focus as the motive.

"If the tests back our suspicions, you can ask him yourself," I said.

He nodded thoughtfully. "Yeah. I'll do that."

CHAPTER THIRTY-ONE

The next morning, I was jogging along the canal in downtown Indianapolis, thinking about how I was going to get the Hammer off Miles' back. I still didn't know the source of friction between the two, but I was beginning to believe it could have something to do with the chairman of the Ways and Means committee—or not. I was allowing my mind to roam.

I had called Mary at home, not long after Miles left, and asked her to run the tag off Hutchins' car. It wasn't his address I needed, it was everything else. Previous encounters with the law, questionable activities, even parking tickets could be accessible from other sources, beginning with the NCIC report of his tag number. Mary agreed and told me she would be coming around about nine that morning. She offered coffee out, and I accepted. I didn't like the growing relationship she had developed with Steve, and I welcomed the chance to spend some time alone with her. It would give me a chance to feel her out. See where they stood. Maybe even...

The run along the canal was a change of pace. Exercise can be boring. The same lifting routine or the same running course can rob the workout of part of its benefit and turn something that is meant to be mentally stimulating into a toxic sleep-inducing waste of time. Since a lack of funds had left me with no choice but to lift in my basement, I could at least alter my running path and enliven my sense of mental well-being. I finished the run and drove back to my house for a shower and change of clothes.

I glanced at my watch as I jogged up the steps to my house. Mary would be by any minute, and I needed to be ready. Like a lot of events in my life, major or minor, I always seemed to be a few minutes behind or a few dollars short.

I dropped my sweats into the hamper and was soon standing in the shower, allowing the water to cascade over me. The run had been invigorating, but it was the shower that rounded out the experience. Kind of like a slice of Key lime pie after a meal of fresh seafood. But I was pressed for time, so I cut the shower short and stepped out of the stall as I reached for a towel.

"Looking for this?" a voice asked.

Before I could turn in the direction of the voice, the towel was thrown over my head, and I was knocked to the floor, where I landed with a thud.

I began to push myself up when someone kicked me on the right side of my ribs. Because of the towel over my face, I hadn't seen the blow coming and didn't have time to brace myself for the assault.

"Get him up," the voice said.

Someone jerked me to my feet and pulled the towel tightly around my face.

"Where's Pork Chop?" the voice asked.

"I don't know—"

Another solid punch. This time to the gut. It managed to knock the wind out of me, and I felt the nauseating taste of bile in the back of my throat. My knees began to buckle.

"Stand him up," the voice said.

The man who had pulled me to my feet put his knee in the small of my back, forcing me into a backward arch as he partially held, partially pinned me against the wall. The man with the voice grabbed a handful of the towel and jerked my head backward as he inched closer to my face.

"We don't play games," the voice said, violently forcing my head backward. "We want Pork Chop, and we know you know where to find him."

I didn't say anything. My mind was racing to catch up, hoping to come up with a plan in what seemed to be a hopeless situation.

"We want him, and you're going to tell us where to find him." Another punch to the gut—another crash to the floor.

I was having a hard time breathing, but my anger was generating enough adrenalin to give me the thrust I needed. I pushed myself back to my feet and grabbed for the towel. Before I could get it off, I absorbed another blow to the jaw. This time though, I didn't crash to the floor. The man standing behind me grabbed me by the towel that was still wrapped around my head, and drove me, face-first, into the shower stall. When I landed, I heard the ratcheting sound of a pump shotgun. The cold gun barrel was driven into my chest.

"We want Pork Chop," the voice said again. "We want him now, or you die now."

I was about to make a grab for the barrel, when the man with the gun forced it deeper into my chest.

"Don't," a second voice said. "We're not supposed to kill 'im. This time was supposed to be a warning."

The man with the gun relaxed. He pulled the barrel from my chest.

"Don't think you're off the hook with us," the first voice said. "We want Pork Chop." He stepped into the shower stall. "And don't think we're above doing you—or that pretty young daughter of yours."

The adrenalin rush turned into a sudden explosion. I slid downward into the stall, and using the leverage of lying on my back, kicked at the man, hitting him in the chest. He fell backward out of the stall and slammed against the opposite wall with a sudden exhale.

I quickly lurched forward, trying to pull the towel off my head as I scrambled to get out of the shower. Just as I cleared the stall door, I was kicked again under the left side of my ribs. I landed on the floor.

The first voice said, "You've got twenty-four hours to give us Pork Chop, or else we come back." He grabbed me by the towel again. "And you can tell your daughter that too."

He struck me on the head with the butt of the shotgun, and everything went dark.

A persistent ringing.

I shook my head. It throbbed.

More ringing.

Another shake of the head—more throbbing.

I pushed off the floor and sat up against the bathroom wall. I pulled the bloody towel off my head.

The ringing kept coming. One ring, then two, followed by a short burst of three.

I stood, using the wall for support, and moved toward the bathroom doorway. I grabbed my robe from the rack and pulled it on as I crept out of the bathroom and into the hallway. The doorbell rang again.

I eased into the living room and opened the front door.

"Hi," Mary said, just as the door opened. "I...Colton! What happened?"

I pushed open the screen door to let her in as I moved toward the sofa. "I fell in the shower," I said.

She helped me to the seat and immediately went into the kitchen and came back with a bag of ice. "Here," she said, placing the bag against the side of my face.

I winced at the contact of the ice against my battered head.

"Sorry," she said.

I held the bag in place, allowing the ice to produce its numbing effect and to decrease the swelling.

"Who did this?" she asked.

"I don't know."

"What do you mean you don't know? How can you not—"

"Mary," I said, slowly turning my head in her direction, "they jumped me. I had a towel wrapped around my face. I couldn't see anyone."

"They?"

I nodded.

"How many?"

I shrugged and felt a sharp pain in my rib cage. "I don't know. At least two."

"Let's see," she said, gingerly moving her hands through my hair, along my face, and along my torso. "Any of this hurt?"

I groaned.

She apologized. "I don't think anything is broken, but I think we should go to the hospital just to be sure."

"No."

"Colton, you could have internal injuries."

I slowly turned my head toward her, while keeping the ice pack pressed against my face. "No."

She sighed.

"What did you find out about Hutchins?" I asked.

"Clean."

Despite the ice pack, my jaw was still hurting. It was difficult to talk. "Not clean," I said. "He's just hasn't been caught yet."

Mary frowned. "Hurt to talk?"

I looked at her in a way that answered her question.

"Sorry."

I needed to tell Mary the whole story. In spite of the pain, I needed to talk. "I'm following a man called the Hammer."

She shook her head. "New one on me."

"Me too," I said. "He's with a group of bikers called Satan's Posse. He met with Rolly Hutchins."

She frowned. "I wondered why you asked me to run his plate."

"If Hutchins is hanging out with someone like the Hammer, he isn't clean."

"I agree."

"The problem is that I don't know how dirty."

"Or what kind of dirt," she said.

"Yes."

We were silent for a moment as she tossed around what I had just said. I eased back onto the sofa with the ice pack pressed firmly to my face.

"You want something?" she asked.

"Yeah. I want you to keep digging. If Hutchins has ever—"

"No, I mean, do you want something for the pain?"

I closed my eyes and nodded slowly. "Aspirin works as well as anything," I said.

She stood and went into the bathroom. From where I sat, I could hear her rummaging in the medicine cabinet. She soon returned with two aspirin and a glass of water.

I lowered the ice pack, took the two aspirin, and washed them down. I handed the glass back to Mary. She set it down on the end table and then sat next to me again on the sofa.

"What am I going to do with you?" she asked.

"Watch my back," I said.

"You're going after them."

"Yep."

She shook her head. "Is it worth it?"

"I was hired to do a job."

"Yes. And you did it."

"Not yet. Not until I know whether Miles is Berger's son."

"And when you find out you can walk away."

"No."

"Colton, don't you think—"

"They threatened Callie," I said.

CHAPTER THIRTY-TWO

Two hours later, I was back at Miles' apartment. He buzzed me in.

"What happened to you?" he asked as soon as he opened the door.

I walked past him and sat on the recliner where he sat the last time I visited.

"What're you doing?" I asked.

He stood in the open doorway, staring at me for a moment, before he closed the door and flopped onto another chair.

"That's my business," he said.

I shook my head. "No. Now it's mine. Two men who are looking for you came to pay me a visit this morning. They threatened me—and my daughter."

He shook his head in disgust as he rubbed his eyes with one hand. "Look, I don't mean for anyone to get caught up in my life. You came looking for me; I didn't come looking for you."

"What do you do?" I asked.

He sighed and hung his head as he paused to think. After a moment, he raised his head. "Threatened your daughter, huh?"

"Yep."

"I don't suppose you can—"

"Nope."

"Okay," he said, with another sigh. "Here's the situation. I don't affiliate."

"You told me that part already, Miles."

"I know. My point is that I don't affiliate, but I know people who do. People from different clubs."

"You told me that too."

"Yeah, well, sometimes they don't all get along. And when they don't, I can sometimes get caught in the middle."

I leaned forward in the chair. "Get to it. What do you *do?*"

"I take advantage of the situation. If I hear of something that's going down, I pass it on to an interested party—for a piece of the pie. I ain't no stoolie. What I do, I do for money."

"Nice to have standards," I said. "But the fact remains, you've crossed the Hammer."

He paused to light a cigarette. "Gee, you think?" he said, blowing the smoke through both nostrils.

I studied Miles for a moment and came to the conclusion that it would be useless to ask him how he crossed the Posse. He didn't have a clue.

"He's a bad dude," I said. "All of the city's law enforcement have an interest in him."

He nodded. "I don't doubt it."

"And that doesn't bother you?"

He shrugged. "What am I going to do about it? Gotta make a living."

I looked around the apartment. "You call this living? Enough living to die for?"

"You ain't living so well yourself." He blew the smoke through his nostrils again.

"Maybe. But no one's gunning for me."

"You sure about that?"

He was right. I did have someone who was after me. The same person, in fact, that was after him.

"So why are you doing this?" he asked.

"It's called honor. When you're paid to do a job, you do it. I've been paid a great deal of money to find out if you're the son of a dying man. I've found you. If I can confirm that you're his son, I need to be able to deliver you to him without fanfare. That means no trail of bikers. Since they've already assaulted me, it's reasonable to assume I can't take you to your father until I can resolve whatever mess you've gotten yourself into."

"And if I'm not his son?"

"Then you're not."

"And you walk away, leaving me to deal with my problems any way I can?" He inhaled on the cigarette, holding it between his thumb and forefinger.

"They're your problems," I said.

"So my problems are your problems as long as you're getting paid to do the job."

"Right."

He smiled. "And the honor thing?" He exhaled.

"The honor comes in doing the job that I'm paid to do."

"It doesn't come in doing the right thing? Whether you get paid for it or not?"

He was beginning to sound like Millikin. "We're going to see the Hammer," I said, tiring of the verbal sparring. "We're going to confront him."

Miles laughed. "Are you crazy? The dude's gunning for me. You think I'm going to just walk in there and say hi?"

"I'll be with you."

He chuckled. "Yeah, you're a real threat to someone like him. You can't even take a shower without getting the snot kicked out of you."

I stood. "You don't know if they're the ones who are gunning for you or not."

"They probably are."

"But you don't know."

He paused to think and then slowly nodded. "This isn't the smartest thing in the world, you know?"

"Maybe not," I said. "But isn't it time to take the fight to them? It's the last thing they'd expect you to do."

He nodded. "Yeah, that's true. They don't get that very often."

"Get your jacket, Miles. I'm tired of running."

CHAPTER
THIRTY-THREE

The weather of late September is usually in a state of flux. This particular September was shaping up to be about the same. The earlier part of the month had been unseasonably warm, but now it was becoming persistently colder.

I stepped outside of Pork Chop's building and waited while he got a jacket.

A van matching the description of the one that was involved in the hit had driven through Miles' complex. Yet someone had felt the need to pressure me to ID his location for them. That meant one of two possibilities. Either there were two groups actively looking for Miles, or one group who wasn't entirely sure if he lived here. In any event, someone knew where I lived, and that concerned me enough to call the Shapiros.

Corrin answered on the first ring.

"You must've been on top of the phone," I said.

"Frank is asleep," she said. "I wanted to get it before it woke him."

The Shapiros constituted the closest thing I had to a family. They had taken me into their lives the minute Anna and I had met, and they kept me there even after her death. Having never had a mother and father of my own, I often turned to them when I needed help or advice. In return, I was there for them as well.

"Everything go okay last night?" I asked.

"Sure. We had a great time. Frank drove her to school this morning and—"

"Great. Listen," I said, "what would you think about keeping her for a couple more days?"

There was a pause. "Sure. Why?"

"I just think she could benefit from it. For one thing, you can cook. For another, you're Anna's mother. I was thinking that a couple of days more might help her."

All of this was true, of course, but I also had need to get Callie away from the house. I needed time to keep her safe while I secured the ten thousand that would make our lives better.

"Sure. That's no problem. I'll just have Frank pick her up at the school when she's done for the day."

I thanked her, and we ended the call just as Miles was coming out of the building. He was dressed in a denim jacket, jeans, and a maroon T-shirt. I could see the bottom end of his shoulder holster peeking out from under the jacket. He tossed a partially smoked cigarette to the sidewalk and ground it underfoot as he turned up the collar of the jacket.

"No time like the present," he said.

We climbed into my car and left the complex as we merged into the flow of traffic on Raymond Street.

"How do you want to play this?" he asked.

"Straight up," I said. "We knock on the door and ask if he has a beef with you."

"Just like that?"

"Yep."

He thought about it for a minute. "Okay."

"Do you know Rolly Hutchins?" I asked as we moved onto I-65 northbound.

He shook his head. "No. Does he have a name?"

By "name," he meant a street name like Pork Chop, the Priest, or Buster. I didn't see a point in telling him that Hutchins' name was Representative Hutchins, chairman of the House Ways and Means committee.

"No."

He shook his head. "Then I don't know him."

We were quiet for the rest of the ride. Thirty minutes later, we were parked in front of the clubhouse.

"I don't want this to turn into something here," I said, "so let me do the talking."

He shrugged. "Sure. But if one of them dudes moves on me," he patted the gun under his coat, "I'm going to do a little talking of my own."

I pulled the Ruger out of its holster and pulled the slide back, chambering a round before allowing the slide to snap back into place. I holstered the weapon and got out of the car with Miles.

Traffic was light but steady, and the neighborhood was quiet as we approached the door.

I knocked, standing to the left side of the door as Miles stood off to my right, keeping an eye open for any activity behind us. It took several knocks before we got an answer.

"Yeah?" A tall thin man with a long beard that was braided on the end answered the door.

"I want to see Percy," I said. From the corner of my eye, I could see Miles shaking his head as he dropped his face into his hands.

"Just a minute," the man said.

"Are you nuts?" Miles asked. "The biggest insult you can give is to not call a man by his name."

"That is his name," I said.

"No, it's not. His name is the Hammer."

Pork Chop was right, but I had wanted to send the message that I was not approaching them from a position of fear.

It was nearly a full minute before the Hammer came to the doorway. He glared at me as he stepped out onto the porch.

"Percy?" I asked. Miles groaned.

"Who are you?" he asked. That simple question answered two questions of my own. The first was that the voice I heard in my shower earlier that morning did not belong to this man. The second was that he didn't know me. Unlike the two in my home who did.

"Colton Parker," I said.

"And that's supposed to mean something to me?" He turned to look at Miles. "I know you though."

Miles maintained eye contact, not backing down.

"I want to know if you tried to kill this man."

The Hammer towered over me. He was a solid man who appeared much more solid when viewed close up than when viewed from a car sitting a half block away.

"If I did," he said, "he wouldn't be here right now."

"If you did," Miles said, "neither of us would be here right now."

The Hammer looked at Miles and grinned. "You haven't left here yet."

I wanted to tell Miles to shut up, but I knew that wouldn't help. Mainly because he wouldn't. But the other reason, the more subtle one, is that it would diminish him in the eyes of his nemesis. And in Miles' world, that sign of weakness would be an open invitation to trouble.

"Any idea who might be gunning for him?" I asked.

He continued looking at Miles for a moment longer, then turned back to me. "Everybody."

"But not you."

"Nope."

The Hammer had a poker face. If he was lying, I couldn't tell.

"Okay," I said. "Sorry to have troubled you."

As Miles and I moved off the porch and toward the car, I saw the barrel of a rifle withdraw from a partially opened window on the second floor.

"What was that all about?" Miles asked when we were in my car.

"A feeling," I said.

"Feeling?"

"Sure. We were being watched. Didn't you hear him say that you hadn't left there yet?"

"Sure. But—"

"But nothing," I said. "I saw someone in the upstairs window. If the Hammer had given the word, we would've been gunned down on our way to the car."

"He can gun us down in our beds. The time to take him would've been—"

"Think about it, Miles," I said. "There are two of us and a houseful of them. He could've done us in, and he didn't."

He paused to think. "So you don't think he's the one who's after me?"

"Us," I said. "After us. And right now, I don't know what to think."

CHAPTER THIRTY-FOUR

We left the clubhouse and began to work our way back to Miles' apartment. For the most part, our conversation centered on things that I considered peripheral to the concerns at hand. My repeated attempts to steer the conversation back to more relevant issues failed as Miles avoided giving direct answers, preferring instead to talk about bikes, guns, or women. The brain-draining talk lured me into a stupor that prevented me from seeing the danger around us.

We were heading south on Emerson, toward Raymond Street, because I wanted to alter the route we took to Miles' apartment. We had just crossed Southeastern when we were suddenly rear-ended. Miles' seatbelt was unbuckled, and the force of the impact shoved him into the dashboard as my seat harness tightened across my chest. Another impact drove us forward and then into the intersection of Raymond and Emerson, again driving Miles into the dashboard.

I glanced into the rearview mirror and saw a dark van. It was the same one I had seen in Miles' complex and matched the description of the van that had been involved in the hit on Milner.

"We've got trouble," I said.

The van rammed us again, and I floored the accelerator, turning west on Raymond.

The Beretta sputtered at first but then lurched forward with the tires squealing against the pavement, leaving a trail of rubber as the car began to build speed. Within seconds, Miles and I were heading west on Raymond with the dark van close behind.

"I can't see who it is," he said, straining to see his side-view mirror.

"Buckle up," I said.

He buckled the harness and pulled the .357 Magnum from its holster as he rolled down the window.

The van veered to my left, attempting to come alongside the Beretta. From the mirror on my door, I could see the window of the van's right front passenger's seat being rolled down.

I veered sharply to the left, forcing the van onto the median. Just as it did, the barrel of a shotgun peeked through the open window and fired. The buckshot skimmed across the top of the car like a bucket of BBs forced through an air compressor. Its trajectory carried it harmlessly into the empty lane on our right.

I turned the Beretta into the left lane in an attempt to further force the van onto the median when it suddenly slowed, allowing me to get ahead of it. As soon as the Beretta's momentum carried it forward, the van moved to our right and began to speed forward.

"They're going to try again," Miles said.

I steered the Beretta sharply to the right and into the lane the van was using. As I did, it moved again to the left, and the driver punched the gas pedal to the floor. The van's engine whined as it lurched forward until its nose was flush with the left side of my rear bumper. I turned in my seat just in time to see the shotgun level at us again.

The blast connected this time, blowing out my left rear window, forcing shrapnel-like shards of glass inward on us. I sped forward again, forcing the Beretta into the path of the van, where I could now maneuver back and forth in front of it, buying time until I could come up with a better plan.

"You okay?" I asked Miles, as I kept my attention divided between the road in front of me and the van behind.

"I'm okay."

I glanced at him. He had the Magnum in his hand, and was trying to stay focused on the van to the left rear of my car.

"Hang on," I said. "I'm going to try to ditch this guy and we'll get—"

Another blast. This one struck the trunk and bumper of the car.

We were within feet of the next intersection when the light turned red and cars began to cross. I punched the Beretta's horn, blaring my way through the intersection and managing to avoid hitting a compact car containing an elderly couple. The van, still in pursuit, clipped the front end of the compact, spinning it in a near 180-degree turn. Our pursuers continued onward.

I steered the car in front of them as I looked for a quick escape. Just as I was coming onto the next intersection, I heard the blast of the shotgun again, followed by a heavy thump as the car settled lower to the left. I could hear the distinctive thumping of a disintegrating tire as it slapped against the pavement in a vain attempt to secure traction.

I steered into their path again as I glanced over my left shoulder. I saw the barrel of the shotgun come out of the passenger door window again, and I ducked just as another wave of buckshot passed harmlessly over the top of the car.

Just ahead, I saw a clear grassy area. Steering the car sharply to the right, I floored the accelerator once again, running the Berretta up and over the curb and into the air.

The car traveled for nearly thirty yards before landing with a sudden thud as I spun it around and faced the oncoming van a hundred yards away. I didn't have to tell Miles what to do.

We exited the car and took cover behind the rear of the vehicle, he on the passenger side and me on the driver side, using the full length of the car and its engine block as a shield. The van continued to barrel down on us, and when it had closed the distance to thirty yards, we opened fire.

I was aiming at the driver's side of the windshield and guessed that Miles was doing the same. We continued to fire as the van's momentum carried it past the grassy area where we were standing. As it sped past, we kept firing at the rear of our pursuer's vehicle and watched as it continued westward on Raymond. We continued watching until it was out of sight.

Miles stood from his shooting crouch and holstered his gun. "Those guys," he said, "the ones that were in your house this morning?"

"What about them?"

"Looks like they found me," he said.

CHAPTER THIRTY-FIVE

We jumped back into the car and sped over to Miles' apartment where we changed the tire. IPD would be all over the area soon, and we wanted to get out of there before we found ourselves in a confrontation that could be detrimental for both of us.

I told Miles that the van matched the description of the one that had been involved in the hit on his friends. When I also told him that I had seen the same van driving through his complex a couple of days later, he was able to draw his own conclusion.

"I need to get out of here," he said.

"Gee, you think?"

"Where am I going to go?"

I opened the freezer door of his refrigerator and grabbed a handful of ice, wrapping it in a washcloth, before holding it to my still swollen face. "Have you got any money put away?" I went back into the living room and sat on the sofa.

"If I did, do you think I'd be living here?"

"Okay, but we need to get you somewhere safe until we can figure out who is after you."

He slunk into the chair. "That could take a while. I've made a few enemies."

"I can see that," I said. I paced the room as I tried to clear my

161

head and think about the possibilities. I couldn't take him home with me because Miles' pursuers knew where I lived. I couldn't take him to the office for the same reason.

"How about a hotel?" he asked.

I thought about it and nodded slowly. "Could work. But we couldn't put you in under your own name."

"I could check in under your name."

I held the bag of ice away from my face so he could clearly see it. "You're forgetting, they know my name too."

"Yeah, but they don't expect you to stay in a hotel. They're not looking for you, they're looking for me."

I pressed the bag of ice firmly against my face as I thought about what he had said. He was right—and he was wrong. They *were* looking for me, even if for no other reason than to get to him. But Miles was right in suggesting that they were probably scouring area hotels for him but wouldn't be doing so for me. Holing him up in a hotel made sense and would be the safest thing to do. It would also free me to go after the men who were after Miles so I could put this thing to rest.

"Okay, pack your things," I said. "And just enough for a few days. That should give me enough time to sort this thing out and find out who's trying to kill you."

"Then what?"

"Then, when we have the test results back, and if they are what we expect them to be, I can take you to your father—if you'd like."

He nodded. "Yeah. Yeah, why not?" He stood. "Give me a few minutes." He went into the bedroom area of the apartment.

"Take your time," I said, more to myself than to him. "I've got to make a call."

I flipped open my cell phone and saw that Mary had tried to call. Judging from the recorded time, she had tried to contact me at the very time I was trying to avoid a face full of buckshot. I decided to not call her back for now and instead punched in Ms. Carmichael's number. She answered on the third ring.

"Colton Parker," I said. " I—"

"Excellent. Are the results in yet?"

"No, but I expect them soon. Actually I'm calling for clearance to get a hotel room."

There was a short period of silence on the line before she said, "A hotel?"

"Yes."

"Which hotel? And for whom?"

"I don't know which hotel yet," I said. "As for whom, it's for Miles. Someone tried to kill him today."

"Kill him?"

"I think that was their intent," I said. "If not, they were sure sending us some mixed signals."

"Oh my."

"You said that I was to contact you for all reasonable expenses. I was pretty sure that this wasn't going to qualify under that definition, so I thought I'd better ask."

"Can't he stay with you?"

"No. Someone tried to kill me today too."

"You?"

"Yes."

"When?"

"This morning."

"Where?"

"My house."

There was silence on the other end again.

"So, how about it?" I asked. "Can I put him up?"

"If you think it's best."

"I do if Mr. Hume wants to see him alive."

"He does," she said. Another period of silence. "I assume, given the circumstances, you won't check him in under his own name."

"No."

Another pause before she said, "Okay, go ahead, Mr. Parker. Do what you need to do."

I ended the call just as Miles was coming back into the room. He was carrying a large plastic bag similar to the kind that most grocery stores use. He had a few clothes and toiletries in the bag.

"You travel light," I said.

He looked at the bag in his hand. "This is light?"

CHAPTER THIRTY-SIX

I checked Miles into the Radisson Hotel on Monument Circle. The hotel was nice—very upscale—and had a good view. It was also close to IPD headquarters and probably the last place anyone would expect to find an outlaw biker with a price on his head.

The lobby was sparse when we arrived, with only a few people moving in and out of the revolving doors that exited onto Ohio Street. Fewer still were coming in by way of the door that led to the attached parking garage.

After completing the check-in process, I pocketed the credit card receipt for later reimbursement, still intrigued by the ways of the wealthy. Hume had once been estimated by *Forbes* to be worth in excess of a hundred million. And while he would drop ten grand to find a man who may not even be his son, he would require an itemized receipt and pre-clearance for any "unusual" expenses. *Just goes to show you,* I thought, *the rich are different.*

"Come on," I said, leading Miles toward a bank of elevators. "Let's get you settled."

We took the elevator to the nineteenth floor and stepped off into a quiet hallway. After checking our key against the room directory, we turned to the left and walked past the first few doors before coming to Miles' room.

"Well, well, will you take a look at this?" Miles said, after I swiped the key card in the door's slot and we entered the room.

"Nice view," I said, opening the draperies. The clerk had given Miles a room that was indeed nice and that looked out onto the War Memorial monument, centerpiece of Monument Circle and of Indianapolis.

Miles dropped the bag of personal effects onto the bed and came to the window.

"This is a good place to be," I said. "With this location, it's unlikely that anyone could get a potshot at you, and they would have to come up nineteen floors if they were going to do the job up close and personal."

He continued looking out the window as he opened his coat to reveal the Magnum. "If they do, I won't be alone."

I handed him one of the key cards. "Stay here, Miles. Give me a chance to find out who is gunning for you. When I do, I promise I'll be back to get you."

He slid the card into his hip pocket. "Make it quick. I can't sit here forever."

I took the elevator down and had just stepped into the lobby when my cell phone rang. It was Mary.

"I've got something for you," she said.

"Shoot."

"Given the circumstances, Colton, that probably wasn't the best thing to say."

Since I hadn't told her about the events on Raymond Street, I assumed she was talking about the assault in my home.

"Your representative is clean," she said. "If he's done anything, it isn't showing."

I wasn't surprised. "He may not have a record, but he isn't clean," I said.

"I agree." She gave me Hutchins' address.

"I'm going back to the stores that I saw him visit and ask around."

"You might want to be careful, Colton. The man has clout. He can create problems for you. Get your license, shut you down— things like that."

"Get my license?"

"Sure. Don't tell me you haven't thought of that."

I hadn't. But now that she brought it up, I was thinking about it.

CHAPTER THIRTY-SEVEN

I stopped at all but one of the stores that Hutchins had visited. None of them could recall why he was there. One of them didn't even seem to know who he was. But considering that all of the clerks were younger than nineteen and more interested in their iPods than in talking to me, I wasn't surprised.

I had crossed them off and was heading toward the last store on the list when I received the third phone call of the day.

"Mr. Parker, this is Janette. I'm the director of testing at GenTec. We have a match."

"Miles Poole is the son of Berger Hume?" I asked.

"With a probability that exceeds ninety-nine percent."

I thanked her for the information and ended the call as I pulled into the parking lot of the last store Hutchins had visited.

I entered the store and found a middle-aged woman with close-cropped gray hair and crinkly eyes standing behind the counter. She was wearing a long-sleeved gray sweatshirt and jeans, and was stacking cartons of cigarettes.

"Can I help you?" she asked in a gravely voice that was reminiscent of the actress Patricia Neal.

I asked her what she knew about Rolly Hutchins.

"Why? Who are you?"

I gave her one of my cards.

"Private detective? I thought you guys were only in the movies."

"Who's your favorite?" I asked.

"Well, let's see," she said, pausing to think. "I think I'd have to say Humphrey Bogart."

"Me too," I said. "Robert Mitchum played the same part, but it just wasn't the same."

"What do you want to know about Hutchins?"

I told her I was working on a case, that I had followed him to her store, and that I wanted to know about her relationship with him.

She laughed. "Honey, I don't have no relationship with him. If you want to know about Hutchins, you need to talk to the owner. Hold on a sec and I'll get him."

I waited at the counter as she went into a back room through a door that stood between the milk freezer and the soft drink dispenser. After a minute, she came out and motioned for me to come back.

I walked past the woman and into the office as she went back onto the sales floor, closing the door behind her.

"Have a seat, please," the owner said in a thick Eastern European accent.

I sat in a chair next to his desk that stood in an office that doubled as a stockroom. Metal shelves laden with paper napkins, soft drink cups of various sizes, and boxes of cigarettes lined the walls.

The owner was a balding middle-aged man with brown eyes and a beak of a nose. He was dressed in a long-sleeved white shirt with gold pinstripes and dark blue pants anchored by suspenders. His shirt pocket was stuffed with a pair of black-framed glasses, a handkerchief, and two cigars that were still wrapped in cellophane. The nameplate on his desk read HIRAM.

"Now, what do you want to know about Hutchins?" he asked, squinting as he read the business card that the woman had left on his desk.

"I want to know how you know him."

"And then what do you do with what I tell you? Who are you working for?"

"I can't tell you that," I said. "But I—"

He shook his head slowly and dramatically. "No, no, no. This man is very powerful. You will not get me on the hook. What do you want?"

I ignored his last question. "Something tells me that you're already on the hook."

"No."

"You're afraid of him."

"No."

"Help me and I can help you."

"I am not afraid of nobody. I came from Romania. As a Jew!" His face suddenly reddened, and his voice elevated as he thumped his forefinger on the desk. "I came here with nothing." His eyes were alive. "And now I have something. I didn't get here by being stupid."

"Times were tough in Romania," I said.

"Yes. Very tough. Very hard."

"A fascist regime who would stop at nothing to line their pockets with money and their corridors with power."

"Yes."

"Evil men," I said.

"Yes, you are right. Very evil. Is why I come here. Now I live in peace."

"You live better, but you're not living in peace," I said.

He seemed confused, as if he hadn't understood what I had said.

"Men like Hutchins succeed when men like you remain silent. You've seen it happen before. Don't let it happen now."

The look in his eyes told me that I had connected.

"Hutchins is working you," I said. "I don't know what he's doing, but he's working you. And he'll keep working you until there's nothing left to work."

He lowered his eyes, then his head.

"What is Hutchins doing?"

He slowly shook his head again. "I...cannot help you."

I sat in his office for a while, hoping he would change his mind. But he continued to sit in his chair with his eyes diverted.

"Okay," I said, standing. "You have my card. If you change your mind, call me."

I went to the door, pausing long enough to look back at Hiram. He slipped my card into his pocket behind the cigars.

CHAPTER THIRTY-EIGHT

I was back at my office making notes of all that I knew so far. I didn't do it because I had to give a formal report to anyone. I did it for the clarity of thought that writing something down can sometimes bring. And what little I knew needed clarifying.

For example, I knew that someone had been sending anonymous letters to Berger. I knew that those letters claimed that he had fathered a son with a woman who had once been his fiancée.

I now knew, thanks to a call from GenTec, that the letter writer had been correct. I also knew that the son, Miles Poole, was an outlaw biker who played both ends against the middle and now had at least one of those ends, if not both, gunning for him. And I knew that he had a daughter with very expensive medical needs. That alone made Miles a suspect as the letter writer, which reinforced my initial thoughts of blackmail as the motivation.

I also knew that at least one of the gangs that may be after him was connected to a powerful state politician. And, despite what Hiram said, I knew that this politician was working some local store owners. How, I didn't know. But I knew fear when I saw it, and I had seen it in Hiram's eyes.

I completed my notes and was about to call Harley Wilkins to prime him for more information about the Priest and Buster when he walked through the door.

"I need to ask you something," he said, sitting in a chair in front of my desk and crossing his legs. "There was a shooting on Raymond Street today. Witnesses say there was a lot of excitement. Shotguns—car chases. We found a lot of buckshot and some spent shell casings from a nine millimeter." He crossed his legs. "You own a nine, don't you?"

I nodded. "I was there," I said.

"Thank you."

"For what?"

"For being straight up with me. It saves us both a lot of time."

"Sure. But you know there are a lot of nine millimeters out there. It's a very popular weapon."

"True, except it's unlikely that any of them were involved in a shootout on your side of town, with a van that matches the description of the one that was involved in a hit—again on your side of town—and that intersects with an investigation you're conducting."

"Kind of narrows it down a bit, doesn't it?" I asked.

"Yep."

"Okay, here's the situation."

He uncrossed his legs and leaned forward as I outlined the whole scenario for him, right down to the conversation I had just had with Hiram. When I was done, Wilkins got out of his chair, walked to the small refrigerator that I kept near the file cabinet, and got himself a Coke. He opened it and took a long drink before sitting down.

"Sounds like Representative Hutchins is into something he shouldn't be into."

"Funny," I said, "but I was thinking the same thing."

He took another long drink of the Coke. "And your guy has some bad dudes who want him dead, and the two are possibly connected."

"I'm starting to think that they are likely connected."

He nodded slowly as he paused to think. "Could be."

"Any more news on the hit on Milner?"

He had been about to take another drink, but he paused. "Now, you know that as a sworn officer of the law, I can't divulge the results of an active investigation to a non-interested party."

"But I am interested," I said.

"Oh, well then, that makes it all different. So if I tell you that we didn't recover any prints at the scene, other than those of the occupants, that would mean something to you."

"A little," I said.

"And of course the fact that one of the witnesses has picked one of the hitters, Leroy 'the Angel' Thomas, from a mug book, might be of interest to you."

"It might."

"And you would certainly be interested in knowing that we tried to make contact with the Angel but haven't been able to locate him."

"Yes," I said, "that would be of interest to me."

He drank some more Coke. "And you might also be interested to know that Mr. Thomas is known to be nonaffiliated."

"Yes," I said. "In fact, I believe I might know someone else who chooses to remain nonaffiliated."

"Yes, I believe you do." He finished the Coke, crushed the can, and tossed it into my wastebasket. "It seems like the Angel was arrested during a raid on Satan's Posse. Possession, I believe. Interesting isn't it?"

"That a nonaffiliate would be hanging around with the same group who are friends with the chairman of the House Ways and Means committee?"

"That is what I was referring to," he said. He stood and buttoned his coat. It barely covered his ample frame. "One other thing though."

"Yes?"

"The Angel?"

"Yeah?"

"His weapon of choice is a shotgun."

"Gee," I said, "I think I already knew that."

CHAPTER
THIRTY-NINE

Callie was still with the Shapiros and would remain there until I could be certain she was safe.

I called prior to leaving the office, and she still seemed down. Something had happened in the restaurant that had affected her. I didn't know what it was, but I was going to have to find out. Her demeanor had been so upbeat lately that I didn't want to lose ground. Before hanging up, I spoke with Frank, and he said she was getting her homework done but spending a lot of time on the phone. That was something new for her, but also something I recognized as a cardinal sign of being a teenager.

I stopped to pick up dinner from Armatzio's and drove home. When I arrived, I was reminded by the For Sale sign in my front yard of my visit with the bank's loan officer. I made a mental note to call her the next morning to check on the loan. I also needed a new rear window installed in my car, and I made a note to do that too. The pockmarks to my car, caused by the buckshot, were actually fewer than I had expected. That meant they could wait. Too many more auto expenditures, and I wouldn't be able to buy the house. *But then again,* I thought as I walked up the steps to the house, *maybe I didn't really want it after all.*

Since the assault earlier in the morning, I had been reluctant to come home. My castle was no longer the same. No longer an impenetrable fortress. Now it was a place like any other place. One where the violence of the world could enter at will. A place to be on guard. A place in which I no longer felt secure.

I entered the house with the Ruger in one hand and the boxed dinner of veal Parmesan in the other.

I set the dinner on the living room coffee table and made a sweep of the house. I checked and rechecked every room, door, and window. The house was secure. I was not.

After eating dinner, I dropped the Styrofoam carton into the trash and got the gun-cleaning supplies from the hall closet. Without Callie the house was quiet, so I left the television on for the noise it provided as I sat at the kitchen table and began to tear down the Ruger. Most of the people with whom I had worked recognized that their life depended on a clean, functioning weapon. I was no exception. Given the incidents of the day, I wanted to begin tomorrow with a reliable gun.

I had just begun to clean the barrel with the brush when the doorbell rang. I rose from the table and went to the front door, pausing long enough at the hall closet to unlock the metal box I kept there and get the Taurus .38 snub I used for backup. When I reached the door, I stood to one side and pulled the curtain back. I saw Dale Millikin standing outside.

"Come in, Dale," I said, unlocking the door for the minister.

He came in and glanced at the gun in my hand before focusing on my face. Although most of the swelling had gone down, the bruises remained. "You okay?" he asked.

"Uh, yeah," I said. "Can I get you something to drink?" I moved back into the kitchen as Millikin followed.

"Got any coffee?"

"I can make some," I said.

He looked at the parts of the Ruger spread over the table. "Looks like you're busy. If you show me where everything is, I'll make it."

I told him where the coffee supplies were and sat down at the table as I put the .38 next to the disassembled Ruger. After Millikin was done filling the basket with coffee and the reservoir with water, he joined me at the table.

"Looks complicated," he said as his eyes scanned my face again.

I smiled. "Can be at first, but like anything else, you do it enough, it becomes second nature."

"I don't know," he said, scratching his head as he watched me clean. "I'd have to do it an awful lot before it would become second nature to me."

"I've done it a lot," I said.

He nodded. "I imagine."

We were silent for a moment as I ran the wire brush through the barrel, forcing the bits of spent powder onto the newspaper I had spread across the table.

"Something I can help you with, Dale?" I asked, holding the barrel up to the overhead light and peering through it.

"I just felt like I should come by."

"Felt like?"

"I know this may sound odd," he said as he continued to watch me work on the gun, "but God laid it on my heart. I guess I just needed to come by and see if everything is okay."

I put a small amount of solvent on the patch and then threaded it through the cleaning rod. "Yeah. I'm okay." I pushed the rod and the attached cleaning patch through the barrel.

"You answered the door with a gun in your hand," he said. "You've never done that before. At least not as long as I've known you."

"I'm in a different business than you are, Dale. That means I have different tools of the trade." Satisfied the barrel was clean, I began to wipe down the frame.

He looked at the gun parts on the table. "That's for sure. But have you ever gotten the sense that something's wrong? That something's impending, and you need to pray about it?"

"I live with a sense of impending doom," I said. "It goes with the job. But I've never felt the need to pray about it." I examined the parts of the Ruger. The barrel, the frame, and the coil were clean. I began to quickly reassemble the weapon.

"I find my security in God," the minister said. "It's how I face the day."

"Coffee's done," I said, hearing the pot beginning to gurgle.

Millikin stood, went to the counter, and got two mugs off the cup tree. He evidently remembered that I took mine black, pouring coffee into both cups and handing one to me before asking if I had any creamer. I told him where it was, and he poured a little into his coffee, stirring as he did. When he was content he had his coffee sufficiently creamed, he came back to the table and sat.

I had the gun reassembled. I slipped an empty magazine into the pistol's butt and pulled back on the slide. I released the lever and allowed the slide to snap back into place with a *clack* that echoed in the otherwise silent kitchen.

"I find my security in this," I said. "Without it, I wouldn't be sitting here with you right now." I set the pistol down and drank some of the coffee Millikin had made. I noticed his slack expression over the rim of my cup.

"Something did happen today, didn't it?" he asked.

"I had a run-in. Couple of them, actually. Just part of the job. If I couldn't handle it, I wouldn't do it."

"That's why you came to the door with a gun in your hand," he said, drinking the coffee.

"Yep." I reached for the Ruger and held it up. "Consider it security."

He swirled the coffee around in his cup as he shook his head. "No. There is no security there."

I smiled. "Thought you'd say that."

"It's true," he said. "Security doesn't come from the end of a gun. It comes from a relationship with Jesus Christ."

"Sure. And don't take this wrong, Dale, but Jesus Christ wasn't being shot at today. I was. And this," I wiggled the Ruger for emphasis, "is what kept me alive."

"Someone shot at you today?" A look of genuine concern lined his face.

"Yeah."

"Want to tell me about it?"

I didn't, but I did anyway. I told him about the confrontation in the house, the assault on Raymond Street, and the shots that were exchanged as a result. When I was finished, the lines of concern on his face seemed to be etched a little deeper.

"I knew it," he said.

"Knew what? How could you have known?"

"I told you. God laid it on my heart to come here."

"If I had been killed today, God would have been a little late in laying it on your heart to come see me tonight, don't you think?"

"God wasn't late."

"You're not making sense, Dale," I said, with a smile. The preacher was an acquired taste. I hadn't liked him much after Anna's conversion, and even less after her death. And we had clashed a few times, to be sure. But over the ensuing months, the man had been a constant in my life. His concern was genuine even if it was cloaked in religion. My problem with him didn't come from belief that there was no God. On the contrary. I very much believed in God, in one form or another. But I had learned long ago that He had abandoned me to devices of my own. And whatever His desire for others, His mercy didn't always extend to me.

I stood to pour some more coffee for Millikin and myself. When I had put the pot back on the hot plate, I set the carton of creamer next to Millikin and sat down at the table.

"There's no need to fear the future, Colton. God is already there. That's why I can say He wasn't late. But there is a need to fear what can come if your trust is misplaced," he said, gesturing toward the Ruger.

"This misplaced trust saved my life today," I said.

He shook his head. "No. God spared your life today." He poured some creamer into his coffee. "The shotgun blasts that were directed your way didn't hit you."

I had to admit that.

"And the men who invaded your home could have killed you."

"True," I said.

"Where was your gun when the men invaded your home this morning?"

"In the bedroom."

"Then isn't it a little foolish to claim security in an inanimate object that was less than twenty feet away but couldn't save you from your predicament?"

He reached for the Ruger and held it up for me to see. "This can misfire, it can get lost, or it can rust. It won't always be where you need it when you need it. Nothing can. Not guns, not money, not the police, not the government, not the FBI. Only God can be in all places at all times. Only God can meet you in the future."

"Didn't Peter carry a sword? Didn't he cut off the ear of a Roman soldier?" I had seen the movies. I had read some of the Bible.

"Actually, it was the ear of a servant," Millikin said. "An unarmed man. But yes, Peter did sometimes carry a sword before he learned to put his trust in Christ. You see, Colton, Peter was like all of us. Fearful. The result of that kind of fear is a need to find security. So Peter, like all of us, sought security in the things in which the world places its confidence. On that particular night it was a sword. On the night he saw Jesus coming toward him, walking on the sea of Gallilee, it was a boat. But then Jesus told him to get out of the boat. When he did, he began to walk on the water as Jesus did because his faith was in the Son of God."

"But then he sank."

"True," Millikin said, "but that was because he took his eyes off Jesus. The result was that his faith faltered, and he began to sink." He drank some coffee. "You see, we have two choices. We can either put our trust in Christ or not. Peter chose not to, and he sank. He chose not to trust Christ in the garden and instead put his faith in the sword." He pushed the Ruger across the table to me. "Later that same night, Peter lost his faith in the sword and denied Christ when he was confronted. It wasn't until Peter—and the other disciples for that matter—placed their faith fully in Christ and were given the Holy Spirit that they became emboldened and no longer lived in fear."

"Was Jesus with the victims of the crimes I've investigated over the years?" I asked.

"Living a life in Christ doesn't mean bad things won't happen. They will. But it means we can trust that whatever happens will work for the good of those who love Him."

"Sure," I said. "But if it's okay with you, I think I'll just continue to carry this thing anyway."

CHAPTER
FORTY

The next morning, I finished my run through the neighborhood and was showered and dressed by seven. By seven thirty, I was at the body shop.

"Yeah, we can get the window. Take about an hour to install it."

I looked at the man's name patch. "Great, Mike. How soon can you get to it?"

He smiled. "Now, that's the problem. The window won't be in for another couple of days."

"Couple of days?"

He must have read my mind. Before I could say I was going to go somewhere else he said, "I checked around after you called yesterday. Nobody's got the window in stock."

"That's just great," I said.

"Hey, it could be worse. It could be really cold."

I searched his face to see if he was serious. He was.

"It's almost October. It isn't going to get any warmer."

"Two days. Give me two days and I'll have it. And I'll put you ahead of the line. Fair enough?"

"I guess it'll have to be," I said.

"What about the holes?" he asked.

"What about them?"

"Looks like buckshot."

"Oh, yeah. Hunting accident. One of my so-called buddies got excited and discharged his gun."

The man grinned. "Your so-called buddy isn't Dick Cheney, is he?"

"He and I don't run in the same circles."

Mike laughed. "So, wanna fix them?"

"Not until I see the damage from repairing the window."

He grinned. "Sure. I'll call you when it comes in."

I left the body shop with plastic sheeting covering my window and headed for one of the snazzier parts of town. I had the address for Representative Hutchins, and I wanted to see what he was up to that could shed light on the mess I had gotten myself into.

I drove east on I-70, bopping along to the tunes of Benny Carter in much the same way I had when I first encountered Miles. Unlike the biker, however, Hutchins wouldn't be interested in gunplay. The tools of the politician's trade would probably run more along the lines of character assassination, innuendo, half-truths, and deception, with a possible license confiscation thrown in to round out the assault.

After a thirty-minute drive along interstates and well-paved roads, I turned into the upscale residential neighborhood and followed the directions I had gotten from a Google map search. A two-story brick home with a heavily wooded front yard matched the address Mary had given me.

I parked several doors down from Hutchins' house and had just turned off the engine when I saw the powerful Ways and Means committee chairman come out of the front door of his house with a leather briefcase in one hand and a travel mug in the other.

I watched as he set the mug on top of his BMW and unlocked the door. After the door was open, he tossed the briefcase onto the passenger's seat, grabbed the mug from the top of the car, and slid into the driver's seat as he closed the door. I waited as he fumbled for the right key and eventually started the car.

He backed out of the driveway and drove past me. I watched in the rearview mirror until he had put a hundred yards between us, and then I started the Beretta and made a broad U-turn as I went after him.

He moved through the winding tree-lined streets of his subdivision, with me in tow, until he reached the main flow of traffic. Despite his influence, the neighborhood bore the same signs of the garbage strike as did the house on Milner. Some things are the same regardless of who you are.

He turned into the traffic flow and picked up speed as he began to work his way onto the interstate. I followed, staying a safe distance behind.

We drove for another twenty minutes, moved onto I-69 heading northeast, and drove for another ten minutes before exiting. I continued following him until we had worked our way into the town of Fishers.

Fishers was once labeled the fastest-growing community in the state but had managed to stay ahead of the tide. By learning from the mistakes of surrounding communities, Fishers had kept the main arteries that led in and out of town wide enough to accommodate the increasing traffic. Now, with an increasing need for a greater tax base, the town was attempting to annex the adjacent community of Geist. The consequence was a growing antagonism between the two previously peaceful communities as one sought to stay independent and the other sought a greater source of revenue.

We turned into the parking lot of a series of upscale offices, and I watched as the BMW parked in a stall that was reserved for Mr. Hutchins. The office had a sign on the door that read HUTCHINS AND GRAY, CERTIFIED PUBLIC ACCOUNTANTS.

I parked several rows and several parking slots down from the part-time accountant–part-time politician. My car continued to run on for a few moments, failing to attract attention despite the obvious misfit with the other vehicles in the lot. I watched Hutchins as he climbed out of his car and went into the office with his briefcase and travel mug.

I glanced at my watch. It was almost nine thirty. I figured I was going to be in the parking lot for a while, so I got out of the car and jogged across the street where I had seen a gas station–mini mart next to a bank. I went into the store and picked up a small black coffee and a package of donuts before going back to the car and settling in for what could be a long morning.

After figuring out how to open the sipper hole in the cup's lid, I set the small package of donuts on the dash of my car and opened them. For the next half hour, I ate donuts and drank coffee as I watched people come and go. I didn't see anyone I recognized.

As I waited, I periodically looked around to see what was happening in the town of Fishers. On at least one of those occasions I saw the woman who had sold me the coffee standing in the lot of her store. She had her hands on her hips and was looking in my direction. I smiled and waved. After that, the morning grew considerably quieter as the excitement waned.

Boredom began to take over, and my eyes were beginning to roll back in my head when I saw Warren Hume and Simon DeGraff come out of the Hutchins and Gray office. My eyes rolled forward.

I hadn't seen them arrive. How long had they been here? When did they enter? What were they here for?

The sight of the two together underscored Mary's statement that Hutchins was powerful enough to get my license. When I tied that to Warren's earlier threats, my eyes began to open in more ways than one.

Warren was not dressed for success. Wearing a light gray windbreaker over a blue knit shirt and gray pleated Dockers, he ambled out of the office like a man who didn't have a care in the world. He wasn't carrying a briefcase, PDA, or any other paraphernalia to suggest he was a modern businessman. Nothing but a cup of coffee in a small Styrofoam cup.

DeGraff was dressed in much the same manner as he had been the morning he showed up at my house with Chang. He seemed quiet as the two moved across the lot.

They walked past Hutchins' BMW, across a couple of rows of parking stalls, and toward a tan Lexus SC430 sport coupe. Warren walked with his head down. The two were not talking.

I watched as they stopped at Warren's car and he performed the same routine that Hutchins had earlier, setting his coffee cup on top of his car as he buzzed open the door with his key fob. After the door was open, he grabbed the coffee and the two of them climbed in, closing the doors behind them.

Since Hutchins seemed to be quietly tucked away, I opted to follow Warren and DeGraff and see who else they knew—and that I knew—who might also know some bad guys.

It's what I do.

I cleared the donut wrapper off my dash and tossed the empty cup onto the back floorboard as I prepared to follow the Lexus. Just as I did, I heard a deafening roar.

CHAPTER FORTY-ONE

The explosion had blown pieces of the Lexus nearly twenty feet in the air, and the car was still burning when the fire department and police arrived. The force of the blast had shattered the windows of Hutchins and Gray, as well as a few other offices. Pieces of the Lexus were lying about the parking lot, and some of the cars parked near the Lexus were also damaged, with missing doors, windows, and bumpers.

I was standing to one side of the lot with a group of bystanders when a police detective came over.

"Anyone see what happened?"

Most of the people gathered were shaking their heads. I was about to speak when the woman I had waved at earlier, pointed to me and said, "He did."

The detective looked at me. "That so?"

"Well, I—"

"He's been sitting there for hours," she said. "Right over there." She pointed to my car. With its sheet plastic covering the shot-out window and the pockmarks left by the buckshot, the car clearly stood out.

"I—"

"He came into my store over there," she said, pointing at the gas station–mini mart. "He bought coffee and donuts, and he's been sitting there ever since."

It might have been the moment, or it might have been the events of the case, but the woman's shrill voice reminded me of Mrs. Kravitz, the nosy neighbor on *Bewitched*.

The detective looked from her to me, back to her, and then back to me.

"Let's see some ID," he said.

As I reached for my ID, I was aware that the people around me had turned their attention away from the burning hulk in the lot and toward the one who seemed most likely to have caused the burning hulk in the lot.

I handed the detective my business card and my driver's license.

"Colton Parker," he said, mostly to himself as he looked at my license. Then, looking at my card, he said, "Parker Investigations."

I smiled.

"What're you doing here?"

I noticed that the others were all ears now, so I motioned for the detective to follow me as I stepped a few feet away. He motioned for two uniforms to come over to where we were standing.

"I'm working a case that involves the men who were killed in the blast."

"That so?"

"Yeah. And I think they may be connected to Mr. Hutchins," I nodded to Rolly, who was standing on the sidewalk just outside his office door. "And I think all of this ties into a couple of rival biker gangs. I'm not sure how all of it ties into my investigation, but I suspect that Warren over there—" I nodded at what remained of the charred corpse that was still strapped in the seat—"stepped on somebody's toes. Somebody who's tied to Hutchins and the biker gangs."

Only when I saw confusion in the detective's face did I realize how crazy I sounded.

"Uh-huh," he said, nodding slowly. "And who is…Warren?"

I pointed to the car. "The dead guy in the driver's seat. Warren Hume. The other guy is Simon DeGraff."

Neither name rang any familiar chimes for the detective. "Uh-huh. I need to see your license, Mr. Parker."

"Well, you see, here's the deal," I said. "I don't have one. It was suspended."

"Suspended," he said.

I nodded. "And I think that—"

He put up his hand. "You know, why don't we just go back to the office, and we can talk there?"

"Sure. That sounds like a good idea."

He nodded to the two uniformed officers who cuffed my hands behind me.

After I was taken to the police station, I called Benjamin Upcraft and told him the story. He said he would be right down and not to answer any more questions until he arrived. When he did, the fun started.

"The license plate survived the explosion, Mr. Parker," the detective said. "And it is registered to Warren Hume."

"I told you that already," I said. Upcraft shot me a glance that told me to shut up.

"Yes, you did. But what I want to know is how long you were in the lot."

I told him. Another detective in the room kept his gaze focused on me but didn't say anything.

"Now, Mrs. Broadbent says you purchased some coffee and donuts from her at around nine thirty."

"Give or take," I said.

"Uh-huh," he said, flipping through his notes as he stood in the interrogation room with one foot resting on a chair. "And you say you were there sometime before that?"

"A brief time," I said.

"And why were you there?"

"I was following Rolly Hutchins."

"Hutchins? Indiana State Representative Hutchins?"

"Yes."

"Uh-huh," he said again, making a note of what I said.

"I told you that in the parking lot," I said.

"Did you?"

"Yes."

"And how does Mr. Hutchins figure into your case?"

I was about to answer when Upcraft placed a hand on my arm.

"Mr. Parker is in my employ. I have been retained by the Hume family to ascertain the whereabouts of one of their heirs. I have tasked Mr. Parker with finding the missing person."

"Uh-huh," the detective said again, making a note of what Upcraft said. "You see, counselor, we have a bit of a problem here. Your client doesn't have a license to practice his trade. So we're going to probably have to charge him on that."

"Do you have any other impending charges on my client?"

The detective looked at the other man in the room, who shook his head.

"No. Not at the moment."

"Then I suggest," Upcraft said, "that you look up the Indiana statute on my client's licensing requirements. If he is in my employ, he is not required to be licensed."

The detective turned to the other man. "Get the prosecutor's office on the horn. See if that's accurate. And call the Humes. I want to see if they've retained Mr. Upcraft's services."

The attorney subtly placed a hand on my arm.

"We'll be back in a few minutes," the detective said. "Would either of you like anything to drink?"

We both declined, and the detective left the room.

"Don't speak until we get out of here," Upcraft said. "Then we can talk."

We sat for another thirty minutes. Just as the hands of the clock pushed close to noon, the detective reentered.

"You're free to go."

I looked at Upcraft, who was smiling. He stood with me.

"That's it?" I asked.

The detective nodded. "That's it, Mr. Parker. For now."

Upcraft drove me back to my car. Arson investigators and the ATF were going over what remained of the Lexus. The bodies of Warren and DeGraff had been removed.

"When you called and said your license had been suspended, I called the Humes. I told them that if they wanted you to remain on the case, I needed a cover story," Upcraft said.

"Did you talk to Ms. Carmichael?"

"Yes."

"Hume said she could be trusted."

"Well, it appears they came through for you."

"Yes. And so did you. I appreciate it."

"No need," he said. "But you appear to have grabbed a snake by the tail."

I nodded. "I've grabbed something," I said.

We watched in silence as the investigators went about their work.

"This is big," I said.

"How so?"

I nodded toward the still smoldering car. "Car bombs aren't usually the modus operandi of street thugs."

"Yes," he said, looking at the car. "I see what you mean."

I turned slightly in my seat to face Upcraft. "Didn't it seem awfully slick back there?"

"You mean that you weren't charged?"

"They let me go. No more questions, no holding cell. They could've held me for twenty-four hours before charging me."

"I have a feeling that one of two things happened back there," Upcraft said.

"The Humes have more pull than I thought?"

"That's probably accurate," he said, "but I doubt they have enough pull to get you out from under an investigation for something like that." He nodded toward the Lexus.

"Agreed," I said. "Or the police have something concrete that clears me."

"Yes."

"Security cameras?"

He nodded. "Could be. Since it would be easy to verify that they arrived here at a certain time…"

"Warren's car would have to have been wired with the bomb after he got here."

Upcraft nodded.

"A security camera caught the perpetrator."

He nodded again.

I turned in my seat to look around. Across the street, next to the store where I had bought my coffee, was the bank that I had seen earlier. It had an ATM.

"I found the camera," I said.

He turned to look. "I believe you did."

"I'm going to need your help again," I said. "Can you dig up some financial information on Hume Enterprises?"

"Something specific?"

"The hotels. I want to know how much money they're losing and when the slide began. I would also like to know who's buying them."

He pulled a small leather notepad from his inner coat pocket and made notes.

The Humes want to unload these hotels for a reason," I said.

Upcraft finished his notes and slid the pad into his jacket. "For a reason other than what they told you."

"Yes."

"It's time to follow the money trail," he said.

"Funny," I said, "but that's just what I was thinking."

CHAPTER FORTY-TWO

I stopped by the Radisson to talk with Pork Chop. Cell phones are not secure, and given the fact that we had now reached a car-bomb level of violence, I was concerned about larger forces being at work. Mob-like forces.

When I entered his room, I saw that Miles had ordered room service—a club sandwich, fries, and a beer—and was watching a game show. He was wearing the same clothes he had been wearing when we checked into the room.

"I need to ask you some questions," I said.

He sat on the edge of the bed and pulled the room service tray close to him. "Sure," he said, offering me half of the club sandwich. I declined.

"Two men were killed today. One was closely linked to your father."

He paused with the sandwich in his hand. "My father?"

I told him that the tests confirmed him as Berger's son.

"Linked? How close?"

"One of his sons."

He nodded thoughtfully as he ate. "That would make him my half-brother, right?" he asked around a mouthful of sandwich.

"Yes."

"How was he killed?"

"Car bomb," I said. "A car bomb that was probably wired to the starter."

He set the sandwich down. "Oh."

"Do you know anyone named DeGraff?" I asked.

He shook his head.

"This is getting serious," I said. "Someone has been after you since this thing started—"

"Before this thing started," he said.

I corrected myself. "And I can't take you to this family until I know I can do it without risk to them."

"Sounds to me like they have their own risks to deal with."

I had to admit he was right. But I had a nagging feeling that the attempts on Miles and Warren's murder were linked.

"So what do you want from me?" he asked.

"Tell me who kills like that."

He sighed as he picked up a French fry from his tray and ate it. "There are a couple of them."

"I'm listening," I said.

"The Hammer is one. He's connected."

"Connected?"

"Mob stuff. He did some contract work for a while. Now he mostly does his own thing."

"He could've killed you the other day."

"You too," Miles said.

"But he didn't."

He nodded. "Yeah, but he don't work like that."

I leaned forward. "Excuse me? This was a man that almost beat an enemy to death with a ball-peen hammer."

Miles nodded. "Yeah, that's true." He picked the sandwich up again and took a big bite. "That's what I mean. He'd just wipe the guy himself. Up close. No explosions. Not anymore. Not unless there was a reason."

"Someone came at me yesterday," I said. "Someone wanting to know where you were. That could be a reason."

He nodded as he chewed.

"Someone who knew how to find me, but not you," I said.

He nodded again.

"Finding me wouldn't be hard, though," I said, "if the person looking for me had my tag number and was connected."

"Connected like the Hammer," Miles said, taking a long swig of beer.

I got off the edge of the bed and began to pace, recalling the figure I saw in the window when we visited the Hammer. Someone who could have copied my tag number. "I would have recognized his voice," I said. "But I didn't. That means he didn't come to the house."

Miles nodded as he downed another French fry. "Doesn't mean he didn't send someone else."

"But why didn't he just kill you then? He had the chance."

Miles ate another French fry. "Who knows. Maybe he didn't want to have to smoke you too. Maybe he wants to do it up close. Maybe—"

"Who else, Miles? Who else in your circle kills with bombs?"

His countenance fell a little. "Freeze."

"You're sure?"

"Yeah. But you can scratch him off."

"How's that?"

"'Cause I work with the guy. He's about business. He ain't gunnin' for me—or anyone else."

"That's it? That's all?"

"It's enough," he said.

"Whoever is after you, got to me."

"I'm sorry about that," he said. "I really am. But no one told you to come into my life."

"I believe you're missing the point here, Miles."

He took another bite of sandwich. The levity of the game show emcee was beginning to grate on me. I turned off the set.

"Hey!"

"Listen to what I'm saying, Miles. Whoever wants you got to me. They got to me and threatened my daughter."

"I'm sorry about that man, I really am. But Freeze isn't—"

"You have a daughter, don't you?"

"Yeah, but..." He paused with the sandwich still in hand.

"You have a daughter, and the men who are after you can get to her like they got to me."

The lightbulb came on. He set the sandwich down and stood. "I've got to get to her," he said, moving off the bed to the chest of drawers.

"No, you don't. You've got to stay here."

"I don't think so." He opened one of the drawers and took out his holstered .357.

"That's what they want."

He had started to slide into the shoulder rig but paused long enough to listen.

"If they knew where she was at they would've gotten to her already. But if you leave now, you'll lead them right to her. Or else they'll whack you as soon as you set foot out of here. If that happens, who will take care of her then? The state?"

For the first time, I saw the hardened biker begin to wilt. His eyes reddened.

"Stay here, Miles. Give me time to check out the Hammer and Freeze."

"I don't know, man. I—"

"Just a little time."

He took time to think, slowly untangled himself from his shoulder harness, and slid the gun rig back into the drawer.

"I'm going to need an address for Freeze," I said. "And Miles? Don't tell him I'm coming."

"He don't like surprise visits. It's just the way he is."

"Then he ought to do something else. A man in his line of work has got to expect the unexpected."

Miles gave me the address. I wrote it down on a piece of the hotel stationery and slid it into my pocket. "Give me a couple of days," I said.

"Okay, man. A couple of days, but that's it. If you don't have this thing wrapped up by then I'm grabbing her, and we're gone."

"That's just what they want you to do," I said. "Get out in the open."

He grabbed the beer off the tray. "I said I'll wait, so I'll wait. But not long."

"I don't have long," I said.

CHAPTER
FORTY-THREE

I left the hotel and called the Shapiros again. They told me that Callie's mood had begun to deteriorate and that she was becoming increasingly upset. They told me that when they pressed her, they discovered she had a boyfriend and that she had seen him with someone else. I recalled the young man in the restaurant, the one with the other girls. I considered him too old for Callie, but I decided that the phone wasn't the right place to have that conversation. I simply wanted to console her for now. I asked them to put her on the phone.

We talked for a while, but I had little to offer. I didn't know about the boy. Didn't approve of it at her age and didn't approve of him. But it had happened. And now she was hurt. Deeply hurt. And all I could offer were platitudes—over the phone.

I promised her I would get her soon. But I knew the promise fell on deaf ears. The pain she was feeling was dulling anything I had to say. And anything I had to say had been said before. Another promise to be there when it mattered—broken again.

I pulled out of the hotel garage and onto Ohio Street, moving east toward Pennsylvania. The traffic was light, and the sun was shining. The day was unseasonably warm again as the September weather continued the same erratic pattern it had followed all month.

Despite what Miles had said of him, Freeze was a suspect until proven otherwise. To clear him, I was going to have to meet with him. It would mean another visit with an outlaw biker on his own turf. It wasn't something I relished, but it was something I needed to do. A simple dialogue over the phone wouldn't work. I needed to see a man's eyes. I needed to see his facial expressions and body language. My years in law enforcement had taught me that a lot of people can lie over the phone. Very few, though, are as convincing face-to-face.

The address Miles gave me was for a house off of German Church Road, near the Paul Ruster park. A nice area that didn't seem to be a natural habitat for a snake like Freeze.

I drove east on Washington Street, eventually turning onto German Church Road, where I found the house. I parked curbside. The neighborhood was neat, quiet, and solidly middle-class. When I knocked on the door, an attractive-looking woman that I placed to be in her late thirties answered. She was wearing jeans and a T-shirt and had a pleasant smile.

"My name is Colton Parker," I said. "Is…Jimmie home?" I had almost asked for Freeze. The double names were becoming confusing.

"Sure, would you like to come in?" She opened the door and stepped aside, allowing me to enter the house.

Two small children, well-groomed and pleasant, were playing video games with a solidly built, tall, bearded man who was dressed much the same way that everyone else in Miles' circle dressed.

"Honey," the woman said, "this man is here to see you. His name is Colton Parker."

The man scored and then stood, setting the remote control on the sofa where he had been sitting. Each of the two kids, a boy and girl who both appeared to be around nine or ten years old, were intent on winning the game they were playing.

"Hey, man," he said, extending a hand. I shook it. His grip was firm.

"Listen, is there a place we could talk?"

"Sure. The garage okay?"

"Fine with me," I said.

The man turned to his wife. "Business."

She smiled. "Okay." Then she turned to me. "It was nice to meet you Mr. Parker."

"Same here," I said, as I followed the man out the door and around the back of the house to where the unattached garage stood.

He unlocked the side door, and I followed him into the garage as he flicked on the light. As soon as we were inside, he swung at me with a right hook.

I blocked the blow and hit him with a straight left that sent him against the workbench to his right. He came at me again with another hook, and I blocked it again, hitting him with a straight left–right hook combination.

I must have rattled his bells because he reached for a crowbar that was laying on the workbench. As his hand came up with the bar, I put the barrel of the Ruger against his forehead. He paused midattack.

"Something I said?" I asked.

"I don't do business in my home."

"I'm sorry about that, but this was the address I was given."

He still had the crowbar in midair, poised to attack. "Who gave it to you?" he asked.

I pushed the gun a little more firmly against his forehead. "Why don't you put that thing down, and then I can put this thing down, and then we can talk."

He was hesitant but slowly lowered the crowbar and set it down on the workbench. I lowered the Ruger and then backed up, clearing some space between us in case he decided to try for another attack. I holstered the weapon.

"What do you want?" he asked.

"I need to know where you were this morning. Between seven and ten."

"Why?"

"Just answer the question," I said. "If it's the right answer, I'm out of here."

He inched toward the workbench. "Out."

I shook my head. "That was the wrong answer."

He leaned against the workbench, with the heels of his hands supporting his weight. The crowbar was close. I moved a little farther to his left, away from him, widening the distance.

"The better answer would've been to tell me where you were when you were out."

"I don't have to tell you a thing."

"True. But you'll tell it to somebody. Might as well be me. That way, you see, if you're clean, no cops show up looking into your business."

He was angry. His face darkened. "Just out."

I glanced around the garage while trying to keep an eye on Freeze. If he had made a bomb in there, I didn't see any evidence of it. But then what was I looking for, exactly? Dynamite? C4?

"I'm going to be blunt," I said. "First, if you touch that crowbar, the coroner will find you holding it in your hand. Second, did you blow up a car in Fishers this morning?"

A mix of confusion and fear erased the look of anger. "Fishers?"

"Know it?"

"Of course I know it."

"Did you?"

"Who told you that?"

"You're not answering my question," I said. "That doesn't look too good."

He moved away from the bench. "I don't care."

"You will," I said, moving toward the door. "And if I were you, I'd consider the police to be my best friend."

"What're you talking about?" He was angry but concerned at the same time.

"Because when your other friends figure it out, you're going to wish you were in jail."

I left Freeze's neighborhood and turned west on US 40. His eva-siveness left little doubt in my mind that he was involved in the bombing. His first reaction to my question had been to ask about the town in which the bomb had been discharged. He almost seemed surprised. Why? And why wasn't he surprised that I was asking about a bomb in the first place?

A light drizzle had begun to fall, and I turned on the wipers as I glanced over my shoulder at the patch job I had done on my left-rear window. I didn't see any leakage.

Unless I was wrong, I thought to myself as I turned to look ahead, Freeze built the bomb but didn't wire it to Warren's car. Meaning that I had just questioned the hired help. The employer was still on the loose.

But who was the employer? And what did he have against Warren? What was he into, and what, if anything, did it have to do with Miles? And did Freeze know the target? Could he have sold Miles out?

So far, the only true connection I had between Warren and the world in which Miles lived was Representative Rolly Hutchins. It was time we talked.

CHAPTER FORTY-FOUR

It was nearing three in the afternoon, and I was guessing that the damage done to Hutchins' office by the exploding car had forced him to take the rest of the afternoon off. To be sure, I called his house. I told the woman who answered that I was a detective and that I needed to speak with her husband. She asked me to wait while she brought him to the phone. I didn't. Anything I had to say to Hutchins was going to be said face-to-face.

I stopped at a Wendy's drive-through, got a single with fries and a Coke, and moved back into traffic.

Hutchins had met with the Hammer. He had probably met with Warren and DeGraff too, unless the two of them had met with Gray. That would seem to be too convenient, which made the connection between Hutchins and the Hume family seem even stronger. When I connected that with the fact that the Hammer was linked to Miles, I had a common link between the Hume family and Satan's Posse by way of one of the most powerful men in Indiana. That made Hutchins the key.

I ate the burger and fries as I moved north of the city and back to the upscale neighborhood where I had started the day. By the time I arrived, the burger and fries were gone, and the drink was down to some melting ice.

I parked in the driveway of Hutchins' home, very aware that my car did not fit with the flavor of the neighborhood. But given what I now knew, neither did Hutchins.

I rang the doorbell and was greeted by an attractive woman dressed in a pink blouse and navy blue skirt. Her hair was nicely done, and her teeth were white and perfectly aligned. Her skin still had the glow of a post-summer tan and a look of genuine concern colored her face.

I handed her a business card.

"Parker Investigations?" she asked, reading the card. From the sound of her voice, I knew that she had been the person I had spoken with on the phone. "What is this about, Mr. Parker?"

"I need to speak with your husband."

"He isn't—"

"Yes, ma'am, he is."

She paused to look at the card again. "You were the one who called, weren't you?"

"Yes."

She sighed as she slumped against the door frame. "My husband has had a difficult day, Mr. Parker. There might be a better time to talk with him."

I shook my head. "No, actually this is as good as it's going to get. I was in Fishers this morning. I saw two men die. Two men who had just met with your husband. I need to ask him a few questions."

She sighed and looked at the card again before looking over her shoulder into the house. Finally, with a sense of resignation, she stepped aside and allowed me to enter.

The foyer was tastefully decorated with forest green wallpaper that was highlighted in a light gold relief, a set of brass sconces on each side of the door, and a large patterned rug that matched the wallpaper in tone and hue. A spiral staircase led from the foyer to a large hallway above.

"Follow me," she said.

I followed her down a hallway to a set of sliding six-paneled doors. She opened them and led me into the den of Rolly Hutchins.

The Ways and Means committee chairman was seated at his desk with a drink in his hand. An opened bottle of scotch sat on the desk.

"Rolly, this is Colton Parker. He wants to ask you some questions about this morning."

Hutchins lowered the glass and looked at me through bloodshot, glassy eyes. He motioned toward a brown leather wingback chair in front of his desk. I sat as his wife left the room, closing the sliding doors behind her.

"Are you a detective?" he asked.

"Private."

He took a long drink, seemingly relieved that I was not with the police.

"What do you want?" he asked. His voice was deep and steady, despite the memories of the morning's events and the liquor he was using to drown them.

"I want to know why someone would want to kill Warren Hume," I said. "I want to know how Simon DeGraff is connected to Warren, and how both are connected to you. I want to know why you were seen with the Hammer, and I want to know what you know about Miles Poole."

He gave me a half-grin as he took another long drink, draining the glass. When he did, he reached for the bottle and poured another four fingers.

"You want a lot."

"You know a lot," I said.

He nodded and took another drink. "Who hired you?"

"That's my question," I said.

His eyes narrowed as he seemed to study the liquor in his glass before taking another drink. The shades had been pulled, making the room dark. Overall, it seemed to reflect the politician's demeanor.

"The good people of Indiana," he said, as his speech showed its first signs of slurring.

"They got burned," I said.

He nodded as he raised his glass. "That they did." He drank again.

"You won't find what you're looking for in that," I said, gesturing toward the bottle.

"And how would you know what I'm looking for?" He looked at me with disdain.

"Because you went into public service with a desire to do the right thing."

He snorted.

"And somewhere, you got off track."

"Story of my life," he said as he swirled the liquor.

"And you won't find redemption in a glass."

He snorted again.

"I saw you with the Hammer," I said. "What do you do for Satan's Posse?"

He drank again, ignoring my question.

"You will have to face this sooner or later, Hutchins. Now, or in court."

He shook his head.

"It won't go away. This thing, whatever it is, has gotten too big for you. It's way out of hand. People are dying. People you know."

Nothing.

"And they're dying in car bombs. This isn't street-level stuff. This is organized crime."

He took another drink.

"Are you shaking down store owners for the mob?"

His eyes rolled from the glass in his hand to me. They looked like misshapen pieces of coal, afloat in pools of blood. I wanted to know what he was doing with Hiram and the other store owners. Given Hutchins' possible link to organized crime, it seemed a topic that was ripe for mining. He said nothing.

"What was your connection with Warren Hume?"

"I don't know him."

"What was your connection to Simon DeGraff?"

He snorted again. "Don't know him."

"And Miles Poole?"

"A usurper," he said. Despite his slurring speech, he had just given me a thread to pull.

"How?"

"He has no right," he said.

"To what?"

"To come in and mess everything up." He took another drink. He was downing the alcohol fast, and it was working on him just as quickly.

"Why was Warren killed?"

He sighed and shook his head. "I don't know."

"Why were you meeting with him this morning?"

He shook his head. "None of your business."

He was drunk and getting drunker. His mental skills were deteriorating.

"You're an accountant," I said. "Are you working on the sale of the Hume hotels? Did he meet with you this morning to talk about the sale?"

"I'm not...talking about...them. I already...told you that."

"Did Warren have something to do with getting my license?"

He downed the glass and poured more.

"Did you?"

He drank some more.

"How far does this thing go, Hutchins? If Chang is involved with DeGraff and DeGraff worked for Warren, does this mean we have just one bad cop, or are there more?"

Nothing.

So far, I had gotten confirmation that Hutchins was aware of Poole, and from what he was saying, his opinion of the biker was the same as Warren's. Miles was an interloper who stood to squelch a multimillion-dollar deal. The information wasn't much and certainly wasn't new, but it was clearly all I was going to get from him.

I stood. He tried to follow me with his eyes, but his head was weaving now, and his lids were heavy.

"There'll be more questions," I said. "Either from me or the police."

His hand trembled as he took another drink and set the glass down on the desk. "No" he said. "There won't."

CHAPTER FORTY-FIVE

I was exhausted by the time I left Hutchins' house. The bombing, the detention at the police station, the tussle with Freeze, and the roundabout with the committee chairman had taken their toll. But I still had another stop to make, and this would be the grand-daddy of them all.

I drove to Hume's residence, where Ms. Carmichael greeted me at the door.

"Mr. Parker." There was no smile. No pleasantries. She was as coldly detached and professional as ever. She allowed me into the house.

"How is he?" I asked as soon as I stepped inside.

"Understandably, Mr. Hume is taking this very hard."

"Could I see him?"

"I'm sorry," she said, "but he's just been sedated."

"I assume Denton is aware of the situation."

"He was the one who informed Mr. Hume."

"And where is Denton now?" I asked.

"He's at the office."

"The office?"

She directed me into the living room, where we sat on the sofa Warren had been sitting on the last time I had been in the house.

"He's burning the midnight oil. The family's business is pressing, Mr. Parker. It doesn't stop, regardless of the disruptions that may occur."

"Disrup—? Ms. Carmichael, Denton's brother was murdered this morning."

"We are very aware of what happened this morning," she said, with an edge to her voice. "But it's not Denton's fault."

"It's somebody's fault," I said. "Warren had enemies."

"The family has enemies. You cannot reach the level of success that Mr. Hume has achieved and not have enemies. There will always be people in our business who will want us out of the way."

"Sure. But what I'm getting at here, Ms. Carmichael, is that Warren had personal enemies. Someone who wanted him dead, not just out of the way. Someone who decided to kill him and not Denton."

She crossed her legs and looked at me in much the same way a microbiologist will look at an amoeba. "I know what you're getting at, Mr. Parker. But if Warren had enemies outside the family context, I'm not aware of them."

"Could he have been working on anything new or personal? Something that may not have been directly related to the family business?"

"Possible," she said. "But that would be his business, and I would have no way of knowing about it. My interests are confined to Hume Enterprises, which, for the moment, means Mr. Hume." She nodded toward the area of the house where Hume's bedroom was located.

"Was Warren political?"

She tilted her head to one side. "Political?"

"Was he involved in local or state politics? Any leanings in that direction?"

She frowned for a moment as she thought. Then, slowly shaking her head, she said, "No, not that I'm aware of, although the family does maintain a hand in the political arena. It's necessary if a business as large as this one is to remain viable."

"How does the family 'maintain a hand?'" I asked.

She cleared her throat as she shifted slightly on the sofa. "Well, for instance, we try to develop and maintain cordial relations with all of the candidates for an office. At least the offices that could affect our business interests."

"Such as Rolly Hutchins?"

"Among others," she said.

"Warren ever spend time with Rolly Hutchins?"

"As I've already stated, if Warren was involved in politics, I'm unaware of it."

"Right. You did say that, didn't you? But the family is involved. Correct?"

"To the extent that they must be."

"And who in the family, specifically, is the one who is political?"

"That would fall to me."

"You're the family's operative?"

"I'm the family's everything. I give advice. I counsel. I take care of Mr. Hume. And, if warranted, I grease the wheel of electoral politics to help those candidates who are friendly toward Hume Enterprises."

"Do you know Rolly Hutchins?"

She nodded. "Yes. Since his ascension to the chairmanship of the Ways and Means committee, he has become someone with whom we would like a satisfying relationship."

"Have you worked with him often?"

She shook her head. "No. Denton has had him to the house for cocktails or an occasional fundraiser, but that's been the extent of it."

"Kind of hard to maintain a satisfying relationship if that's all the time you spend with him, isn't it?"

"In politics, Mr. Parker, it's the fundraisers that seal our mutually satisfying relationship. Money is the mother's milk."

"Sure. It takes money to make money."

She nodded slowly. I still had that amoeba-like feeling.

"How was Warren connected to Simon DeGraff?"

"I don't know Simon DeGraff," she said.

"He was killed along with Warren this morning."

She shrugged. "I'm sorry for his family, but I don't know him."

"Do you know Chang?"

"Who?"

"Never mind," I said. "Probably not important in the scheme of things. Do you have any idea why Hutchins would be meeting with Warren?"

"No."

"Would Denton?"

"You'll have to ask him, Mr. Parker." She stood, signaling that it was time for me to leave. "We appreciate the fact that you came by, and I'm truly sorry you were unable to see Mr. Hume."

I stood and followed her to the door.

"Mr. Parker, we didn't hire you to delve into the family's political or business affairs. We hired you to find Miles Poole, determine if he is Mr. Hume's son, and then arrange for the two of them to meet."

"That's what I'm doing, Ms. Carmichael. And doing it will require me to delve into the family's political and business interests. It's what you're paying me for."

"We know what we're paying for." She opened the door. "And the family always gets its money's worth."

CHAPTER FORTY-SIX

Despite the fact that I had managed to alienate my employer, the day wasn't a total loss. I now knew that Hutchins was connected to the Humes and that the family's political fortunes were important enough that they didn't want me involved in them—even if the politician they were involved with was friendly with an outlaw biker gang that might be responsible for murdering a member of their family.

I was climbing into my car when the phone rang.

"Upcraft here," the attorney said as soon as I answered the phone. "I have some interesting news."

"Shoot," I said, backing around the family's trash cans as they sat at the end of the driveway.

"I've done some checking on the Hume family's financial picture, as you requested."

"And?"

"It would appear that the family is quite sound, financially speaking. Given their corporate stock, real property, and other investments and holdings, they are estimated at a net worth of just under a hundred million."

"No news there," I said.

"No, but here's the interesting part," Upcraft continued. "Hume

Enterprises isn't faring as well. The major drain on the business is coming from the hotel chain."

"That isn't exactly news either," I said.

"Maybe not. But the hotel chain just took out a thirty-million-dollar loan for a new face-lift. A complete renovation. Plans include updating all—and I want to stress *all*—of the rooms in the hotels. There will be a new pool in ten of the facilities, new landscaping for all of them, and an aggressive advertising campaign that includes discounts for those patrons who use a specified travel agency. Also, in those areas where it's legal—for example, Indiana—they have applied for gambling permits."

"Maybe they're trying to spruce up the place. Attract some business."

"That might be a legitimate approach if they were intent on keeping the hotels. But didn't you tell me that the family is within a few weeks of selling them?"

I pulled the car alongside the curb several doors down from the Hume residence. "Yes, I did." I paused to think. "Why would someone invest that much money and go into that much debt to renovate something that's losing so much money they feel the need to sell it as quickly as possible?"

The attorney cleared his throat in an outlandishly audible way. "Now, do you see what I mean by interesting?"

"I'm beginning to," I said. "How did you find all of this?"

"I drove by the hotel in Richmond. I wanted to see one of the hotels up close and talk to the manager. I was intent on asking about occupancy, average length of stay, that sort of thing. But when I got there, I saw a major rehab underway. There was construction going on everywhere, along with the delivery of new furniture and what appeared to be a gaming table that was still in the crate. Of course, I changed the tack I was going to use when I talked to the manager. Instead of asking about average lengths of stay and that sort of thing, I asked about the renovation. He was excited and spilled the beans. When I called the other hotels, I got the same reaction. But, and here's the truly interesting part, none of this has been publicly released."

"Why?"

"No reason given. But nearly every one of the Hume hotel managers I spoke with told me they were ordered to begin the face-lift. In the case of the Richmond hotel, they were told to order new gaming equipment but to sit on it until they got the green light."

"In two weeks," I said.

"Exactly."

"That probably corresponds to the time of the sale."

"I would agree with that."

"And they had no problem telling you this over the phone?"

"I told them I represented the buyer. That I wanted to know how the renovation was going."

"You know who the buyer is?" I asked.

"A group calling themselves Oro. They have corporate papers filed in New Jersey, but other than that, I don't know anything about them."

"Me either," I said. "Never heard of them." I paused to think about the gambling motif that the hotels were adopting. "Hutchins could push through a gambling permit, couldn't he?"

"Absolutely."

I thanked him for his help and ended the call before turning in my seat and looking back at the Hume home. The trash cans and bags that I had nearly run over as I had backed out of the driveway were standing curbside, just outside the wrought-iron gates.

Ms. Carmichael had told me the hotels were losing money. In fact, both Denton and Warren had confirmed that fact, and both were concerned that the Miles Poole incident be resolved before the deal was inked. And yet the family was spending millions to refurbish a losing proposition just prior to selling. I didn't like the feeling I was getting.

I studied the trash cans. I certainly had more important leads to check out. Leads that translated into strong suspects, given the nature of their lives and their proclivity toward violence. Men like the Angel, for example. But suspicions that are aroused in cops—ex or otherwise—tend to lead to concern. And concern leads to questioning. And questioning leads to more investigation, and more investigation leads to facts. And facts never lie.

I backed the car to the curb where the trash cans stood and got out. I picked up the plastic bags containing their two-week-long accumulation of garbage and put it in my trunk.

Evidence comes in all shapes, sizes, and wrapping. Sometimes, it can even come in a garbage bag.

CHAPTER FORTY-SEVEN

I slept fitfully that night, mostly due to the home invaders of two days before, but partly due to the issues at hand. After rising early, I checked the door locks and found them as secure as they had been the night before.

I took a shower with the holstered Ruger hanging on the nearby towel hook. When I was done, I dressed and went into the kitchen to get the coffee started. I flicked on the small television in the kitchen and tuned in to one of the local channels before going back to the front door and getting the newspaper off the stoop.

I brought the paper back into the kitchen and dug out the Home and Garden section. I opened that section of the paper and spread it out onto the kitchen floor. When that was done, I opened the first of Hume's trash bags and spilled the contents onto the floor. I promised myself that if I found what I was looking for, I would never complain about a garbage strike again.

I found an eclectic collection of old newspapers, coffee grounds, cans, and milk cartons. Everything but what I was looking for.

I rolled up the newspaper along with the contents I had dumped onto it and put the whole thing back into the garbage bag before opening a second bag and tossing the contents onto the City section. The results were no better.

I did this two more times before finding what I was looking for in the fifth and final bag. Lying on the Classifieds, among empty cans and bottles, were the pieces of the drinking glass I had broken in Hume's bedroom.

I stood and went to the kitchen counter, where I got a ziplock plastic bag and a pair of kitchen tongs. Gingerly, I picked up the pieces of broken glass and placed them into the plastic bag before rolling up yet another newspaper section full of garbage and placing it back into the Humes' trash bag. When I was done, I poured myself a cup of coffee and called Mary at home. She answered on the second ring.

"I need a favor," I said.

"It's seven thirty in the morning. I was just on my way into the office. Can it wait?"

"Not really."

She sighed. "Okay, what is it?"

"I need some prints run."

"Off what?"

"A drinking glass. Well, actually, pieces of a drinking glass."

"Who handled it?"

"Berger Hume, his assistant Elizabeth Carmichael, and me."

"Do you have the glass with you?"

"Yes. But it's been sitting in the garbage for a few days."

She sighed a long heavy sigh. One that was meant to telegraph me on how much I had annoyed her. I got the message.

"You know that getting prints off of this glass is going to be difficult, if not impossible."

"I know it's a long shot," I said.

"And you know it could take a while to get these back."

"Yes. Could you make it a priority?"

There was a long stretch of barren silence.

"Mary?"

"Colton, how am I supposed to log this? How do I tell the bureau that this matters to them? Which case do I file this under?"

"That's the favor part," I said.

She paused before sighing again. But this time, it was different. More like a sigh of capitulation.

"Okay, I'll come up with something. But you know, you could ask one of your other friends. Dave Chastain or—"

"Yes, Mary, I could've done that, but it would ultimately have to go through the FBI's database anyway. Right?"

"Yes."

"Can I bring it to you today?"

"Okay. But get it there before noon. I have to be in court."

"I'll have it there in an hour. And Mary?"

"Yes?"

"If I'm right, you'll have a case to file this under. A big case." I balanced the phone between my ear and shoulder as I glanced at the television while moving to get another cup of coffee. To the anchor's left was a picture of Rolly Hutchins. Before I could turn up the volume, the news had changed to a car accident on the interstate.

"Big case? Why? What's going on?"

"Uh, I'm going to have to call you back."

"Colton, what's happening? What do you mean by big case?"

"Mary, I've got to go," I said, flipping the channel dial. "I'll see you in an hour."

I hung up the phone, turned up the volume, and began frantically flipping the channel. When I landed on the local ABC affiliate I heard, "After the break, news of a pile up on I-69, and a powerful local politician is missing."

I flipped the channels again and found that all of them were on commercial breaks as they advertised breakfast cereal, floor cleaner, and shampoo. I decided to flip back to the ABC affiliate and wait it out. Just as I finished pouring the cup of coffee I had started earlier, I saw Hutchins' picture flash on the screen again.

> Indiana state representative Rolly Hutchins, chairman of the Ways and Means committee, has disappeared. Family members say Representative Hutchins was home all evening

but could not be found this morning. His car is missing, and no one has heard from him since he was discovered to be absent from the family's near north side home at around six this morning. You may recall that yesterday a car bombing was reported near the representative's office in Fishers, but at this time the police aren't saying whether the two incidents are linked. The investigation is continuing.

The anchor turned to the weather reporter, and I flicked off the television.

I could link Hutchins to Warren Hume and to Satan's Posse. Warren was dead of a car bomb blast, and now Hutchins was missing. That left Satan's Posse in place.

CHAPTER
FORTY-EIGHT

I handed the bagged pieces of drinking glass to Mary and gave her the rundown of what I knew so far.

"Sounds like you've got a bunch of pieces." She held up the bag containing the sections of the broken drinking glass for emphasis before setting it on her desk. "And when you get it all put together, you'll have that big case you were talking about this morning."

I shook my head. "On the contrary. *You* will have a big case. This will reach the bureau, and I'm not with the bureau anymore, remember?"

"I remember."

Mary and I had often worked together on some of the Indianapolis office's most complex investigations. When I was fired, she was severely reprimanded for leaving me alone with the perpetrator—something that was very much against bureau policy.

"Anyway, can you speed this thing up?" I gestured toward the bag.

"I don't know," she said, matter-of-factly. "But I'll see what I can do."

I told her that I truly appreciated all of her help. But the words rang hollow. I owed her a lot. It was a debt that would be difficult to pay.

I left the federal building and saw that the late September weather had waffled again. The sky had turned a dusky gray, and the temperature had taken another dip, becoming decidedly chillier. I ran the zipper up on my jacket as I walked to my car.

I needed to make contact with the Hammer. He seemed to be the key to the whole sordid affair, being as connected to the missing state representative on one side as Warren had been on the other. And Hutchins was missing, and Warren was dead.

But that was going to mean isolating him, getting him away from his gang. Judging from what I had seen of the man so far, that wasn't going to be easy. But as I drove away from the curb I began to think, and by the time I reached the Posse's clubhouse, I had a plan.

I parked near the same spot I used the last time I was at the clubhouse. The engine continued to run on for a few seconds, forcing me to make a mental note to have that problem looked at—after I got the left rear window replaced and after I had the damage from the buckshot repaired.

I spent the next few minutes observing the house and the nearby traffic. All appeared quiet, including the window that had been opened and manned with a rifle the last time I visited. Figuring it wasn't going to get any better than this, I got out of the car and opened the trunk.

I got the lug wrench, closed the lid, and walked to the car I had seen the Hammer riding in a few days before. I was careful to keep the wrench down at my side and my eyes open. I took some comfort in the weight of the Ruger under my left arm, but I also knew that a covert gunshot from an open window could come quickly, eliminating any chance at retrieving the nine millimeter in time to be useful. I recalled Millikin's comments about the dependability of my gun.

The car was parked curbside, and I knelt on the side of the vehicle that faced the street, away from the house. The car didn't have hubcaps, which was going to make my job a lot easier.

I loosened all the lug nuts on the left front tire and removed all of them on the left rear tire. When I was done, I pocketed the nuts, stood with the wrench down at my side as I had done before, and calmly walked back to my car. After I tossed the lug wrench into the trunk, I got back into the Beretta and called Chastain. He was out, but the sheriff's dispatcher offered to page him. He returned my call in less than five minutes.

"I need some help," I said.

"Yeah. I've heard that before."

I ignored the jab. "I'm sitting in front of Satan's Posse's clubhouse. I need to get the Hammer alone for a few minutes."

The other end of the line was silent for a moment before Chastain said, "I told you to stay away from that guy."

"Yes, you did."

More silence, followed by a sigh of exasperation.

"Clearly, you are not listening," Chastain said.

"Clearly."

More silence.

"Tell me what you want, and I'll let you know if I can go along with it."

"I need a couple of patrol cars to begin driving past this place sometime in the next thirty minutes. Maybe even park out front for a minute or two. Then circle around the block a couple more times."

"Why?"

"I need to get the Hammer out of the house."

More silence.

"The clubhouse is in IPD's jurisdiction."

"I know. But with the merger and all, I didn't think it would make a difference." The Indianapolis City-County Council had recently voted to merge the Indianapolis Police Department with the Marion County Sheriff's Department. It was a cost-cutting move that was truly annoying to the departments' rank and file.

But my request would send a clear signal to Chastain that I wasn't a junior leaguer. I wanted him to know that I could deal with the

Hammer. If we were ever going to work together again, Chastain needed to know that.

"Okay," he said. "But they're only going to make a show. If you get into trouble on this, you're going to be handling it out there all by yourself."

"Wouldn't have it any other way," I said.

We ended the call, and for the next thirty minutes, I sat and watched the clubhouse. There was no sign of activity until I saw a sheriff's department patrol car park curbside in front of the house. It was soon joined by another, which parked nose-to-nose.

I flipped the cover of my phone open and called the clubhouse. I had gotten the number from the crisscross directory after I located the clubhouse's address. The phone answered on the third ring.

"A word to the wise," I said. "You're about to get raided." I pushed the End button on my phone and waited for the rats to jump.

CHAPTER FORTY-NINE

The Hammer was the first to come out of the house. He was accompanied by one of the two thugs I had seen him with the first time I followed him. Soon after, small groupings of three or four walked out of the house very casually and hopped on motorcycles or got into cars.

One of the patrol cars had already left, and the other was preparing to make a lap around the house before leaving. As the deputy started the car, the bikers began to leave with haste. I started the Beretta as I prepared to follow the Hammer and his bodyguard.

They pulled away from the curb and moved north on Tibbs, toward Sixteenth Street. When they reached the intersection, they turned left and began to pick up speed. From my position several car lengths behind, I could see the Hammer's left rear tire. It had already begun to wobble. I had left the lug nuts on the left front tire to avoid an accident, but I needed the car stopped, and this was going to get it done as safely as possible.

The biker and his bodyguard drove for another two miles before reaching the eastern edge of the Indianapolis Motor Speedway. They were driving cautiously, staying within the posted speed limit and desperately trying to maintain a law-abiding appearance. They also were maintaining a vigil in the rearview mirror.

They stopped at a red light on westbound Sixteenth Street. I stopped several car lengths behind. As the light turned green and they started to move, the left rear tire slid into a lopsided position, causing the left rear of their car to drop. The driver glanced back at the tire before he pulled the car against the curb and came to a stop. The other cars that were between mine and the Hammer's began to slowly move around them and into the flow of traffic in the left lane. It only took a few seconds for all the cars that were between us to start moving along, but it was enough time for the bodyguard to get out of the car.

I watched as the driver shook his bandanna-covered head and looked at the front tire, which had also become very lopsided. The Hammer remained in the front passenger seat with his arm hanging out the window. He flipped the ash off a cigarette.

The other man moved from the front of the car to the open driver's side window and said something to the Hammer before moving to the rear of the car again and opening the trunk. It wouldn't be long before he discovered that they had been set up.

Assuming he was armed, I was going to have to move quickly and get to him before he figured out what had happened.

I sped up and came to a stop behind their car, flicking on my emergency flashers as I did. I was pleasantly surprised when they worked.

I got out of the car as the biker-bodyguard eyed me. Just as I approached the car, he seemed to recognize me and began to slide his hand under his leather jacket. I pulled the Ruger from under mine, holding it in my right hand and keeping it low against my waist to shield it from onlookers as they drove past on my left.

"Keep your hands down to your side and put the wrench back in the trunk." From the perspective of passing motorists, I was here to help. I didn't want the man to appear to be under duress.

The biker tossed the wrench into the trunk as I motioned for him to follow me to the right side of the car, curbside, and away from prying eyes. I was concerned about the traffic that was moving along and the fact that a well-intentioned witness could provide me with unwanted trouble. The position between the car and the shoulder of the road could offer a shield against that intrusion.

"Unzip your jacket," I said after we had moved to the other side of the car. I continued to keep my gun low as I smiled. Colton Parker—roadside Samaritan.

At first the man hesitated, but finally he relented and unzipped his jacket. As he did, I glanced toward the front seat. The Hammer hadn't yet noticed what was taking place outside the car.

When the jacket was opened, I saw a holstered .45 under the man's left arm. I moved in such a way as to position the man so that his back was to the traffic. I told him to remove the gun from his holster with his left hand, using two fingers. He glared at me but slowly removed the pistol. I reached and took it from him and tucked it in my belt underneath my jacket.

"Move to the front of the car," I said. As he did, I kept the Ruger low against my side.

The man moved toward the front of the car as he was told but didn't take his eyes off me. It wasn't until he moved past the open passenger's window that the Hammer seemed to notice that anything was amiss. He gave the man a puzzled look before turning in his seat to look at me. His arm was still hanging out the window, and he was still holding the burning cigarette.

"Put your other hand out the window," I said to him. "I want to see both hands."

He glanced at the gun in my hand, dropped the cigarette, and slowly did as he was told.

I motioned toward the other man. "Open the door." I kept the smile on my face to help divert any unwanted attention from passing motorists.

He opened the passenger door as the Hammer shot him a glance.

"Take off your jacket and raise your shirt," I said. The Hammer did as he was told. He wasn't carrying a weapon, so I slid mine into my jacket pocket.

I told both men to move toward my car. The Hammer and I would sit in the back while the other man drove.

Once we were in the car, I extracted the Ruger again and told both men to take off their boots. They glanced at each other and then at the gun in my hand before doing as they were told. The Hammer had a knife in his, and the man with the gun had a barber's razor in his. I took the weapons from them.

"Get on US 40 and drive west until I tell you to stop," I said.

The man who was driving glanced over his shoulder. "You better be ready to use that thing," he said.

I recognized the voice. "Say that again," I said.

He glanced at the Ruger and turned around to start the car. I leaned forward and rapped him hard between the shoulder blades with the gun. "Say it again."

He said it again.

I settled back in my seat with a smile. "Start driving," I said.

CHAPTER FIFTY

We drove for forty minutes, finally turning onto a narrow gravel road that ran between two fields of corn. The stalks were tall, which afforded a nice cover. After we had driven for nearly a quarter mile, I saw a small turnaround just ahead that was cut into the field on the left. It was probably used by the farmer as he turned his combine around. I would use it for interrogation.

The driver pulled the Beretta off to the left side of the road and parked, turning off the engine. It ran on again.

"You willing to die for a piece of junk like this?" the driver asked.

"Are you willing to die for a piece of scum like this?" I asked, nudging the Hammer with the barrel of the Ruger.

I ordered both men to get out and to lean against the driver's side of the car as I stood facing them with my back to the field. I holstered the Ruger and pulled the .45 from the small of my back. The movement wasn't lost on the two bikers.

"You're going to shoot us with our own gun," the man with the familiar voice said. "Try to walk away from it."

"You've been quiet," I said to the Hammer. "Time to start talking."

He told me where he would like for me to go. I rapped him across the mouth.

"Now," I said, "let's get down to business. What is the nature of your relationship with Rolly Hutchins?"

The men looked at each other before the Hammer said, "None of your business."

I rapped him across the face with the pistol. "Wrong," I said. "It is very much my business."

He wiped blood from his mouth with the back of his hand. "You better kill us, 'cause you ain't going to live if you don't."

"I am going to kill you," I said. Then I turned to the guard. "But you first. You were stupid enough to come into my home and threaten my daughter." I saw a subtle shift in the man's demeanor. "And nobody does that."

There are very few people who truly have no fear of death. Few, anyway, who live the lifestyle that these men did. For all of their pretense, all of their bravado, when faced with the prospect of leaving everything behind and stepping into an unknown world, they begin to lose their grip. Like all gangsters, their strength comes in numbers. Isolate them, and they begin to wilt.

I turned to the Hammer. "What do you do for Rolly Hutchins?"

He continued to look at me without expression.

I grabbed the first man, the one who had invaded my home, and pulled him several feet away from where the Hammer stood. I forced the man to his knees.

"Hey man, wait. Wait, you don't want to do—" the man began saying.

"Yes I do. *You* have to die, no matter what. You threatened my daughter." I put my foot on his back, forcing him to the ground facedown. I knelt over him, keeping my knee in his back. "I can overlook a lot, but no one threatens her." I cocked the hammer on the .45 and put the barrel against the back of his head. I turned to the Hammer.

"Watch closely. You will go the same way if I don't get what I want."

The man was shaking. His veneer of macho had melted.

I leaned forward and whispered in the man's ear. "Say goodbye."

"No! Don't! Please don't!" he was crying. "Hutchins hired us to—"

"Shut up!" the Hammer said.

"He hired us to find Pork Chop."

The Hammer began to move toward us. I pointed the .45 at him.

"You'll get your turn," I said.

"No!" The man said again. "I'm telling you everything I know."

"Keep talking," I said.

"Shut up!" the Hammer said again. "He's just bluffing."

I leaned forward and spoke into the man's ear again. "You willing to die to prove him wrong?"

"I don't want to die, man," he said.

"You threatened my daughter. I don't know who the other man was, but I recognize your voice. You'll have to pay for him too."

"It was the Angel," he said. "He was the one who threatened your daughter. I'm the one who stopped him from shooting you."

The man was right. It was the second voice who had stopped the other man from killing me.

"Shut up!" The Hammer began to move forward again. I wasn't going to be able to fight him off and keep control of the situation at the same time. I needed to gain the upper hand.

I pointed the pistol at the Hammer's left foot and fired. He went down as the man under my knee began to sob uncontrollably.

"Stay put," I said to the Hammer. "All I want from you is information. My beef is with this dude here." I drove my knee deep into the man's back.

"Tell me about the Angel," I said.

"He's an independent. For hire," the man said, still sobbing.

"Hutchins hired him to look for Pork Chop?"

"No. Hutchins hired us to find Pork Chop."

Things were starting to clear up. If Hutchins had hired Satan's Posse to find the Chop, Warren was probably at the root of it. After all, he stood to lose a great deal in the sale of the hotels if Miles showed up claiming his inheritance.

"So the Angel and you came to my house to find Pork Chop."

"Yeah, that's right."

"You're dead, man," the Hammer said from the ground.

If Hutchins knew who to call when he needed a job done, like getting rid of Pork Chop, then what else had he done with Satan's Posse? What was the extent of their relationship?

"Where did you find the Angel?"

"He used to hang around. Did some work for us a few times. Used to hang with a gang on the west side. But he's independent now. He left the city. Works out of Chicago."

"When were you hired to find Pork Chop?"

"Shut up," the Hammer said.

"Stay put," I said to the man.

I walked over to where the Hammer was laying. "Take off your socks," I said.

He hesitated. I struck him with the gun. "Take them off—now."

He removed the dirty, wet socks—one of them bloody—and handed them to me.

I rolled them into a ball. "Open your mouth," I said.

He hesitated, but opened his mouth just as I was about to hit him again.

I stuffed the socks into his mouth and forced him facedown into the dirt. I pulled the bandanna the other man had been wearing off his head and went back to the Hammer. I forced my knee into his back and tied his hands behind him with the headband.

"Now, that ought to keep your trap shut. After I'm done wasting my buddy over there, I'll come back and have some fun with you."

The Hammer raised his head to momentarily glare at me. Unlike the gangster I was interrogating, Percy was hard-core. He didn't need a gang for strength. Just protection.

I moved back to the man I had been interrogating and placed my knee in the small of his back. He continued to heave with sobs.

"When were you hired to find Pork Chop?" I asked again.

"I don't know man, I—"

I dug deeper with my knee and the man cried out in pain.

"I don't know, man, I really don't. Six, maybe eight weeks ago."

"Eight weeks?"

"Yeah man, maybe."

"Could it have been later than that?"

"No. I know it was at least that long ago because I started looking for him right after the fourth, but we couldn't find him. He went underground."

"Underground?"

"Yeah, man. He don't affiliate. He makes enemies. This time, he must've gone too far. We got close to him a few times but couldn't find him anywhere. That's when Hutchins told the Hammer to hold off. He didn't want too much of a stir or to start a gang war. He said he would find somebody else to find him."

Things were beginning to take shape.

"Did you say the fourth?"

"Of July."

That would have made it almost three months. Yet Ms. Carmichael said the letters hadn't begun arriving until about a month ago. Meaning that the Humes must have known about Miles before they hired me to find him. Before the letters began to arrive.

"How much did Hutchins pay you?" I asked, driving my knee even deeper into the man's back.

"I don't know, man. A lot I guess. He brought us a gym bag full of cash."

"Hutchins brought the money?"

"No…yes, he came but he wasn't alone. It was the other guy. He brought the money."

"What other guy?"

"I don't know his name, man, I really don't."

"What did he look like?" I asked.

"Rich, man. He looked rich. Suit, nice watch."

"Young? Old?"

"I don't know, I didn't look that close. He was maybe in his forties. Dressed real nice. Nice car."

"What kind of car?" I asked.

"A Mercedes. A big black one."

Denton drove a black Mercedes, and Denton dressed well. Had a nice watch too. The pieces were coming together, but the picture still wasn't complete.

"Now," I said, "tell me about the Angel."

CHAPTER FIFTY-ONE

The man told me that Miles was difficult to find. That was undoubtedly due to his constant moving. Satan's Posse had come close to finding him on several occasions, but that only served to drive Miles farther underground and fuel his paranoid personality.

The Angel was imported talent. He had come into the scene after I was hired to find Pork Chop. Find him and lead Satan's Posse to him so the Angel could do the hit.

I still had a lot of loose ends. Like why did Hutchins stop the Posse from pulling out all the stops?

I left the two bikers where I had interrogated them, knowing they would work free and manage to get back to Indianapolis.

I decided to keep their .45. It had undoubtedly been used in one crime or another, and I would turn it in to Chastain when all of this came together. I would also have to answer questions about my assault of the two, but right now that really didn't rate that high on my list of things to worry about.

I started the Beretta and drove to US 40, where I turned and headed east, back to the city.

The man who had threatened Callie was deeply involved in all of this, but I couldn't prove it unless I got corroboration from Denton, and that wouldn't come easy. Men who made the kind of money he did and who had been as successful in business as he had been didn't succumb to pressure very easily. He had gone back to work right after his brother's murder, so his love of the buck clearly surpassed his love for family. Or maybe even his own life. After all, Ms. Carmichael had pointed out that the family had enemies too, and my assumption that Warren had been killed by a personal enemy could not yet be substantiated. That meant that the man who killed Warren may also be gunning for Denton.

Or I could have one brother who sought to eliminate the other. Men have done stranger things for the love of money.

I continued driving east on US 40 as the thick layer of dusky clouds that had been in place all day finally broke, allowing a brief reprieve of sunshine.

I dialed the Radisson Hotel and asked for Miles' room. The phone rang several times without an answer. He could be in the shower of course, I thought, but given what I knew of him, I quickly dismissed the notion.

I dialed again, and again, no answer.

I drove another ten minutes and called again. Again, no answer.

I had the Hammer walking on foot, a wounded foot, several miles behind me. But the Angel was still out there, still looking for Miles. And Miles wasn't answering his phone.

I arrived at the hotel and parked in the garage, taking the elevator to Miles' floor. I used my key to open the hotel room door and drew my gun as I entered the room. It was empty. The few clothes that Miles had brought with him were still in the chest of drawers, and a discarded room service tray sat on the table beside the bed. The television was playing. There were no signs to indicate a struggle, nor were there any indications that he wasn't coming back.

I sat on the edge of the bed and used the television remote to call up a current list of room charges. After a short delay, the list of charges appeared. Except for the recorded costs of the room, tax, and meal charges, there was nothing out of the ordinary.

I picked up the phone receiver and called the front desk. "This is Mr. Parker," I said. "I've been out for a while. Are there any messages for me?"

I was asked to hold while the operator checked. Miles had been registered in my name. If all was well, he shouldn't have any messages.

"Yes, sir," the operator said, coming back on line. "I have a message for you. It says, 'tell Parker, you lose.'"

"When did that come in?"

"Let's see...just about an hour ago."

"Any return number? Name?"

"No, sir. It appears to be a telephone message, but we were asked to write it down rather than post it to the room."

"Anything else?" I asked.

"No, sir."

I thanked him and hung up.

When I had been attacked in the shower, I hadn't been able to see either man. But I knew the voices. I had already encountered one of them and left him in a cornfield. The other knew that I would be able to pin him down when I heard him speak.

I looked at the message in my hand. The *written* message. The message that the caller had not wanted to record.

"Tell Parker, you lose."

CHAPTER FIFTY-TWO

I drove back to the house where Chastain and I had made our initial contact with the biker world. The man I had interrogated in the cornfield had said the Angel liked to hang out with a gang on the west side. I was betting it was at this house.

Just as before, the house was dark and the curtains closed. Unlike before, the piece of plywood that covered the doorway in the building's reinforced front porch was standing open.

I approached the fence as I had done the last time with the lug wrench in hand and began to beat on the chain link. This time, though, no dogs came charging.

I paused to listen. The house and the yard were silent. I began beating the fence again. Again, no dogs.

I tossed the wrench back into the trunk and vaulted over the fence, pulling my Ruger from its holster as I landed on the other side. Still no dogs.

I crept around the house, keeping my attention focused on the doors and windows. I saw no movement of the curtains and heard no sound.

"Hello," I said as I paused at the opening in the porch's barricade.

No answer.

I stepped through the opening, keeping the gun in both hands, barrel pointing upward. I strained to listen for any noise from the house. Still I heard nothing.

I moved across the porch and toward the front door of the house. The screen door was hanging by a single hinge. The wooden front door itself was decayed. Apparently, most of the gang's security was coming from the concrete wall that surrounded the front porch.

I stood cautiously to one side and knocked. No one answered.

I leaned across the doorway to peer in the window that was on the other side of the door. I saw two men. One was lying on the sofa, the other on the floor. Both of them had pillows covering their faces. I kicked the door in and entered the house.

The pillow over the man on the floor was blood soaked. I uncovered him and saw him to be the same man I had talked to the last time I was at the house. He had taken a shotgun blast to the head. There wasn't much left.

I moved to the sofa and uncovered the other man. He appeared to be the younger of the two, the same one who had spoken with Chastain and me. Like the older man, he had also taken a shotgun blast to the head. Both murders were recent. Neither body was in rigor.

Wilkins had told me that the Angel's preferred weapon was a shotgun. Since he was still on the loose and was most likely the one who left me the message in Miles' empty room, it was safe to assume he was responsible for the hit.

I went out onto the front porch and called Chastain.

The red lights from the squad cars cut a swath through the room. They didn't mesh well with the nauseating smell of dried blood.

"Can we talk outside?" I asked.

Chastain was kneeling over the body on the floor. He had the pillow lifted back. "Sure." He re-covered the head of the victim and stood. "This way," he said, moving through the front door, across the porch, and into the daylight. I followed.

"What do you think?" I asked.

"Probably someone they knew." He nodded toward the house. "With all that security, they were afraid of someone. Which means that whoever got close enough to do this was someone they didn't fear. When did you discover them?"

"About five minutes before I called you," I said.

He looked at the flip-over spiral notebook in his hand. "Right." He made a note of what I had just said.

"Whoever hit these two used a shotgun. Just like the Angel," I said.

"That makes him the most likely suspect," Chastain said. "These two were tortured too."

"Tortured?"

"Yeah. Didn't you see their hands tied behind their back?"

"I just assumed it was an execution."

He frowned. "Not hardly. You don't have to tie someone up for that. Not when you're using a shotgun. Besides," he lifted a small evidence bag that contained several teeth, "we have these. Whoever did these guys wanted information. He tied them up and pulled their teeth out, probably one at a time, before wasting them."

"I think he's got Miles too." I told him about the message and the empty hotel room.

"If he does, you can write off your friend."

"The hotel clerk said the message came in about an hour ago. Given the time for me to drive here, discover the bodies, and call you, we're probably looking at almost two hours ago." I gestured toward the house. "Those bodies are still fresh."

He nodded. "Yeah. But it takes time for rigor mortis to set in. He could have hit them and been back at the hotel before you arrived."

I shook my head. "Not likely. If he hit Miles, he lured him out of the room. Miles was armed and not afraid to use it. His guard was up. He wouldn't have been taken by surprise."

"You're convinced Miles is in danger?"

"Aren't you?"

He thought for a minute, then nodded. "Yeah, I do. If he's still alive."

"I've got to find the Angel," I said.

"Well, if what you're telling me is true, I would say that he—" He was interrupted by his pager. He slipped the device off his belt and read the number. "Hold that thought a sec." He used his cell phone to call the number.

"Who?" he asked the caller. "When?" There was a pause as he made a note in his notebook. "Where?" He made another note. "Okay, I've got two here, but we're about done. The lab's here now, so I should be there soon." Another pause before he ended the call.

"Busy day?" I asked.

"You could say that."

I had known Dave Chastain for a long time. He was part of my poker group and had been one of the first to see Callie after she was born. I knew the man. Knew his face. And what his expression said wasn't good.

"We've found Rolly Hutchins."

CHAPTER
FIFTY-THREE

The lifeless body of Rolly Hutchins was sitting in the front seat of his BMW, held upright by the car's safety harness. He had a gunshot wound to the right temple, and his eyes were fixed in a vacant stare. A .380-caliber handgun was on the front seat.

"Who found him?" Chastain asked the deputy who had phoned in the discovery.

He nodded to a young couple who looked to be about high school age. "They came here to be alone and noticed the victim slumped in the seat. The boy there," he gestured toward a nervous-looking young man, "thought the victim was watching them. He didn't like it, so he went over to the car to say something. When he did, he saw our victim here. That's when he called us."

I leaned into the car. Unlike the bikers, Hutchins' body was showing signs of rigor.

"Suicide?" I asked Chastain as he peered through the passenger's side window.

"Probably."

"He was despondent," I said. "Drinking pretty heavily when I left him."

Chastain nodded. "Drinking a depressant when you're depressed is never a good idea."

242

"Note?" I asked.

Hutchins cupped his hands around his face and looked through the window. "I don't see any."

"If they're going to leave a note, they'll usually leave it where you can find it," I said.

"Yeah. Doesn't look like he left one though," he said, coming around to join me at the driver's side of the car.

Neither of us wanted to contaminate the crime scene. Our assumption that Hutchins' death was self-inflicted could be wrong, so any effort on our part to examine the car for a note would wait until the area was properly processed.

I stood by my car while Chastain talked to the kids who found the body. While I waited, the lab arrived and immediately began taking pictures and processing the scene. The deputy coroner arrived a few minutes later.

I remained by my car until Chastain finished questioning the kids and came back to where I was standing.

"Kids say they come to this park a lot. Kind of a lovers' hangout. They were here yesterday evening, but the car wasn't."

"He probably drove around town for a while, trying to figure a way out. When he couldn't, he decided to do it this way," I said.

Chastain nodded. "Maybe. But maybe not. This could be arranged to look like suicide."

"True."

"If it is, we'll find out." He turned to look at me with a bit of pride in his face. "We're very good at what we do."

"How soon will you know anything?"

He shrugged. "Soon. Depends on what the coroner says."

"This guy was into something," I said.

"Figures. Why else would a successful, upwardly mobile politician like him kill himself?"

We didn't talk for a minute as we watched the lab technicians lift the mannequin-like body of Rolly Hutchins from the car and place it into a vinyl bag.

"I've done this job a long time." Chastain said, "I've seen more than my share of people leave in one of those, and it never fails to make me think."

"About life after death?"

He shook his head. "No. About the brevity of it all. Why we spend so much time running on the wheel, round and round like a hamster, chasing after our pot of gold when we aren't here long enough to enjoy it."

"Hutchins wasn't chasing a pot of gold," I said. "He was chasing truckloads of the stuff. And my guess is that he tangled with someone else who was chasing after the same truck."

"Like you said, he was probably trying to figure a way out. He was probably chin deep in something and didn't know how to extricate himself."

"But the suicide victims I've seen usually leave a note. Especially if they're trying to run from someone. It's a chance to even the score."

Chastain crossed his arms as he leaned against his car. "That's true if the victim *can* even the score. But what if he can't?"

"I don't follow," I said.

"Hutchins is dead. He can't be killed twice. So if he were to leave a message or in some other way exact his revenge on whoever drove him to this, he would be endangering those who *can* be killed."

"You mean the people he's running from can no longer harm him, but they can harm his family?"

"Right."

"So we may have cause for alarm for the man's family?"

Chastain shook his head. "No. He didn't leave a note, so here we stand none the wiser about what he was up to. Whoever drove him to do this is safe. For the time being. Like I said, we're very good at what we do."

We watched as the gurney bearers struggled to lift Hutchins' body onto the gurney.

"Which brings me to another point," I said. "The car bombing in Fishers was caught on the bank's ATM camera. Chances are the one who wired the car is on the tape."

"Okay. I'll look into it," he said. "ATF is probably all over it by now, but I'll see what I can do." Then he turned his attention from Hutchins' body to me. "You're in something deep on this one."

"You think?"

He smiled. "Be careful. I don't want to have to cart you off in one of those things."

"Me either," I said. "That would ruin the whole day."

CHAPTER FIFTY-FOUR

I left Chastain and drove toward Biker Haven. Ernie had consistently been the best chance I had of finding Miles. And now I needed to find Miles more than ever.

But I also had concern for Ernie himself. He knew too much. And he was too connected, however loosely, to Miles and the other bikers who had been murdered. If the Angel put it all together, Ernie could be in big trouble.

Hutchins had restrained the Posse from going after Miles with everything they had. Now, with the murder of the two men in the house and Hutchins' suicide, there was no restraint on the Angel. His hunt for the Chop could lead him to Biker Haven. And if it did, we could add Ernie to the growing body count.

I was moving up the entrance ramp and onto the interstate when my phone rang.

"Mr. Parker? This is Jim Dimond, with the bank."

"Yes?"

"I'm pleased to tell you that your request for a loan has been approved."

"Thank you," I said, glancing over my shoulder as I eased into traffic. "Why the turnaround?"

"Your credit has always been good with us. We try to extend some

246

leniency to those we feel are good risks and who are businessmen in our communities. Call it the long-term view."

Whatever he called it, I was appreciative. "When do I come in to sign?"

"No rush. I have an opening early next week."

"That'll be fine with me too."

"Okay, then. Why don't we plan on seeing you Monday morning, say at nine?"

"I'll be there," I said, welcoming the first piece of good news I had received in days.

"You'll need to bring your check for the down payment, of course. Since you bank with us already, that will speed everything up."

"Sure," I said. "Keep it simple."

We agreed to the meeting time, and I ended the call. The day was looking up, and as I sped along toward Biker Haven, I slipped a Benny Carter cassette into the player, hoping the day would end that way too.

I pulled into the lot of Biker Haven, turning off the cassette player and the car simultaneously. When I got out of the Beretta, I was greeted by the same whirring sound of the pneumatic wrench I'd heard the first time I came. And as before, Ernie was hunched over a bike as he worked on its rear tire. I tapped on his head and he turned around.

"Don't run this time, okay? I just need to ask you a question."

He sighed as he set the pneumatic wrench on the garage floor and straightened to his full height.

"You're always asking questions," he said. "What do you want this time?"

"Pork Chop is on the run."

He looked at me in disbelief and then broke into laughter. "On the run?" He shook his head. "Are you for real, man? He's always on the run. I told you that before."

He walked past me and out to the parking area. He shook a cigarette out of the half-empty pack he had taken from his shirt pocket. I followed him outside and waited while he lit the smoke.

"He's in immediate danger," I said. "There are some very heavy professionals who are after him."

He blew smoke. "He's always had people after him. It's the way he lives."

"He won't be living long if you don't help me."

He looked at me for a minute, studying me to see if he could believe what I was telling him. He took a long drag on the cigarette and began coughing.

"You're not going to live long either," I said, "if you don't give those things up."

He continued while his face turned a deep purple. It was a few seconds before he could gain control.

"I'm not going to live long anyway."

If I had been talking to someone else, I would've assumed he'd meant cancer. But given that it was Ernie, and given his circle of associates, I could assume he meant his life would be cut short in much the same way the others' had been. I decided to use that to my advantage.

"Some friends of yours were hit today."

"Who?"

I gave him the address of the house. His face registered immediate concern.

"They gave me your name when I was looking for Pork Chop. Now he's missing again, and I think the man who killed your friends is looking for him. That means he may be looking for you too."

He took a couple more drags on the cigarette before flipping it to the ground and crushing it under his oil-stained work boot.

"They were tortured before they were killed. They may have given you up."

The concern on his face took on a different hue.

"What do you need?" he asked.

"Pork Chop. I need to know where he might be."

He sighed. "There's a place some of them use when they need to hide."

"Let me have it," I said. "And Ernie…?"

"Yeah?"

"It's time for you to hide too."

CHAPTER FIFTY-FIVE

According to Ernie, Miles could be in a safe house. A place that was often used by the men who had been tortured. Their need for security prompted them to find a safe place to go when under immediate threat. If they had given the place to Miles, he could be there. If not, it was probably too late, and his body would soon turn up somewhere.

I followed the directions Ernie gave me to a brick building located on the near east side of town. In its previous incarnations, the building had housed a mom-and-pop shoe store, a laundry, a donut shop, and finally a massage parlor before closing altogether. Now it was vacant with plywood over the windows and gang graffiti spray painted over the brick. I must have passed it a hundred times in recent months but hadn't noticed that it was now abandoned. Like all of us, when it died it was seemingly forgotten.

I parked alongside the building in front of a tan Buick and paused to study the layout. It was two stories with a front door on Washington Street and a second-story side door on Monroe. A staircase must have once run alongside the building to the door on the second floor because the struts were still there. The staircase, though, was gone.

The front door of the building, like the windows, was covered in plywood. The door on the second floor wasn't covered.

I got out of the car with the Ruger in one hand and a flashlight in the other. I moved around the structure to each piece of plywood, testing them to see if any were loose enough to allow me to pass. After a couple of failed attempts, I found a board that was partially nailed down over a broken window. I forced the wood back and entered the building. As soon as I was inside, I called out to Miles. He was on the run, which meant that despite his bravado, he was scared. Scared men are dangerous men. I didn't want a repeat of the gunplay we had experienced in the alley.

I didn't hear an answer.

I called again.

Again, no answer.

I moved forward, shining the light along the periphery of the building's interior. As I stepped forward, I heard a squeal and jerked the flashlight downward just in time to see a rat scurry out of the ring of light.

I raised the beam and moved forward. I called his name again.

No answer.

The building had the musty smell of a waterlogged basement. Miles Poole's lifestyle was a long way from his brothers'.

I ran the beam clockwise around the base of the room. As I did, the flashlight ran across a staircase that led to the second floor. I inched toward the staircase and crossed my hands at the wrist. The position allowed me to use the flashlight and the gun at the same time.

When I reached the bottom of the staircase, I shined the beam upward, keeping the barrel of the Ruger aimed at the area that was illuminated. The door that led to the second floor was open, and I could see a lightbulb screwed into a socket that was in one of the rafters. A pull-string mechanism was attached.

I called to Miles again but got no reply.

I began the ascent up the staircase. It was the kind that is attached to a pull-down door. The type of staircase that is often used in homes to access the attic. It creaked with each step and sagged under my weight as I kept the flashlight focused on the opening above.

During my years with the Chicago Police Department, I often had need to go into unknown places. Dark alleys, closets, attics, and basements always held the potential for sudden danger. But it was part of the job. The part that kept it interesting, alive. Given the chance to run down a dark alley or complete a stack of reports, I'd take the alley anytime. I didn't like the unknown, but I did thrive on risk. Now, a few years older and wiser, my attitude had changed. I would rather not have to stick my head through an unknown opening and die in this vacant building as a result. It could be weeks or months before I would be found. And while I didn't relish the idea of a body bag, it seemed a lot more hospitable than to lie in a discarded building for an undetermined amount of time. After all, body bags don't have rats.

I shined the beam around the attic, just over the rim of the door. Seeing nothing, I pivoted to shine the light on the other side of the attic as I moved upward another step. Just before I cleared my head over the rim, someone fired at me.

CHAPTER FIFTY-SIX

I tumbled off the ladder and thudded onto the floor like a two-hundred-pound sack of flour. The flashlight rolled from my grip, and my gun clattered as it slid away, lost somewhere in the darkened room.

Above me, I could hear the shooter scurrying to his feet as he made his way to the opening in the attic floor. From where I was lying, I was an open target. He would be able to shoot downward at me, point blank. If he did, the day would not have ended as well as I would have hoped.

I scrambled to my feet and grabbed the attic ladder, folding it into the door and pushing the door back into the ceiling. Just as I cleared the zone of fire, a shotgun blast tore a hole through the door, sending a hail of buckshot ricocheting around the room.

The flashlight was on the floor, thirty feet away. Without it, I had no chance of finding my gun in the darkened building. Yet leaving the door for long, would mean he would have it opened in seconds and could fire at me unabated.

He kicked at the door, nearly pushing it open, before I was able to force it closed and take cover against the wall just as another shot was fired.

Going for the flashlight was a chance I was going to have to take.

I could reasonably assume he thought I still had my gun in hand. That meant that while he might fire blindly, he would not charge down the steps as soon as the door was open. On the other hand, if I didn't return fire soon, he would figure out I didn't have a gun and would come down the ladder.

I raced toward the flashlight as two more blasts tore through the wood-framed door.

I grabbed the flashlight and scanned the floor with it until the familiar form of the Ruger came into view. It was on the other side of the room, ten feet from where I had landed.

Two more shots were fired through the door as he began to push it open.

I ran back to where I had been standing and flipped the door closed on my way to the Ruger. He fired two more shots, each penetrating the door and sending buckshot that bounced off the concrete floor.

I grabbed the Ruger from the floor and in one fluid motion fired five shots upward through the attic door. He fired once more, and I answered him with another volley.

I ran for the north wall, several yards away from his zone of fire, and waited. The gunshots had been deafening. I could still hear the traffic outside, but I couldn't hear the softer sounds inside. Unable to hear if he was moving, I now had to rely on the motion of the ceiling above me. The door remained in place, but I could see the ceiling above me sag with each step he took. I moved myself away from his direction of movement, keeping the Ruger pointed upward.

I watched the ceiling as it sagged in small increments from the attic door to the eastern wall of the building. After the movement reached the end of the room, it stopped.

My ears were still ringing from the gunshots, preventing me from hearing anything, and now I couldn't see the movement along the ceiling either.

I kept the flashlight focused above me for a moment and then remembered the door that led to the outside from the second floor. The one where the outside staircase was missing.

I ran to the window through which I had entered the building and pushed the plywood covering aside just in time to see a tall man wearing a ball cap jump from the opened exterior attic door and land on top of his car. I couldn't see his face, but he had a shotgun in his hand.

I began to push myself through the opening, but he turned and pointed the shotgun at me. I ducked back into the building as he fired two shots, blasting large holes through the building's deteriorating brick facade.

I cautiously peered through the opening with the Ruger in hand. The man had started the car and was moving away from the curb. By the time I pushed the plywood back and crawled through the window, he was driving away from the building. I was still able to read the car's tag number.

I called IPD and asked for Wilkins. While I waited for him to come on the line, I jiggled my finger in my ears to stimulate the return of my hearing. Although it was improving, it was still not up to par.

When Wilkins answered, I told him what happened. "If you get an APB on this tag, you might get him before he leaves the area."

"Let's have it," he said.

I gave him the plate number and the description of the tan Buick.

"What was he doing in the attic?" Wilkins asked.

That was a good question.

Wilkins told me to hold while he called the dispatcher. I went back into the building and reopened what was left of the attic door and ladder.

"It's on the wire," Wilkins said as he came back on the line. "I gave them the description of the car too. By the way, some of the neighbors heard the shooting. A couple of our guys are on the way there, so it might be best if you didn't come out of the building with your gun in your hand."

"It's already holstered," I said. "Hang on, though, and I'll see what he was after."

I climbed the ladder and peered my head over the rim of the attic's opening. I shined the flashlight along the western side of the room, back toward the center where the door was at, and around toward the eastern edge where the shooter had jumped to his car. The flashlight's beam and the bit of light that was shining through the opened exterior door revealed more than I wanted to know.

Miles Poole was sitting against the eastern wall with his feet straight out ahead of him. Part of his head was gone.

CHAPTER FIFTY-SEVEN

Two IPD uniformed officers arrived at nearly the same time. I was sitting on the hood of my car when they pulled up with their light bars flashing.

"You Colton Parker?" one of them asked as he got out of his car.

"Yep."

The patrolman was young, maybe midtwenties, with close-cropped hair and the build of an NFL lineman. He said, "Captain Wilkins hit us and said to be on the lookout for you."

"Thanks," I said. "It's nice to not be shot at twice in the same day."

The second officer was female, about thirty, with blonde hair and blue eyes. She did not have the build of an NFL lineman.

"I'm officer Reeves," she said, "and this is officer Lloyd."

I nodded. "There's a body inside. Upstairs in the attic."

"You know who it is?" she asked.

"Yeah. Name's Miles Poole. He also goes…he went by the street name Pork Chop."

The two officers glanced at each other.

"He's a biker," I said.

"Gang?" Lloyd asked.

I shook my head. "Unaffiliated."

Reeves studied me. "You hurt?" she asked.

"No."

"You've got blood on your forehead."

I reached my hand to my forehead and brought it down with blood on it. Sliding off the hood of the car, I leaned down to look at the passenger's side-view mirror. There was a small cut. Probably due to the fall, I thought. Or maybe a splinter from the door. Or buckshot.

"I'm okay," I said.

"We can call an ambulance if you'd like," Lloyd said.

I shook my head.

"We got a call on gunfire," Reeves said.

"Yep."

"We're going to need your gun."

I reached under my jacket and pulled the Ruger from its holster. I handed her the gun, butt forward.

"The captain says you're okay, but we've got to check it out," she said.

"Man's dead. We've got to know where the shot came from," Lloyd said.

"Sure," I said.

Lloyd was about to speak, but he was interrupted by his radio. He reached for the mike on his epaulet and said, "Say again?" He turned the volume up on the radio's receiver unit, which was attached to his gun belt. His eyes widened. "Ten-four."

"What's up?" Reeves asked.

Lloyd directed his answer to me. "They've got your guy. Corner of New York and Parkview."

That was less than two miles from where we were standing.

Reeves said, "Detectives are going to want to talk to you. We can't let you leave."

"No need," Lloyd said. "They're bringing him back here. They want to see if you can identify him."

The detectives and the lab unit arrived at nearly the same time that another uniformed patrolman turned up with the suspect.

"Recognize him?" one of the uniforms asked. The officer's name-plate identified him as Gilkey.

I leaned down to a place that put me eye to eye with the shooter. "No." I said. "He was pointing a shotgun at me when he turned around, so it took precedence over his face. But he's wearing the same clothing as the shooter. And he was wearing that cap," I said, motioning toward the Cubs ball cap he was wearing. "And I can tell you he got away in a tan Buick."

"We nabbed this guy in a tan Buick. And," he said, "he had this." He held out a sawed-off twelve-gauge pump shotgun with a modi-fied pistol grip.

"I do recognize that," I said.

"Is this the one he pointed at you?" Gilkey asked.

"Yeah. I'll bet it's the one he fired at me too. And I'll bet it was involved in a shooting on Milner. Some bikers were whacked there. I know a man who can ID him." I was thinking of Ted Michaels.

"Really?" Gilkey set the shotgun down on top of the squad car and retrieved a note pad and pen from his shirt pocket. "What's the name?"

I gave it to him. "You might also want to talk to Dave Chastain. He's a detective with Marion County. Some bikers were hit in a house on the west side. They were killed with a shotgun too."

After making a note, the officer led me back to the grouping of other officers just as Wilkins pulled up in an unmarked squad car. The gaggle of police, along with the teams from the lab and coroner's office, were beginning to attract a crowd.

"Got to love a parade," I said to Wilkins as he slid his ample frame from under the steering wheel.

"These things always turn into a three-ring circus," he said. "It's why I like to fill out reports. Less excitement." He motioned for me to stay put while he talked to Reeves, Lloyd, Gilkey, and then the other detectives. After a minute, he motioned for me to join them.

"We're going downtown," Wilkins said to the other officers as he gestured toward me. Then turning to me, he said, "And your shooter is going too. It's time to get to the bottom of this thing."

"I'm afraid it's going to be a long drop," I said.

CHAPTER FIFTY-EIGHT

I spent nearly two hours talking to Wilkins and other detectives after our arrival at IPD headquarters. Most of their questions centered on the shooting in the abandoned building, but some began to dance around the investigation itself. I reluctantly told them about my conversation with the Hammer's bodyguard and how he was hired by Hutchins. I told them that a man matching Denton's description paid them in cash.

"If that's true, then we've got him on conspiracy," Wilkins said.

I shook my head. "He's only part of it. I think his father's executive assistant is involved too." I told Wilkins about my suspicions and the prints that were being run by the FBI. "If they come through," I said, "we'll know more about her."

"If they don't," Wilkins said, "we're still going after Denton."

"Sure," I said. "At this point, with Miles dead, I failed in the job I was hired to do anyway."

We were quiet, mulling over the situation, when an attractive female clerk entered the room.

"Detective Wilkins, the man's ID comes back as Leroy Thomas."

Wilkins glanced at me.

"The Angel," I said.

Wilkins thanked the clerk and led me down the hall to another interrogation room. When we entered, the Angel was sitting with a uniformed officer and drinking a Diet Sprite.

"Excuse us for a minute, will you please?" Wilkins said to the officer.

After the uniform left, Wilkins started the recorder as we sat at the table across from Thomas. He looked first at Wilkins but then fixed his gaze on me.

"You missed," I said.

He grinned. "I don't know what you're talking about."

Wilkins sighed and said, "You know, I've been doing this for almost three decades. And every time I sit here with some punk like you, I get the same answer. And every time I tell some punk like you that I might be able to help you with the prosecutor's office, I get the same answer. When're you people going to learn?" He leaned across the table. "Let me make sure that you hear this. We have your gun. You're going down for murder. Premeditated murder. Death penalty kind of stuff."

"In other words," I said, recalling the message he had left for me at the Radisson, "you lose."

I waited for a response, verbal or otherwise, but none came. I glanced at Wilkins who rolled his eyes in near resignation. But then I recalled my conversation with Miles. I remembered his comment that in his world, "if you play, you pay." The Angel wasn't the only one playing, but he would be the only one paying—unless I could work on his warped sense of honor.

"The Hammer doesn't," I said. "He wins. We can't hold him on anything. He gets to keep the money and walk while you go to prison and fight off unwanted advances for the rest of your life."

"Until you're executed," Wilkins said. "Like I said, this is death penalty stuff."

The Angel drank the remainder of the Sprite and set the empty can down on the table. He sat slumped in his chair as he twirled the can. He seemed oblivious to his situation.

Wilkins looked at me and shrugged. "Okay," he said. "Let him rot. We can get at the Humes in another way."

We stood to leave.

"Wait," the Angel said.

Wilkins and I paused at the door.

"What kind of a deal?" he asked.

"That depends on what the prosecutor offers," Wilkins said. "But I can tell you that if you help us, I can try to help you."

"That's it?"

Wilkins nodded. "Yeah, pretty much."

He thought as he continued to slowly spin the can. He was about to answer when my phone rang. I stepped out into the hall to answer it.

"I've got the picture," Chastain said. "The one from the ATM in Fishers."

"Can you fax it over?"

"Sure. Where are you?"

I told him and asked him to fax it to the attention of Harley Wilkins. After we ended the call, I went back into the room.

"How much?" Wilkins was saying as he scribbled notes.

"Twenty thousand," the Angel said.

Wilkins shook his head in disbelief. "That's a lot," he murmured.

The Angel grinned. "I guess they wanted it done right."

Wilkins turned to me. "Denton Hume paid for the murder of Miles Poole. Twenty grand."

"Must've wanted him dead a lot more than he was letting on," I said, fully aware that the killer had been paid more to eliminate Miles than I had been to find him in the first place. But why had I been hired to find Miles? Why hire me when he had already hired two others? I recalled the man in the cornfield who told me they had been looking for Miles for more than two months before the letters began arriving at the Hume residence.

"You couldn't find him," I said. "Is that why the Humes came to me?"

He shrugged. "I don't know, man. I didn't even know they hired you until they told me. I was hired to do the hit. That's all. The Hammer didn't want any of the Posse doing the shooting. That's why they hired me."

"When did you come into the picture?" I asked.

"Not too long ago. They was having trouble finding the Chop. So someone hired you to find him for us. Then I was supposed to do you both. The Posse wasn't ever supposed to whack the dude. That was always going to be my job." He shook his head. "We almost had you once. Followed you to some apartment complex, but then we lost you."

I recalled the van in the complex.

He redirected his attention to the empty can as he resumed spinning it around with his finger. "We kept losing you early on. We kept looking for your car, but you got a new one, and that threw us off for a while."

"Did you hit us on Raymond Street?"

He nodded. "Yeah, that was us." He grinned. "We were going to take you at that lab you went to, but the Hammer said if we played it right we could make it look like an accident. You know, run you off the road." He shrugged again as he spun the can. "But you got away from us, so we decided to do it the old-fashioned way." He grinned.

The room was quiet as Wilkins and I glanced at each other. His expression told me how close I had come to getting my family killed. If Callie had been home the morning they had invaded…

"Who gave you the instructions?" Wilkins asked.

"Like I was telling you," he said, "I don't know his name, but I know what he looks like."

"Was he alone?" I asked.

"Yeah."

More silence as Wilkins made notes.

"How did you get Pork Chop out of the hotel room?" I asked.

He looked up at me from the spinning can. "Man, that was easy. I paid a call to Wild Bill and Hog Master. I told them—"

"Who?" I asked.

"I'll bet they're the two guys who were killed at the house you and Chastain went to this morning," Wilkins said. "I know the names."

"Yeah, anyway," he continued, "they weren't close friends of Pork Chop, but they did business with him sometimes. It was in their interest to maintain the relationship with him. So, I persuaded one of them to—"

"By pulling their teeth out?" I asked. Wilkins winced.

"Yeah." He grinned. "I started with Hog Master, and that convinced Wild Bill to go along. But," he quit spinning the can, "after that, I just yanked on both of them."

"Go on," Wilkins said, clearly angered.

"Anyway, like I was saying, I persuaded Wild Bill to call Pork Chop." He paused to look at me. "We knew where he was, man. You ain't that good at hiding stuff." He grinned. "But we couldn't get to him, you know? So Wild Bill called and told Pork Chop that his little girl was going to be hit if he didn't get her out. He told the Chop that they already had her and took her to their safe house and he could meet them there."

"And he bought that?" Wilkins asked.

The Angel shrugged again. "Sure, why not? He knew we could get to her, and he knew that Wild Bill and Hog Master were looking out for their own business interests by taking care of the girl, so why not?"

"How was Pork Chop involved with the Priest?" Wilkins asked.

"The Chop was working both ends. He supplied inside information to rival gangs. Sometimes it was useful, most times it wasn't. The Posse had some guns they wanted to unload. The Feds was on them, but they had a good place to stash them. When Pork Chop found out where the guns was hidden, he gave the information to the Priest for a piece of the pie."

"That could explain the hit on Milner," I said. "The Priest was trying to unload the guns. The Hammer was hoping to kill two birds with one stone."

The Angel shook his head. "Huh-uh. Whacking the Priest and Buster was a bonus. It was the Chop that we were after."

"Could be why they didn't shoot the place up sooner. Or tear the town apart looking for Miles. Hutchins and Denton couldn't afford for a gang war to get started," I said, recalling what I had been told during my interrogation of the Hammer's guard.

Wilkins paused to think. "Could be. The Humes had some other reason for all of this, and their reasons didn't intersect with the Posse's."

"So the Posse had to lay low and work out the situation for Hutchins and Hume before they could take care of their own business."

"Explains why a lot of people didn't start turning up dead sooner." Wilkins turned to Thomas.

"Where are the guns?" Wilkins asked.

He shrugged. "Don't know. Like I said, we were after the Chop. When we wasted the other two, I knew then that the Hammer was going to be mad." He shook his head. "We should've took the time to work on those two for a while. Find out where the guns were. You know?"

"Why didn't you go to Wild Bill and Hog Master a few days ago?" I asked.

"Because we didn't know where the Chop was at. So we figured you must've stashed him somewhere. A hotel seemed like a logical place. The Hammer began calling places and asking if you were registered there."

"Me? Why me?" I was curious how the Hammer knew to call in my name.

The Angel shrugged. "I don't know, man. I just do the job. I don't ask no questions."

"So you found me. Then what?"

"Then, when that politician turned up missing, we knew it was time to move. That's when I went to the west side."

"Wild Bill and Hog Master were friends of yours," I said.

He nodded. "Yep. But I don't let friendship stand in the way of business. Business is business. You know?"

I wanted to steer the conversation back to Miles. "And Miles was willing to let these two guys get his daughter out of Hope House to keep her safe from you?"

"He didn't have no choice, man. We told him it was a done deal."

Wilkins looked at me. "He probably didn't figure those two guys to be the more immediate threat. He reacted like you or I would have done under the same circumstances."

The Angel's face flushed with anger. "We don't do no kids. But the Chop didn't know that. So we used what we had."

"You threatened mine," I said.

He grinned again. "That was just to work you up, man. And it worked too." The annoying smirk remained on his face. I knew how to remove it, and restraining myself was becoming increasingly difficult.

"Why are you giving all of this up so easily?" I asked.

"I don't affiliate, man. I just do a job. I'm not going down so the Hammer can keep twenty grand of my money."

The door opened, and a young woman came in asking for Wilkins. When he went to the door, she handed him a large manila envelope and walked away. Wilkins opened it, looked inside, and motioned for me to join him in the hallway.

Once we were out of the room, he handed me the envelope without a word. I opened it. Inside, were the faxed pictures from the ATM camera. They were grainy, but each showed the photo of an elderly woman as she stood at the machine. Over her shoulder was the unmistakable image of the Hammer, as he was kneeling beside Warren's Lexus.

"Now," Wilkins said, "we've got the Hammer too."

"Miles said the Hammer wouldn't do this. That he would kill up close."

"Looks like Miles was wrong," Wilkins said.

Wilkins was right, but so was Miles. "He came to the house one night. Told me he felt like he would die soon."

Wilkins nodded. "Well, he was right about that."

I flipped through the others and found a clear shot of Warren getting into the car. Simon DeGraff was in the picture too. I handed the photo to Wilkins.

"There's Warren getting into the car. The guy had about fifteen seconds to live."

Wilkins looked at the picture and frowned. "I know this guy."

"You know Warren?"

He shook his head. "No, not him. *Him*," he said, pointing to DeGraff.

"That's the guy that got my license. He was with Chang, a state trooper."

"I don't know Chang, but I know this guy, and his name isn't DeGraff. It's Morgan. Paul Morgan. He used to be a cop, but now he's retired. Last I heard he was working in corporate security somewhere."

"He's with Warren. Think he could've been working for Hume Enterprises?"

Wilkins slid the photos into the envelope. "Sure. I'd bet that Warren, here, wanted you out of the way. Didn't you tell me that he didn't want Miles found?"

"Yes."

"He probably put his guy DeGraff on it, and DeGraff worked with Chang, and the two got your license." He paused. "Which, by the way, we will get back for you."

"So Chang is dirty too."

Wilkins smiled. "You have a firm grasp of the obvious. Use the power wisely."

"So now we have The Angel, Denton, Warren, Chang, DeGraff, and the Hammer."

"We better not let him know," Wilkins said, nodding toward the closed door of the interrogation room, "or he'll back out on us. The only reason he's cooperating now is that he thinks the Hammer is going to walk away with the money."

"I agree. And you might want to talk to a guy named Jimmie Rossi. Goes by the name Freeze. I think he's responsible for making the bomb that the Hammer used."

"Okay," Wilkins said, "I'll check it out." He placed a hand on my shoulder. "I'm going to wrap up here, and then we're going to get a warrant for Denton." He smiled. "Nice work for a private detective."

I left the interrogation area and took the elevator downstairs. Things seemed to be coming together all right, but I still had a nagging feeling that all wasn't what it should be. It was intuition. Cop's intuition.

How did Denton find bikers who were willing to execute a hit? How did he know where to go? Did Hutchins guide him? Who was pulling the strings?

Certainly, Ms. Carmichael was educated. She was smart enough to pull it off, and was probably involved. But I doubted she was connected enough to know who to call. And why would she risk jail time for Denton? And did Denton have anything to do with the murder of his brother?

I left IPD headquarters and stepped outside. The day had grown colder. I zipped up my jacket as I climbed into my car and pulled away from the curb.

Carmichael had lied. Her statement that the letters began coming in only a month ago didn't jibe with the statement that the bikers had been hired three months ago to begin their search for Miles.

But there were other things too. Denton had referred to Ms. Carmichael by her first name. The only one who had done so.

Were they romantically involved? Or was he using her for cover? Or for that matter, was she using him?

I had a lot of questions. Too many, in fact. That meant the picture was unclear. But I knew where to go to bring it into focus.

CHAPTER FIFTY-NINE

The Indianapolis office of the FBI is located on the sixth floor of the federal building in downtown Indianapolis. It's less than two miles from IPD headquarters, making my drive from Wilkins' office to the FBI a short one.

I called Mary as I drove to the bureau's office to be sure she was still working. She was. And by the time I entered the suite, she was waiting for me behind the wooden gate that separated the reception area from the rest of the office. She buzzed me in, and I followed her down the long hallway that led to the largest of the agents' squad rooms. As we walked, she seemed preoccupied, not saying a word.

"What's up?" I asked.

"What do you mean?"

"I mean you're awfully quiet. What's up?"

She stopped midstride. "It didn't work out between Steve and me," she said. "It's over."

"I'm sorry," I said, wondering if it sounded genuine. The relationship that had begun to develop between Mary and Steve had gnawed at me. I didn't like it, yet I had no right to feel that way.

"Yeah, well, I'm kind of bummed out, but I'll be okay," she said as we resumed our walk.

As we entered the squad room she said, "Over here. They've moved my desk again."

The room was large and rectangular. It held the largest grouping of agents in the building, with a large number of desks facing forward. Along the periphery of the room were a number of individual offices in which supervisory special agents sat as they delegated tasks to their individual squads. Mary's desk had been moved to the rear of the room.

She sat at her desk, and I took the seat next to it. Most of the agents were out, but the couple who were still in the office came by to make small talk before moving away.

"Okay," she said, turning to her monitor, "you want the prints on the glass."

"Right."

"You're lucky," she said. "They had just come in when you called."

"And?"

"And the report says that some prints show up. They're a match for an Angelina Russo."

"Russo?"

She nodded. "And that's it. No prints for Hume. But then, if he hasn't been arrested, served in the military, or had some other reason for his prints to be in the database, they wouldn't show up."

"I saw Carmichael pick up the glass."

Mary nodded. "I don't doubt that you did. But either her prints aren't showing up or someone else is in the house."

"Or she's going by another name," I said. "Does Russo have a record?"

Mary scanned the monitor. "Yep. Arrested in Trenton."

"Can we...you...get hold of them? Get some detail? Maybe a mug shot?"

"No problem." She glanced again at the monitor and began dialing the number she saw on the screen. After a minute, she was talking with someone at the Trenton PD.

A couple more agents came into the room, but I didn't know them. The bureau is notorious for its transfer policy. The two guys who came in had probably been transferred to Indianapolis after I had been fired.

"Okay," Mary said. "I appreciate it." She hung up.

"What did you find out?"

"Angelina Russo is the granddaughter of Carmen Russo. Know him?"

I ran through my mental database and came up empty. "No."

"At one time, years ago, he was head of the Valerio crime family in New Jersey. That is, until he was assassinated. Trenton intelligence believes the family is trying to go legit."

"You're kidding."

"Well, as legit as they can. They're not squeaky clean."

"What legitimate areas are they getting into?"

"Gambling."

"It's becoming the quick way to a buck," I said as things became more clear.

Mary nodded thoughtfully. "Maybe the better way to say it is, 'the quick way to *maybe* making a buck.'"

"Sure. Maybe for the player, quick way for the host."

"Anyway," she said, "to make a long story short, Angelina was once married to a man who managed a casino in Atlantic City."

"Was?"

Mary nodded. "Until he died. Then the casino was bought by a group of investors calling themselves the Oro Group."

"That's the same group that's made the offer for the hotels," I said, recalling the information Upcraft had given me.

"Oro is Italian for gold," Mary said.

"How did her husband die?"

"No one knows."

"What do you mean, no one knows?"

"I mean that no one knows the cause of death. He just got sick and died."

"Just like Berger."

She nodded. "You were right, you know," she said. "This thing is going to reach the bureau."

"Can I get a copy of the mug shot?"

She glanced at her watch. "It ought to be coming in now."

She got up, and I followed her back down the hall we had come from earlier, into a similarly designed but smaller squad room that housed the clerks and other support personnel. A fax machine stood on a table near the center of the room.

"Here it is," Mary said, pulling the fax off the printer and handing it to me.

The black-and-white photograph showed a front and side picture of Elizabeth Carmichael. Just under her chin was a placard that identified her as Angelina Russo.

"We've got to get her out of that house before Berger dies."

"I agree. But so far, we only have a criminal record and some suspicions."

"We have more than that," I said. "We have Denton."

CHAPTER SIXTY

Corporate headquarters for Hume Enterprises was located in a near north side building that looked more like a center for the arts. The lobby was ornately done in marble with a free-flowing fountain in the center. Original works of art lined the walls, and a bloodred, heavily padded carpet covered the floor. I recalled what Ms. Carmichael—or Angelina, depending on what name she preferred—had said about Denton frequently burning the midnight oil. It was something we had in common. The day had been long, and I was tired. But I needed to find Denton, and corporate headquarters seemed like a good place to start.

A balding, middle-aged security guard sat behind a tall marble counter that gave him the perspective of looking down on whoever entered. In this case, he was looking down on me.

"We're closed," he said matter-of-factly.

"I'm Colton Parker," I said. "I'm employed by Mr. Hume. May I speak with him?"

He didn't say a word but picked up the phone and punched a button. After speaking into the receiver in hushed tones, he hung up.

"You can take the elevator over there." He pointed to a marble-covered door that stood separate from the bank of other elevators.

"Fourth floor. It will take you directly into Mr. Hume's reception area."

I thanked him and took the elevator to the fourth floor. When I stepped off, I found myself in a reception area that was considerably less garish than the one below.

"Mr. Parker?" an attractive receptionist asked.

"Yes."

"Go right in, sir," she said, gesturing to a solid-looking cherry door. "Mr. Hume is waiting."

I entered the room and found Denton sitting behind an ornate desk that stood before a wall of floor-to-ceiling windows. Heavy draperies were opened, allowing for a panoramic view of the city.

Hume was on the phone and motioned for me to have a seat. I sat in a soft leather chair.

"Okay, sounds good," he said into the phone, winking at me. "Great. I'll talk to you later." He hung up and said, "Mr. Parker, how is the investigation going?"

"I wish I could say that it's going well, but I've run into a bit of a snag."

He leaned back in his seat and clasped his hands behind his head. "Oh? How so?"

His demeanor didn't fit that of a man who was losing a father and who had just lost a brother.

"Miles is dead."

"Really?" he seemed mystified. "How did that happen?"

"The guy you hired to kill him did his job," I said.

His demeanor remained intact. "Excuse me?"

"You hired Satan's Posse to find Miles. But they couldn't find him, so you and Carmichael hired me. You set me up."

"You better have a very good attorney, Mr. Parker. You're making some—"

"Stop," I said. "The threats don't work." I stood and came around to his side of the desk. He remained seated with his hands behind his head. He seemed as though he didn't have a care in the world.

"You and Carmichael friendly?"

"That's none of your business."

"Yes it is," I said. "And now it's police business too."

He smiled. "I'm not worried about the police."

"Oh yeah, that's right. You're connected."

He continued to smile.

"But so was Rolly Hutchins."

"He was a good and decent public servant," Hume said. "And a close family friend."

"He's dead."

"I believe the police are calling it a suicide."

"Yes. And the note he left tells us a lot about you," I lied.

He smiled. "There was no note."

"How do you know that?"

His expression changed, revealing that he was concerned about the misstep.

"Actually, there was a note," I lied again. "It's the one that relieved his conscience of its burden. The one he mailed to his attorney. You see, like most men who know they're about to die, he wanted to unburden himself." I sat on the edge of his desk. "But his burden is now yours."

"Look around you, Simple Simon. Do you think all of this falls out of the sky?"

He rose out of his chair and stood to gaze out the window. "It comes from hard work. From being tough."

"From selling your own father out and murdering your brother?"

He turned from the window, his hands clasped behind his back. "My father?"

"How much is the Oro Group offering for the hotels?"

He turned to look out the window again. The twinkling lights of the Indianapolis skyline were just beginning to assert themselves.

"Millions? Tens of millions? And why would you take out massive loans to reface a business that's going bankrupt?"

He shook his head as he continued to gaze out the window. "I don't have time to give you a lesson on the intricacies of high finance. In fact, I don't have time for this at all."

He moved to his desk and picked up the phone. "Ms. Worth, could you have security come to my office, please?" There was a pause. "No, I'm fine, but I want them to remove this man from my office." He hung up.

"You may or may not know that the Oro Group is a front for the Valerio crime family."

He went back to the window and resumed gazing.

"You may also want to know that they're heavily into gambling."

He said nothing.

"And that Elizabeth's real name is Angelina Russo. She's the granddaughter of Carmen Russo."

He said nothing but glanced at his watch before resuming his stare out the window.

"She probably had your brother killed too. He was interfering with my investigation. She had to stop him so I could find Miles and bring him to you."

Nothing.

"She's probably the source of your father's illness."

He turned to look at me. "What do you mean?"

"Her husband died of an illness that's similar to your father's. A sudden, unexplained illness. I'm willing to bet she poisoned him, took over the casino he managed, and sold it to the Oro Group. Don't you see a pattern here?"

His eyes shifted to the floor for a moment before returning his gaze to the scene beyond the window.

"Are you in love with her? Did she promise you something? Are the hotels really losing money, or did the two of you doctor the books?"

He continued to maintain his fix on the city's skyline.

"The police are on their way," I said. "The man you hired to kill

Miles is in custody. He's going to ID you as soon as you're taken downtown."

He said nothing.

"And she will have gotten away with it. You and everyone else involved will go to prison, and she will kill your father and walk away with everything he built. Unless you help me," I said, hoping that he had the same sense of honor the Angel had.

The door opened, and the receptionist came into the office. Her face was drawn, and she seemed confused. "Mr. Hume, security is here, and so are the police."

He continued to stand at the window as the rest of us stood quietly. Finally, he turned to the woman. "It's all right, Ms. Worth. Have security stand down, and show the police in."

CHAPTER SIXTY-ONE

"He spilled everything," Wilkins said to me in the reception area as Denton was led away in cuffs.

"Did he know about Carmichael?"

Wilkins shook his head. "No, and neither did I until he told me what you said."

"Sorry," I said, "but I just found out the news myself. I wanted to move on it."

"It's okay—this time," Wilkins said. "It gave us leverage. He's involved with her, and now we have leverage there too."

That explained the familiarity I had seen earlier. "We need to get Berger out of that house," I said.

Wilkins nodded. "We are. We're going there now. In fact, Mary is going to meet us there. I telephoned her from Hume's office and gave her everything we have. She's going to the US attorney, even as we speak, to obtain a warrant for Carmichael's arrest. Trenton PD and the New Jersey state police have a renewed interest in her too."

I watched through Denton's open door as a team of detectives and uniformed officers began placing the contents of his desk into boxes.

"We got a warrant to seize his records and the records of Hume

Enterprises," Wilkins said. "If this guy was doing the stuff that we know about, what else was he doing that we don't know about?"

"You might want to talk to some store owners too," I said, giving him Hiram's name. "If Hutchins is tied to this family, and they're trying to use his influence for gambling, maybe he was involved in other stuff too."

"Care to speculate?"

I shrugged. "Could be anything. But given the gambling operations that this family is involved with, maybe he was trying to skim off the lottery sales."

Wilkins nodded thoughfully. "Could be," he said. "Or worse. He could've been rigging the machines, or forcing the store owners to buy the mob's machines."

Wilkins was probably closer to the truth than I was. Using the mob's machines would mean that they would print out tickets that were similar to those from the state but that were counterfeit and therefore worthless. All proceeds would go to the mob, and no one would be the wiser.

"After all, it's like you said," Wilkins continued, "Hutchins was in Hume's pocket and Hume was getting in bed with organized crime."

"Hutchins was probably doctoring the books of the hotels, making it look like they were losing money. Warren was none the wiser. He got in the way of his brother's plans when he started interfering with my search for Miles. So either Denton or Carmichael gave the order, and the Posse took him out."

Wilkins nodded. "Until then, Hutchins could restrain the Hammer. But after the bomb went off—"

"In Hutchins' parking lot," I said.

"In Hutchins' parking lot," Wilkins echoed, "the whole thing began to fall apart. The restraint that Hutchins or Hume had exercised over the Posse began to decay."

"Hard to domesticate an animal from the wild."

"Sure," Wilkins said. "Sooner or later, a snake lives true to its nature."

We watched as the officers began to cart the boxes to the private elevator. I stepped aside in the small reception area to allow them room to pass.

"Why the need to find Miles?" I asked Wilkins

"Hume said that his father's will states that any living heirs must share equally in their father's estate. And that if Hume Enterprises or any of its subsidiaries is sold, the sale must bear the signature of the immediate, living members of the Hume family. Specifically, Berger Hume and his immediate descendants."

"That explains why they needed to find Miles before Berger died," I said.

"Yes."

"And killing Berger outright could turn Denton against her plans, and it would still leave Miles out there somewhere."

"Yes. She needed at least one of the brothers alive. If too many of them turned up dead, she would risk suspicion," Wilkins said.

"But the fact remains that she was trying to kill Berger. Probably the same way she killed her husband."

"I have two theories on that," Wilkins said, as he crossed his arms and sat on the edge of the receptionist's desk. "First, she may not have known about Miles. But somewhere along the line, as she became more familiar with the will and other documents, she decided to check. That would be especially true if she knew about Berger's prior engagement to Marian Collins."

"Sure," I said. "That makes sense. That would make her the writer of the letters."

"Exactly, which is my second theory. She tried to find him for almost three months before you got involved. Since that didn't work, she could slowly poison the old man. Knowing how he constructed the will, and how that reflected his love of his family, she could take her time killing him while she worked on him with a series of anonymous letters."

"She couldn't afford to kill him if she needed him to change his will."

Wilkins nodded. "Right. If Miles couldn't be found, she would have an alternative plan to use Berger to alter his will."

"Her plan worked well because it led to Berger using his influence to find a PI who he felt could keep quiet."

"Right. He couldn't take a chance on hiring just any schmo."

"So she hired me and then used me to lead her to Miles."

"Yep."

I recalled telling her that I had a lead on Miles. Telling her that I had an address for him on Milner, only to have the house assaulted shortly after.

I recalled telling her that I was taking Miles to the lab, and I remembered the Angel telling me he had picked me up at the lab but decided to attack Miles and me later as we were driving on Raymond Street. And I recalled how I had called for permission to put Miles in a hotel.

"It's all adding up now," I said. "All the things I should have seen but didn't."

Wilkins put a hand on my shoulder. "We all do that. Don't sweat this one, Colton. You opened up a network of corruption that extends all the way to state government. There'll be local and federal investigations on this until long after I've retired."

"Sure," I said. "And as long as people love money enough to kill for it, or steal for it, or betray for it, you won't be able to retire."

He nodded. "Drives the system, doesn't it?" He slid off the desk. "Listen, Mary is heading to the Hume home. If you want to be there when she arrests Carmichael, I would suggest you get going."

"I am," I said. "But first I need to make a stop."

CHAPTER SIXTY-TWO

By the time I reached the Hume residence, a long day had turned into night, and the wrought-iron gates had been flung open, allowing easy access for the cluster of police cars—marked and unmarked.

I eased into the compound and parked between two squad cars. Mary was leading Carmichael out of the house in handcuffs.

"Stay here for a second, okay?" I said to my passenger as I climbed out of the car.

Carmichael had her head down, but raised it to look at me as I approached.

"Doggedly determined and will get the job done," I said, reminding her of our first conversation.

She gave me a wry smile. "I should've paid more attention."

I shook my head. "No. Berger should have."

Mary steered the woman to a nearby squad car and placed her hand on top of Carmichael's head as she eased the woman into the car. After closing the door, she tapped on top of the roof, and the car drove away.

I watched as the car pulled out of the Hume compound with Carmichael secured in the backseat. When I considered charges like solicitation for murder, fraud, and possible attempted murder, not to mention the federal charges she would face, I knew that Carmichael would be going away for a long time.

"Come to see your handiwork?" Mary asked, smiling.

I glanced around the compound and saw a repeat of the scene I had witnessed at Denton's office. Uniformed officers, detectives, and FBI agents were swarming all over the house, carrying boxes and bags of evidence to their respective vehicles. An ambulance was parked near the entrance.

"For Hume?" I asked, nodding toward the ambulance.

"Yeah. We thought we'd check him out. Chances are, though, if he was poisoned, the damage is done."

"Come on," I said, leading Mary to my car. "I have someone I want you to meet."

When we reached the car, Mary said, "Who's this?"

"I'm April," my passenger said. "What's your name?"

"I'm Mary."

"Hi. I'm April."

Mary looked at me.

"She's Miles' daughter. She's the only living relative of Berger Hume who isn't dead or going to jail."

Mary smiled. "Well, she's also going to be a very rich little girl."

"Want to meet your grandpa?" I asked April.

She said she did, and we got out of the car.

"I'm going to let her meet him before he goes to the hospital. Is that all right?" I asked Mary.

"Sure, if I can go with you."

We led the twelve-year-old into the Hume home and back to the bedroom, where I had last seen Berger. Paramedics were checking his vitals and preparing him for transport. A gurney that was unfolded to its full height stood next to the bed.

"Wow," April said, clutching my hand with one of hers as she pushed her glasses up with the other. "This is big." Her eyes were as wide as the room she surveyed.

Berger was weaker and more sallow than when we had first met. He turned his head on the pillow to look at us.

I walked April to the bed. "Give us a minute, will you, guys?" I asked.

They looked at Mary who nodded.

"Sure," one of the medics said, motioning for the other one to join him in the hallway.

"Berger, I couldn't save Warren or Miles. And Denton's going to jail."

Tears began to well in his eyes.

"But I do have someone I want you to meet." I moved April closer to the bed. "This is your granddaughter."

His eyes shifted to the little girl and then to me.

"She's Miles' daughter. She lives at Hope House."

"I'm April," she said as she pushed her glasses up again. "What's your name?"

He tried to talk, but his moving lips were silent. His frail hand gestured for me to lean forward.

"She's beautiful," he whispered.

"Are you my grandpa?" she asked.

He turned his head on the pillow and looked at her through eyes that were more alive than I had seen since we met. He held out two thin, feeble arms in an embrace. The girl hugged him in return.

"We're going to leave you two alone for a while," I said, motioning for Mary to join me.

We left the house and stepped outside into the cold air as the last of the detectives and agents drove away with their boxes of evidence. The paramedics remained in the house with Berger and April.

"That was nice, Colton."

"Miles told me about her. He did what he did partly to provide for the expense of her care."

Mary looked back at the house. "That won't be a problem anymore."

I shook my head. "Funny, isn't it? How all these people were scrambling and killing and jockeying for Berger's money, only to have it all fall into the hands of the most innocent of them all."

She put a hand on my arm. "That's where it belongs, isn't it?" She kissed me on the cheek. "I've got to go. Work to do."

"Sure," I said, "I'm going to hang around. Take her back home as soon as Berger is on his way."

I watched as Mary drove off, thinking of my own little girl, whom I had not seen in days because I had been too busy. Busy earning thousands of dollars that I thought was going to change our lives. But which, of course, wouldn't. It would take something far more meaningful to do that.

I looked around the Hume compound. The spacious grounds, sprawling home, and manicured gardens had not provided happiness for them. They had wanted more, and more would never be enough.

Like all of us, they wanted what money couldn't buy.

EPILOGUE

A gentle rain fell on the morning that Miles was buried. He was laid to rest next to his mother in a simple graveside ceremony. There were few in attendance.

Ernie stood next to me, smoking, with head bowed as he listened to Millikin say a few words over a man that he had seen only once and had never met.

April was there too. Wilkins had brought her. She didn't understand the full impact of what had happened. But then, that was probably a good thing.

Berger would survive Carmichael's attempt to end his life. It would take time, but he would recover. And when he did, April would live with him.

The brief ceremony concluded with a short prayer by Millikin, and we began to disperse.

I wrapped an arm tightly around Callie. We would go home. Home to a house we now owned. But lessons had been learned. Time spent chasing my own rainbow had blinded me to the real needs of those about me. Just like the Humes, I had allowed the value I placed on money to cloud my judgment. And others had paid.

It was a cost that had been too high. And as I looked at my daughter, I knew it was a cost I would never pay again.

© Susan Gerth 2005

MEET
BRANDT DODSON

Brandt Dodson was born and raised in Indianapolis, where he graduated from Ben Davis High School and Indiana Central University (now known as the University of Indianapolis). A creative writing professor said, "You're a good writer. With a little effort and work, you could be a very good writer." That comment, and the support offered by a good teacher, set Brandt on a course that would eventually lead to the Colton Parker Mystery series.

A committed Christian, Brandt combined his love for the work of writers like Raymond Chandler and Dashiell Hammett with his love for God's Word. The result was Colton Parker.

"I wanted Colton to be an 'every man.' A decent guy who tries his best. He is flawed and makes mistakes. But he learns from them and moves on. And, of course, he gets away with saying and doing things the rest of us never could."

Brandt comes from a long line of police officers, spanning several generations, and was employed by the FBI before leaving to pursue his education.

A former United States Naval Reserve officer, Brandt is a board certified podiatrist and past president of the Indiana Podiatric Medical Association. He is a recipient of the association's highest honor, the Theodore H. Clark Award.

He currently resides in southwestern Indiana with his wife and two sons and is at work on his next novel.

You can reach Brandt Dodson at www.brandtdodson.com.

MEET COLTON PARKER, P.I.

Original Sin
ISBN13: 978-0-7369-1809-1
ISBN10: 0-7369-1809-4

Colton Parker was just fired from the FBI and has a teenage daughter who blames him for her mother's death. Now that he's hung out his shingle as a P.I., his first paying client—Angie Howe—has enough money for only one day's worth of investigating. But Angie looks as if she could use a friend, so Colton has his first case.

When the mystery is finally resolved, Colton is resigned to improve his parenting skills with his daughter—and while the pair still struggle with each other, hope finally gets a chance to grow.

Seventy Times Seven
ISBN13: 978-0-7369-1810-7
ISBN10: 0-7369-1810-8

Lester Cheek had everything a man could want. A beautiful home, a thriving business, and money to burn. But he was alone—very alone. Until he met Claudia.

The attractive and effervescent Claudia was everything that Lester could hope for. But she mysteriously disappears, and Colton Parker is hired to find her.

Suspense...intrigue...high drama in the tradition of Dashiell Hammett and Raymond Chandler.